Secrets of the Heart

Gilda O'Neill was born and brought up in the East End. She left school at fifteen but returned to education as a mature student. She is now a full-time writer and *Secrets of the Heart* is her fourteenth novel. She has also had six non-fiction books published including the highly acclaimed *Sunday Times* best-sellers, *My East End* and *Our Street*. She lives in East London with her husband and family.

Praise for Gilda O'Neill

'A treasure . . . Every page is a delight. Every chapter made vivid by a writer who has poured heart and soul into her book' *Daily Mail*

'A thumping good read' Lesley Pearse

'A rich tapestry . . . a finely detailed examination of our not so distant past. Her book is as much a piece of history as the accounts it contains' *Time Out*

'A cracking read' Martina Cole

'Her vivid, flint-edged picture of London's East End . . . leaps off the page with its sardonic dialogue and sharply realised characters . . . you'll find it very difficult indeed to put this one down' *Crime Time*

'Compelling' *Daily Express*

'A sharp eye, a warm heart and a gift for storytelling' Elizabeth Buchan

Also by Gilda O'Neill

Gilda O'Neill
Secrets of the Heart

arrow books

Published by Arrow Books 2008

2 4 6 8 10 9 7 5 3

First published in Great Britain in 2008 by
Arrow Books
The Random House Group Limited
20 Vauxhall Bridge Road, London, SW1V 2SA

www.randomhouse.co.uk

Addresses for companies within The Random House Group Limited can be found at: www.randomhouse.co.uk/offices.htm

The Random House Group Limited Reg. No. 954009

A CIP catalogue record for this book
is available from the British Library

ISBN 9780099492320

The Random House Group Limited supports The Forest Stewardship Council (FSC®), the leading international forest certification organisation. Our books carrying the FSC label are printed on FSC® certified paper. FSC is the only forest certification scheme endorsed by the leading environmental organisations, including Greenpeace. Our paper procurement policy can be found at www.randomhouse.co.uk/environment

Typeset by SX Composing DTP, Rayleigh, Essex
Printed and bound in Great Britain by CPI Cox & Wyman,
Reading, RG1 8EX

For Vivian Archer
And everyone at the wonderful
Newham Bookshop
With love and thanks

Prologue

Apart from going hop-picking, she'd never been to the country – and certainly not alone.

'This is it.' The Greenline bus driver didn't bother trying to conceal his distaste as he pulled the vehicle to a halt in the dark lane. They had stopped a few yards from the only light, a dim, caged bulb over a pair of plain metal gates set in a high brick wall.

'Are you sure?' the girl asked timidly, unable to believe that her mum would have sent her to such a forbidding-looking place.

'It's where your mother said to drop you when she put you on the bus. So, if you don't mind moving yourself, you'll get off now. I've not got all night and there's other passengers, you know.'

Slowly, she trudged along the verge to the gates, her thin-soled town shoes slipping on the wet grass. She watched as the bus disappeared around a bend in the lane, willing it to stop and turn around and take her back home. But it didn't.

Now she really was alone.

She reached up and tugged at the old-fashioned bell pull.

The girl stood in front of the elderly nun's desk with her head bowed, the raindrops dripping from the brim of her hat mingling with her tears. She was holding a cheap pressed-cardboard suitcase. She had never had anything like it before, and at any other time she would have been so proud – having something as elegant as luggage – but now all she felt was scared. No, not scared, it was far worse than that. She felt terrified. In fact, apart from that one terrible thing that had happened to her, she could not remember ever feeling such fear.

She replied to the final question so quietly that she had to keep repeating her answer to try to make herself heard. Though she did wonder if the nun was simply choosing not to hear her. She seemed like that sort of a person – stern, unforgiving, deliberately difficult and unwaveringly judgemental.

'So, that at least is completed.' The nun put the final full stop after the girl's details – or rather the few details she had wanted to know about her – on a series of forms, and then, licking her dry, wrinkled finger, she separated each of the triplicate sheets.

'Now, you will go through to the dormitory

with Nurse – and you will hurry up about it. We're busy people here. No time to waste. Go on . . . move, girl, move!'

The girl would have liked to have asked what a dormitory was, but she felt too intimidated by the woman's posh, clipped vowels to dare do such a thing. She'd never spoken to a nun before and had been surprised by the woman's accent. She'd thought that all nuns were Irish, like the priests in her neighbourhood, but this woman's accent was definitely not like any Irish person's – priest or otherwise – that she'd heard before. She sounded more like the ladies on the wireless.

The nun stood up, scraping her chair back across the bare floorboards. Through her wet lashes, the girl could see the heavy wooden crucifix bouncing on the woman's flattened bosom. The image added to her fear; she had never understood why religious people displayed such visions of torture and pain.

Someone tapped the girl sharply on the shoulder, and a voice snapped from behind her: 'Come on, come with me. And don't dawdle, some of us have better things to do with our time.'

The girl turned to see who had spoken to her in what – in other circumstances – she would have found a woefully inept attempt to copy the nun's genteel accent. It was a tall, broad-beamed woman that she saw, tossing an impatient look back over her shoulder as she marched away along the corridor.

'And, I should add, *decent* things. Now there's a lesson you'd do well to learn.'

The girl was momentarily distracted from her feelings of utter dejection – and from her tears – when she saw that the dormitory the nurse had led her to was nothing more than a long, narrow room. Despite her anxiety about where she was going, she had somehow imagined that it would be something different, something unlike anything she had seen before. Yet all it was was a room decorated in an ugly, institutional green paint that had a slight gloss to it, making the place look unpleasantly clammy, with a row of narrow, iron-framed beds lining one side. Most of the beds were occupied; all had a locker on one side and a wicker crib on the other. The lighting in the room was miserable, as dim as the bulb outside the gates, and there was the faint sound of a whimpering baby and a louder sound of someone mumbling fitfully in their sleep. The room stank of disinfectant with a sickly under smell that the girl couldn't quite put a name to, but that, for some reason, made her start crying again.

Or maybe it wasn't the room and its disagreeable smell, but the realisation of the enormity of what was happening to her. She couldn't deny it any more, not even to herself. Her family had abandoned her.

'Will you hurry up and stop complaining, girl?' The nurse pushed her down on to one of the few empty beds. 'I am becoming increasingly bored by girls like you. Think about things for once, will you? It's too late for tears, and that's the end of it. It's not even as if you have anyone to blame for all of this but yourself.'

The girl began to cry louder – heart-breaking, chest-heaving sobs. She had never, ever felt so alone. 'Please, I want to go back to my family. Please let me.'

'Well, we can all want things, but I don't suppose *they'll* want anything to do with you. Not now they won't. Not after the shame you've brought to their doorstep.'

'I only want to go home. I know he'll change his mind when he sees me.'

'You want too many things, my girl. That's the trouble with the likes of you. Because that, young woman, is what gets you into trouble in the first place – wanting things you shouldn't have. Now stop making all that noise, get into your night things and go to sleep before you wake the others. I'll give you your full examination in the morning.' She looked at the wretched young thing – up and down, very slowly, her gaze fierce with disapproval. It was as if she was assessing horse flesh and the poor animal had proved itself to be more than wanting. 'So make sure you bathe thoroughly beforehand.'

The girl swiped the back of her hand across her nose. 'How will I know what time to get up?'

'You'll know, my girl. Oh, believe me, you'll know.'

The girl lay there in the dark, listening to the unfamiliar sounds of the countryside creeping in from the fields that surrounded the building, but mainly wondering what new horrors a 'full examination' might hold. She badly needed to go to the lavatory but was far too frightened to get out of bed in case the nun or the nurse was watching her. Who knew what sort of punishment might result?

Her eyes gradually became accustomed to the low lighting and she could now make out the sleeping bodies around her more clearly. They mostly seemed to be as young, if not younger, than she was. The one who had been mumbling was quiet now, but the baby was still grizzling wretchedly to itself. The whole place seemed awash with unhappiness.

Why had they done this to her? Why had they been so determined to hurt her even more than she had been already? It wasn't her fault that it had happened to her. She'd tried to make them understand how terrible it had been. But no one would listen. No one.

When she tried to tell them again, they just carried on shouting at one another, ignoring her as if she wasn't there, so she had gone to her room and she too had shouted – the words so loud she thought her head would split open. How could they believe her when they wouldn't even listen? Then, when they had calmed down a bit, and her mother had stopped crying, they came into her room, told her to be quiet, and said that she was going to be sent to this place – this cold vile place in the middle of nowhere – because *it was the best thing for everyone*.

So here she was, and here she had to stay, but it wasn't fair. All she wanted to do was to go home and be with her family. Why should she be punished for what had happened?

The next morning, the full examination that the nurse had promised her had been even worse than she had imagined – almost worse than what had happened to her before – and now she lay on her bed, sore and humiliated, while the other residents of the dormitory were somewhere down at the bottom of the cast-iron staircase, eating their breakfast and doing whatever else went on in this desolate place.

The girl stared at the wall, trying to rid herself of the image of the nurse coming towards her with that glare on her face as she snapped on those thick rubber gloves, when one of the others, the one with long fair hair pulled into two thick plaits, came back upstairs. She was alone.

The girl watched her over the edge of the bedclothes.

Her face and eyes were red and swollen from crying. Without a word she pulled a straw shopping bag from under her bed and began savagely stuffing it with the contents of her locker, her plaits swinging about her face as if she were a schoolchild playing a skipping game.

Raw and uncomfortable as she felt, the girl in the bed propped herself up on her elbows.

'Are you all right?' she asked the girl with the plaits. 'Is anything wrong?'

'What do you think?' The other girl didn't look at her.

'I don't know. I was only asking. I thought—'

'Well, if you're so busy thinking, I don't know why you haven't worked it out for yourself, but I'll tell you, shall I?' Tears ran down the fair-haired girl's face as she sobbed out the words, the straw bag dangling from one hand, and the index finger of the other jabbing towards the door. 'Them – them bastards down there – they took her away from me. My baby. Just now. She's going to some rotten rich bitch and her ugly old man. They just took her off me. Aw, yeah, they've got everything, them two. They've got a car; a special basket thing to carry her around in; dinky, little shoes; pretty clothes. All shop-bought, of course, nothing home-made or second hand for them. Everything, they've got. Everything them stinking nuns say *I* won't be able to give her.'

She dropped the shopping bag on the floor, her few possessions spilling out across the cold linoleum. 'But I'd have loved her, I really would. Only they didn't care what I had to say, did they? She's my baby, I kept telling them, mine, not theirs – that rotten, rich, stinking bastard pair, taking her off me. *She's* not got milk leaking out of her breasts. *Her* gut doesn't ache from wanting to hold her child. *She* hasn't got a single idea what it all means, what she's doing to me . . .'

'I'm sorry.'

The other girl's head snapped up, her plaits making her look oddly innocent even as she spat out words full of fury and venom. 'Don't waste your pity on me, you stupid, bloody cow. It'll be your turn soon.'

The days passed, each much the same as the other, but with nothing becoming any easier. The girl just wanted to fall asleep – maybe never to wake up – because now she knew what the girl with the plaits had meant. Even though her words had been so harsh and crude she had been talking nothing but the truth. But she and her anger-fuelled words were long gone. Now there were only the sounds of snuffling and wakeful stirrings from the cribs that had her stomach knotting and her breasts throbbing. She had been here for five weeks now, and – like that poor girl had said before she had left for who knew where – it would soon be her turn to have the heart ripped out of her.

Maybe it would have been easier if the girls could have talked more to each other. But how could they, when it might have meant someone wanting to talk about what was happening to them, about what *had* happened to them to bring them here? Worst of all, it would have meant admitting what was going to happen to them. How could any of them stand saying those things out loud without losing their minds?

She had just fallen into a shallow slumber that

had brought cruelly happy visions of her old home and family, sitting around the Sunday dinner table – all laughing and arguing, nudging and pushing, pinching bits of food off each other's plates – when she was suddenly brought back to the awful reality of where she was and what was going to happen to her.

There were voices coming from the hallway that ran alongside the dormitory, one of which was so familiar she'd have known it anywhere – although she could hardly believe she was hearing it now. Was she still dreaming?

She rolled herself out of bed and padded over to the doorway. No, she wasn't dreaming. It was her. It really was.

'Mum? Mum, what are you doing here?'

The woman cleared her throat, straightened her hat and lifted her chin in the air. 'I've decided he can't do this to you, love. I can't let you go through with this just because of him.'

The girl flashed a look at the puce-faced nun standing beside the unexpected visitor, who clearly wasn't impressed with this unexpected intrusion on to her territory.

The woman saw her daughter's unease and turned to the nun. 'If you wouldn't mind leaving us for a minute? In private.' It was an order rather than a request.

Her mother was being the bravest that the girl

had ever seen her. And she was doing it all for her.

Mother and daughter stood there, waiting for the nun to finish snorting angrily at this audacity.

'Well?' said the girl's mother.

With her eyes narrowed to convey open disapproval of the situation, the nun turned on her heel and deigned to glide along the hallway out of earshot. It was more of a disconcerting trick than a natural way of moving. The girl had grown used to it, but it could still unsettle someone unfamiliar with it – someone like her mother.

'She's a piece of work,' said her mother, when she was sure the nun couldn't hear her.

'You should see her when she's in a really bad mood. She's frightening.'

'No, thanks.'

They stood there in silence for a while, oddly embarrassed in each other's company.

Eventually the girl spoke. 'How about . . . him?' Her words were cautious, her voice uneven.

'Don't worry yourself about that.' The woman was still staring at the nun who was by now at the far end of the corridor.

'But, Mum . . .'

She turned to face her daughter. 'He's gone away.'

'Where?'

'I don't know.'

'Is it because of—?'

'Look, stop worrying, will you?' Her mother fiddled around with her hat, and then hitched her handbag higher up her arm. 'I'm going to sort this out.'

'But, Mum, how will I manage?'

'We'll find a way.'

'What happens if he decides to come back?'

'Don't you worry about that. I told you, don't you worry about anything. Now, you go and get some sleep, and I'll talk to the people here and get it all organised.'

The girl grabbed her mother's hand. 'Can't I come home with you now?' she pleaded

The woman tried to summon a smile. 'Sweetheart, I wish you could come with me – right now, this minute – and that I could take you home, put you to bed and give you a cup of hot milk and a great big cuddle. But it's not as easy as that, is it? Like I said, I'm going to find a way, but I've got to have a bit of time to work it all out. But – and I mean this – it won't be long, I promise you. We'll be all right. We will. And they'll look after you here until I work out what we're going to do.'

She pressed her lips to her daughter's

forehead – the first time she had kissed her in such a long time – and unshed tears burned in her eyes.

1940

Chapter 1

Puffing from the effort of climbing the five flights of stairs to the top floor of Turnbury Buildings, Wapping, Kitty Jarrett handed the baby to her daughter. 'Here, Grace, take little Bobby for me while I find the key.'

Freddie, Kitty's sixteen-year-old son, put down the two pillowcases full of bedding he'd been carrying on the bare concrete landing.

'Blimey, Mum. I know we should be grateful that they found us a place so quick, but this is gonna do us all in. Five floors?'

'That's enough, thank you, Freddie. And watch that language of yours.'

The door to number 56 – one of the three flats leading off the landing – was flung open, and a short, fat, grumpy-looking woman, arms folded and head bristling with curlers, appeared framed in the doorway.

'Be nice,' said Kitty under her breath. 'And, apart from being polite, keep your mouth shut. Especially you, Grace, or you'll get all nervous and start gabbing.'

'Well, I suppose we're going to be neighbours.

I'm Ada Tanner. Who are you?' the grumpy-looking woman demanded.

Grace stared down at the landing floor as she scrubbed listlessly at the tiles. Would they ever be able to tell him the truth? Who he was? What he really meant to them? Or was it going to be like this forever?

She blinked back her tears. It was all so sad. If only they could forget all about the secrets and lies and just be honest. But she knew that could never happen. If anything, things were getting harder for them by the day. It was all one great big mess.

Grace sploshed the scrubbing brush into the bucket, sending a spray of soapy water all over her as she swiped the tears away with the back of her hand. She looked through tear-blurred eyes at the bit of landing she'd cleaned outside the door of number 55. She hadn't done a bad job. With a bit of luck, her mum would be pleased and have nothing to complain about when she got home from work. It wasn't fair. Her big brother Freddie got away with everything, running around all over the place. If their dad was here it would be different, but after what had happened, and him walking out on their mum like that, they'd probably never see him again.

'Huh!' Ada Tanner was standing at her door, glaring at Grace, who was still on her knees.

'That's very nice, I don't think.'

'Good morning, Mrs Tanner,' said Grace flatly, pushing her brown hair off her forehead with the back of her hand. Despite being new to the ins and outs of the top floor of Turnbury Buildings, she had quickly become accustomed to this woman's often breathtaking rudeness.

'Don't know about no *good morning*,' the woman went on. 'But it wouldn't have hurt you to scrub the landing outside here while you had that brush in your hand. When I was young we showed our elders a bit of respect.'

Grace said nothing. Instead she got up off her knees, picked up the coconut mat she'd been kneeling on and took it over to the rubbish chute. She pulled down the metal door and whacked the mat across the opening. Dust rose up in a puff of dirty, cough-inducing air, and came sprinkling down like filthy snow to cling to the front of her damp cardigan.

'That was stupid,' sneered Ada Tanner, watching as Grace tried to flick off the dust with her wet hands. 'How old are you?'

'Fifteen, Mrs Tanner.'

'And how long have you been in number fifty-five now?'

Grace tried rubbing the dust away, but only

succeeded in making it worse, smearing it into the pink wool. 'I don't know, Mrs Tanner. A few days?' She spoke without looking up, wondering why she had the cardigan on in the first place – it might have been September but it was sweltering, and had been all week.

'A few days? And you don't even know how to use the chute or beat a mat. And how long do I have to wait before you ask if you can go and get a bit of shopping for me?'

'Mrs Tanner, I don't want to sound cheeky—'

'No?'

'No. And I really don't want you to take this the wrong way, but since we got bombed out and moved here and had to scrub the place out from top to bottom, and Mum had to go and work in the factory and I have to look after myself and our little Bobby, and now Mum's got even more worries about our Freddie getting called up next – well, I reckon we've got more on our minds than washing your part of the landing and doing your shopping for you.'

'You've got a nice way of talking, I don't think.'

'Have I? I'm sorry, I don't mean to. It's just that—'

'And how come it's your mother going out to work? Isn't your father's pay from the Merchant Navy enough for her? Women nowadays want it all. Working in factories, I ask you! *And* I've seen her in slacks. It's like the world's gone mad. But even if she is acting like a bloke, I bet she'd still help a neighbour out by fetching a bit of shopping for her. And, while we're at it, why don't you go out to work? Girl your age, you should be grafting by now. And come to think of it, why does that brother of yours keep such funny hours? What's he up to then, eh?'

'Do you know what, Mrs Tanner? Mum says that what we do is our business. So perhaps you should mind yours. Then everyone would be happy, wouldn't they?'

'Well, that's charming, that is, coming out of the mouth of a young woman – notice I didn't say young lady. I think I'll have to have a word with your mother about that tongue of yours.'

'But, Mrs Tanner, I never meant—'

'And, while we're on the subject, I saw you talking to my granddaughter this morning. Well, I'll give you a bit of advice: I don't want you mixing with her no more. So if you know what's good for you, you'll keep your distance else you'll have me to deal with. There's families and there's families . . . a good girl like my Bella shouldn't be keeping bad company.'

Grace dropped the mat on the floor. 'Bad company?' Her voice rose as she stepped towards Ada. 'What do you mean by that? Are you talking about me? Because, if you are, just say so. And as for *your Bella*, you should hear the half of what she has to say for herself! She uses words I've never even heard before. Think about it, I've only known her for a couple of days and—' She paused and shook her head. 'Aw, never mind, I'm wasting my time. People like you never listen. Well, you do – but only to yourselves.'

Ada took a step back, clearly shocked that anyone – especially a quiet-seeming girl like Grace – would dare talk back to her like that. 'All right, keep your hair on.'

But Grace moved even closer to her, trying desperately not to cry again. 'And while we're at it, why can't you do your own shopping and cleaning? It's not like you're an invalid or anything, is it?'

'I've never heard anything like this. The sort of people they let in Turnbury Buildings nowadays . . . it's a disgrace, that's what it is. These flats had a bit of class about them when they first put 'em up. But then we got stuck with the bloody Flanagans and all their carrying on. Then we had to put up with the Harrises and all their comings and goings to bloody evacuation, like a lot of flipping yo-yos, and now you. Who'll they shove in here next? Hitler?'

A poorly disguised splutter of appalled

laughter had Grace Jarrett and Ada Tanner turning towards the stairway.

Grace sighed with relief; it was the two nice women from across the landing – Nell Lovell and her mother-in-law, Mary. They were standing at the top of the steps leading up to the landing. If they hadn't turned up when they did, who knew what she might have wound up saying to Mrs Tanner?

Nell – tall with naturally curly blonde hair, and, despite being in her late twenties, still refreshingly unaware of her own good looks – had a toddler on her hip and was holding a young girl by the hand. On the lapel of her navy polka dot blouse there was a pearl and gold brooch in the shape of a capital N; it gleamed in the afternoon sunshine that flooded in through the tall window lighting the landing.

Mary, a greying, comfortable-looking, middle-aged woman, with an easy smile and a friendly way about her, was toting two bulging bags of shopping.

Ada narrowed her already piggy eyes. 'How long have you been standing there ear-wigging?'

Mary adjusted her amused expression to one she hoped looked like friendly concern. 'Hello, Ada. Grace. Tell me, love, how are you settling in to life in the Buildings?'

Grace took a deep breath, doing her best to calm down. 'Not too bad, thank you, Mrs Lovell, but I can't quite get the hang of that chute.' She brushed at the messy smudges across the front of her cardigan, making them worse than ever. 'Look what I've gone and done.'

'Off that, I suppose,' said Mary, raising one of the bags in the direction of the coconut mat that was still lying in the middle of the landing.

'Yeah. I made a right mess of it. Look at me.'

'Well, you'd have been better off giving that a good beating down in the courtyard. Out in the fresh air. It's what most of us do, especially on a beautiful day like this. It lifts your spirits, seeing such a gorgeous blue sky. Especially at this time of year. You'd never think it was the end of summer.'

'I suppose I was being a bit lazy, Mrs Lovell.' Grace managed a weak imitation of a smile. 'Because Mum's not here to see me, I thought I'd get away with not having to go up and down all those stairs. Five flights. It feels like they go on forever. I don't think I'll ever get used to them. Even our Freddie moans about the climb, and he's as fit as a fiddle. Why Mum had to say yes to a place on the top floor, I'll never know.

'It was ever so good that they offered us somewhere so quickly, though, because the rest centre was really rotten. Not hygienic at all. Mum reckons it was because we've got little Bobby. But none of us has been up this high before. Ever. Our old house was ordinary, with just the one set of stairs – and we only ever went up them when it was time to go to bed.'

She stared down at her cardigan and made another attempt to wipe off the mess. 'And if I'm honest, I get scared down in that courtyard because of all them planes going over. Since we got bombed, they really frighten me.'

'Well, let's start at the beginning. First, I don't think you're lazy, Grace. I know what a terrible state that last mob, the Harrises, left number fifty-five in, and you've had your work cut right out, getting it nice again. It's a shame you never saw it when Nell lived there. Like a little palace she used to keep that place.'

Mary smiled down at ten-year-old Dolly to reassure her, knowing that she must have some terrible memories of those dark days when Flanagan had been around.

'Second, you'll get used to the stairs in no time. And third, those planes are up there in the sky to take care of us – keep the other lot away or, with a bit of luck, shoot them down in some field out in Kent somewhere, before they drop any more of them stray bombs on families like yours.'

Grace looked up at her, still unable to summon a proper smile. 'I suppose.'

'And, last of all, just look at yourself. You're such a pretty girl, and that's nearly a smile. You should try it more often. It makes that face of yours light up.'

'*Light up?*' hissed Ada. 'What is she – a blooming lamp-post?'

Mary put down her shopping bags and took her door key out of her handbag. 'And it's ever so nice having good people back in fifty-five again. It puts a bit of life back in the place. Since the Harrises were evacuated back out to Oxford, it's been strange not having someone living in Nell's old flat.'

'Nell's old flat.' Ada was talking again. 'Now there's a story.' She jabbed her thumb at number 55. 'If you knew the half of what's gone on in that place over the years, you wouldn't be able to sleep of a night. Not a wink. And if you did, you'd have nightmares. 'Cos Flanagan, he was a nightmare in himself, that one.'

Nell shook her head. 'Don't you think the country being at war, and us having to worry that we might be bombed to Kingdom Come, is bad enough, Ada, without you gossiping and making life worse for everyone?'

'Bombed to Kingdom Come? If you're worried that things are going to get so bad, then why don't you evacuate those kids of yours? Plenty of others have been sent away. That Mrs Brown down in the old terrace, she sent all three of hers away to the south coast.'

Mary rolled her eyes. 'Yeah, and what a good idea that was. So many dog fights, they all had to come back home. Families should want to stay together, any decent person knows that.'

Grace blushed but no one noticed, all too busy with their own concerns.

Nell leaned closer to Mary. 'Not if Ada was my mother-in-law, I wouldn't,' she said quietly. 'I'd run like the flipping wind.'

'What's that you're whispering about?' Ada really didn't like missing out on anything, especially if it was supposed to be private.

'I said, Ada, that some of us like to stick together, with the people we love.' Nell turned to her mother-in-law, signalling to her with her eyes – flicking her gaze towards Grace, and then towards the door of number 57. 'Give me the key and I'll go in and put the kettle on, all right, Mary?'

'Good idea, Nell.' Mary looked directly at Ada, her expression impassive. 'I know you've always got so much to be getting on with indoors, Ada, what with you being so house proud and everything, but how about you, Grace? Fancy coming in for a quick cup, do you?

We can explain all about beating mats and how to use that rubbish chute over there – without covering yourself in dust and dirt. It takes some getting used to.'

'I don't know . . .'

'Come on. And fetch your little brother over – Dolly and Vicky can keep him entertained. They love babies.'

'So tell me, how's Kitty getting on at the factory?' Mary pushed a cup of tea across the kitchen table towards Grace, and, without a second thought, the sugar basin. 'It must all be so strange to her. First she moves into the Buildings, and then she has to start work. Six full days as well. I know the Buildings have got all mod cons, and that life's a lot easier for us here than for most people round these parts, but that's still a lot of change for one person to be faced with. Her head must be spinning.'

Grace hesitated for a brief moment, her spoon hovering over her cup, but then she couldn't resist: she helped herself to some sugar from the bowl. 'Mum's not the type to say too much about how she is or isn't, Mrs Lovell, she likes to keep herself to herself, but she always made most of our clothes when we were growing up – still does – and she's a right fast machinist so she can earn plenty, seeing as it's piecework. And at the rate Bobby's growing, and with the amount our Freddie eats, she says the money's going to come in right handy.'

Grace stirred her tea and took a sip. 'Not that there's always that much to spend it on lately. Mum says the shops are getting emptier every day. But I think she's more concerned about what our Freddie's up to.' She put down her cup and added hurriedly: 'What with him working on the railways.' Another sip of tea. 'And now she's even more worried about whether she should evacuate me and Bobby again rather than about having to work herself. Us being bombed and that, well, it makes you nervous.'

Nell frowned. 'Freddie works on the railways, you say? But I thought I heard you tell Ada your mum was worried he'd be called up. That won't happen if he's on the railways. And I'm sure they wouldn't let a little one as young as Bobby be evacuated – not without his mum. I know everyone's in a right two and eight at the minute, but you should tell her to stop worrying herself.'

Grace flashed a look towards Bobby, a serious-faced little boy with blondish-brown hair that hadn't quite decided its final colour yet. He was sitting on the floor next to Nell's youngest daughter, Vicky. They were both transfixed as Vicky's ten-year-old sister Dolly demonstrated her skills in building houses out of playing cards. Vicky, exercising all the restraint of her almost three years, was demonstrating her maturity by preventing Bobby from grabbing the cards and stuffing them in his gummy mouth.

'I only said that about Fred to Mrs Tanner to shut her up,' Grace said quickly. 'And I'm not sure what the evacuation rules are.' She forced a brief smile. 'Mum says everything has to have a piece of paper to back it up nowadays.'

Nell looked really puzzled. 'But the little one couldn't have been much more than a baby when the war broke out.'

'You're right. He was tiny.' Grace looked distracted. 'Far too young to know much about it. But I know I hated every minute of it. Them horrible people down in the country – they covered us in Keating's powder because they thought we were cootie. Know why? Just because we were Londoners, that's why. Cheeky so-and-sos! I wouldn't mind, but they were the ones who were soapy. All that dirt down their nails, and scraggy, greasy hair. They all wore Wellington boots and clothes that looked fit to put on a Guy on Bonfire Night. It was horrible, I hated it there. Every minute of it. I was so glad when nothing was happening in London and Mum fetched us back.

'But then, when we got bombed out last week – even though we never got hurt or anything – she got ever so nervous again. It was just my luck that one of those stray bombs had to hit *our* place in Poplar. What did they want to bomb us for? It doesn't make any sense to me. I'm telling you, that's why she makes us go down to the laundry here of a night.'

Grace stared into her empty cup. 'Do you know what? I hate that basement. It stinks of damp washing, like when I used to come home from school on a wet Monday when I was little. Mum would have all the wet washing draped over the clothes horse, steaming in front of the fire. And the camp beds down there . . . they're so narrow, and ever so uncomfortable; you feel like you're going to fall out every time you turn over. And when Bobby piddles his nappy, it's even worse.'

'Well, we're a lot better off in these good solid buildings with their deep basements than in those little terrace houses down there. You know, where the Browns live that Mrs Tanner was talking about?' Mary nodded towards the kitchen window that overlooked the street, five floors below them. 'And your mum's only doing what she thinks is for the best, Grace, because believe me, mums never stop worrying. We always try to do the best for our kids, darling, no matter how old they are. And even if they don't realise it.'

Mary looked across to the stove where Nell was topping up the teapot with more boiling water, making full use of the tea leaves. 'I see it every day, Nell fretting about her Tommy, Dolly and Vicky. I know she wonders if she's doing the right thing, keeping them up here in London. Like you said, you see those planes up in the sky and you can't help but wonder. But I know why Nell stays here. She wants to make sure we're all together and that she's keeping me company.'

Nell put the teapot down on the table and Mary patted her daughter-in-law's hand. 'She's a good girl to me is Nell, a right good girl. But maybe it'd be different if our Martin wasn't working down the docks, and if my Joe wasn't doing his coal and ambulance-driving jobs. Perhaps then we could all leave London together.'

'Martin? That's your son, isn't it, Mrs Lovell?'

'Yeah, that's right, love, he's my son and Nell's husband.' Mary put down her cup and looked off into some distant place that no one else could see. 'We were all so proud when he took himself off down the Labour Exchange to join up. He would have looked so handsome in a uniform.'

Nell refilled their cups. 'Thing was, when we got married he left the brewery where he used to work, because the wages in the docks were so much better. Gave up a proper office job, didn't he, Mary? Even though he was the first one in the family to have a job like that. But he insisted on going into the docks. Wanted to make sure we all had the best.'

'But what difference does that make?' asked Grace. 'Him being in the docks?'

'It's a reserved occupation, love,' explained Mary. 'Like your dad being in the Merchant Navy, and your brother working on the railways.'

'Right,' said Grace, turning her head away to check on Bobby again. 'Working on the railways.'

'Still, at least it means Martin's here with his family. I can't imagine how worrying it must be for your mum, having to wave your dad off to sea all the time. Shipping's been taking a right pasting lately.'

'No, you're right.' Grace sounded completely preoccupied. She didn't look at Mary as she spoke; instead, she focussed her attention on Vicky, Nell's youngest child. 'She's not very old, is she, your Vicky? Away for long was he, your husband?'

'No, Martin never went anywhere in the end.

Reserved occupation, remember?' Nell was smiling but she was colouring from her chest up into her throat as she pulled her crossover apron more securely around her. 'And our little Vicky's almost three. Born long before the war started.'

'Sorry, Nell, I was just wondering. It's all so strange being in a new place. I get, you know, nervous. I didn't mean any offence.'

'And none taken, Grace. Here, drink your tea before it gets cold.' Nell pushed the refilled cup in front of her, not knowing quite what else to do or say.

Grace soon filled the void. 'You work in the corner shop sometimes, don't you, Mrs Lovell?'

'That's right, love. I do a couple of days and the odd afternoon for Sarah Meckel, the lady who owns it.'

'Her husband's the one who's not right in the head, isn't he?' She looked away then, embarrassed. 'Well, that's what I heard.'

Mary almost choked on her tea, leaving Nell to answer. 'Grace, you should know that Mrs Meckel's husband suffered a lot in the Great War. He was in the trenches and saw some terrible things. He hasn't been the same since. Now, what with everything that's going on, he's started to feel really poorly again.'

'He doesn't go right barmy or anything, does he?'

'No, Grace, he doesn't. Mr Meckel's unwell, that's all, but he'll always be all right while he's got his wife looking out for him, because she's a good, decent and kind woman who wouldn't harm anyone, and who keeps smiling even though things are really hard for her. In fact, that woman's an example to us all.'

Mary took her cue and smiled kindly at Grace. 'Here, you've not got a job, have you, love? Perhaps Mrs Meckel could find you a few hours. What would you say to that?'

Grace turned away again and looked at the children playing on the floor. 'Your Vicky and Dolly don't look very alike, Nell. And your Tommy's got really dark hair, hasn't he?'

'You've noticed a lot in a short time, Grace,' said Nell, widening her eyes at Mary who was dabbing at her lips with a handkerchief, trying her best to compose herself.

Grace looked shamefaced. 'To be truthful, Nell, Mrs Tanner's granddaughter . . . you know, her Bella . . . she mentioned how you were . . .' She paused, weighing up her words. 'You know . . . married to some bloke before you married Martin. I shouldn't have said anything. I'm ever so sorry, I can't help it. When I get nervous, I sort of open my mouth and out it all comes.'

'That's all right,' said Mary, before Nell could

say anything. 'Nell's first husband died. But that was all years ago.'

'And now I'm married to Martin, and I'm very happy,' said Nell with a brisk smile. 'And I bet you're glad you've made friends with Bella. It's always nice to have someone your own age to talk to, especially when you're new to a place. You can go to the flicks and dances and that. You'll have a right good time.'

'You'll have to keep an eye on her, though, sweetheart,' said Mary with a wink. 'A forward girl like Bella will be after a good-looking young chap like your brother Freddie like a rat up a drainpipe. You'll have to warn him about her or he won't stand a chance.'

Grace gulped down the last of her tea. 'Mrs Lovell?'

Mary picked up the girl's empty cup. 'Yes, dear?'

'Bella's got a brother, hasn't she?'

'A brother? Oh, yes, that's right, dear. Alfie his name is. He'll be about . . . what? . . . eighteen now. A couple of years older than your Freddie, I reckon. Something like that.'

Nell grinned. 'Here, are you after finding yourself a young man, Grace?'

The girl's face darkened. 'No. Mum wouldn't like that. She doesn't approve of girls doing that sort of thing. She says we should keep ourselves to ourselves or it leads to all kinds of trouble.'

Nell dropped her grin. 'Well, you know what mums are like. They worry themselves. But if she's a bit strict with you – say, more than usual – it'll be because you're her only daughter. I don't think mums worry quite so much about their boys. They can look after themselves better.'

It was as if Grace hadn't heard her. 'Bella says her brother never comes round to see his nan and granddad like she does, but she didn't say why. Maybe they had a row or something. Something that made him walk out.'

Mary looked at Nell, shook her head almost imperceptibly then smiled pleasantly at Grace. 'I don't really think that's for us to wonder about, do you, dear? Like you were saying earlier, it's always best to keep out of other people's private business. Now, when you're ready, I'll take you out and introduce you to the mysteries of the chute. Who knows? If you do a good job, your mum might not mind you getting yourself a nice young feller one day.'

Grace looked at Mary as if she'd said something completely ridiculous. 'Oh, no, she'd never let me do that, Mrs Lovell. Mum doesn't approve of that sort of thing. Like I said, she thinks it leads to all sorts of problems, and we've all got more than enough of those to be getting on with. And now we're having to live up here.' Grace's eyes began to glisten with tears. 'And I think that Mrs Tanner's a really spiteful old woman.'

'Look, Grace, we all know Ada can be a right sour old girl at times and she can upset people without even trying, but she's not had it so easy herself. Her Albert's a nice enough man, if a bit quiet at times, but she's had a lot of – I'm not sure how to put it – let's say, disappointments with her family, in one way and another. Well, that's how she sees it anyway, and we can't be sure how we'd behave in the same circumstances ourselves, now can we? So we should try and be a bit understanding.'

Grace stared down at the table.

Mary patted the by now weeping girl's hand, very aware of Dolly and Vicky casting curious glances over towards her. 'Here, come on, let's cheer up,' she said comfortingly. 'How about a drop more tea?'

Chapter 2

'Grace seems like a nice type of a girl,' said Nell. She was still sitting at the kitchen table with Vicky on her lap, and Dolly was sitting on the chair next to them, dealing out the playing cards ready for a game of Snap.

Mary was putting the washed cups and saucers back in the glass-doored dresser that ran the width of the far wall. She laughed kind-heartedly as she closed the door and wiped the glass with the tail of her apron. 'Even if she does bunny more than our Tommy having a row with a couple of talking parrots.'

Nell laughed in return. 'I wouldn't have believed anyone could talk more than our Tom till I met that one. She's a proper little chatter-box. I don't know about you, Mary, but I think she was being honest, saying it was down to her nerves or it seemed like that to me. It was like she couldn't have shut up for a single minute, even if she'd wanted to.'

'You're right, Nell. Still, getting bombed out like that by them stray bombs, when hardly anyone else is getting hit, and then having to move to a strange place, it'd be enough to make anyone's nerves bad.'

Mary dragged the potato bag from under the sink and filled a saucepan with water. She then spread a sheet of newspaper on the table, sat down and started peeling the vegetables. 'But it does seem like a strange set up, her staying at home to look after her baby brother while her mum goes out to work. I mean, she's what – fifteen years old? I'd been at work for a good two years by the time I was that age.'

'But she did say how good a machinist her mum is though, Mary. So if that's true, she would be able to earn more on piecework than Grace could, which makes it sensible for them to do it that way round.'

'Perhaps.'

'Or maybe the poor girl's health's not the best? When you look at her, she is a bit peaky. Here, perhaps that's why she finds the stairs such a struggle. '

'If you want the truth, Nell, the answer is – I don't know. Maybe you're right, but whatever her story is, you can be sure that Ada will find out the strength of it, sooner rather than later.'

'And if not she'll make something up. That's what she usually does.'

'She might not have to, not now her granddaughter's got thick with Grace. I agree with what you said – it *is* good for youngsters to have friends their own age. 'Course I do, why wouldn't I? – but she's always been a bit of a sly one, that Bella. And just as nosy as Ada.' Mary let the curl of peel drop onto the newspaper, chopped the potato in half and dropped it into the saucepan. 'Remember what Grace said about Sarah's David?'

'I was a bit shocked by that to be honest, Mary. I mean, it wasn't very nice, was it? *Not right in the head.* Like he was a raving lunatic or something.'

'No, it wasn't nice, but you can guarantee that those ideas didn't come from her. You could practically hear Bella's voice while Grace was mouthing the words. Like a flipping ventriloquist's act from up the Empire. You'd think even the Tanners would stop spouting all their nonsense and be kinder to people, what with all this . . .'

She stopped herself from saying any more, looking at Dolly who was concentrating on dealing the last of the cards, counting them out quietly under her breath, breathing out on each number as she laid it down. 'You know, this . . . lark going on around us.'

'You're right what you say, Mary, of course you are, but I really don't think you need worry about Bella feeding Grace too many daft ideas. It seems to me like she's already got more than enough of her own.'

'I know. That was a bit strange, wasn't it? Whatever was she going on about when she was saying how she was evacuated with her little brother? And then when she said she didn't know anything about reserved occupations – yet her dad's a merchant seaman and her brother's working on the railways.'

'You have to remember, Mary, she might be old enough to work, but, like you said, she's still only a kid who's not long been bombed out of her home. She'll have got a bit mixed up, that's all. It's hard enough for grown ups having to go through that sort of thing, but kids having to suffer it, it's not right.' Nell pressed her lips to Vicky's thick, red-brown curls. 'And now I can't stop worrying myself about what's going to happen to our Tommy.'

'Tommy would never bring any trouble home to you, Nell. You know that. That boy's an angel.'

'I don't mean that, but think about it – he's getting on for fourteen years old, and if this lot doesn't finish soon, it'll be kids of sixteen being called up next. And before we know it, it'll be our little Tom.'

'Mum?' Dolly picked up one of the hands of cards and pushed the other in front of Nell. 'Do you think a bomb's gonna come and drop on us, like it did on Grace's house?' She paused, thinking. 'Did anyone get killed?'

Nell grimaced at Mary. ''Course not, you daft thing, that bomb that hit Grace's house was an accident. You wait and see, all this'll be over in no time. Before Christmas, I shouldn't wonder.' She squeezed her daughter close to her. 'Here, just think, I know it's ever so warm, but Christmas won't be long, will it? I wonder what Father Christmas is going to bring you this year.'

But Nell's attempt at distracting her daughter didn't work.

'I'll be glad when it's over and then we can give our gas masks back. They smell horrible! And I don't want them to make our Tommy have to join the army and go away and leave us.' Dolly's voice grew softer. 'And I don't want to get blown to Kingdom Come.'

Mary reached across the table and touched the cheek of the young girl she had come to think of – and to love as dearly – as her own granddaughter. 'No, of course they won't do any of that, darling. And now Tommy's helping Granddad Joe out on his coal lorry as a van boy, everyone can see what a good worker he is. Soon as he's old enough they'll find him something in the docks, then he won't have to worry about being called up, will he? He'll be able to work with your dad, because he's not like one of those horrible kids who spend all day running wild about the place collecting shrapnel 'cos the schools are closed. Their poor mums never know where those boys are, but we always know what Tommy's up to. Your mum's done a right good job bringing up you three, you should all be very proud of her.'

Nell couldn't look any of them in the eye; instead she pretended to concentrate on organising her cards into a neat pack. 'So you think the docks are safer than the army, do you?'

Mary plastered on a smile for Dolly's benefit. 'Will you stop worrying yourself, you two? Everything's going to be fine. When you think what life could be like, we should be counting our blessings. Like Grace said to Ada earlier, there's enough trouble and heartache for everyone to fret about without us finding more things to get us down.'

She unhooked her handbag from the back of her chair and took out her purse. 'Here, Dolly, why don't you leave that game till later? You know how Granddad Joe loves a game of cards; he'll play with you when he gets home tonight. Go and take Vicky back round to Sarah's and see what you can get for tuppence.'

Immediately distracted by the prospect of yet more goodies – she and Vicky had already had half an apple each when they'd been round to Sarah's earlier for the shopping – Dolly took the cards from Nell's hand and stacked them on top of her own before Mary had a chance to change her mind. 'Thanks, Nanny Mary.'

'Remember what I told you the other day though, kids, she might not have a lot in, but you can still go and see what there is. I know Sarah will find you something. So go on, go to the shop, and I'll be along in a bit, all right?' She looked at the clock. 'My goodness me, will you look at the time. I'm going to be late if I don't get a move on.'

Mary went over to the sink, turned on the tap and started splashing her face.

'Chatting with Grace has made me lose all track,' she said, eyes screwed up against the water. 'Sarah and David have to do all their special things on a Saturday, and if I don't get there soon that dopey girl who helps out of a Saturday afternoon will probably just walk out and leave the shop unlocked when her shift's over. Tell Mrs Meckel I'm having a quick cat's lick and a promise and I'll be round there in no time, because we mustn't let people down, must we, Dolly?'

'Nanny's right, we have to take care of one another, don't we, sweetheart?'

'Yes, Mum.'

'Good girl.' Nell pulled up her daughter's snow white ankle socks and straightened the cuffs. 'And you make sure you hold Vicky's hand all the way. Nanny won't be long.'

As soon as she heard the sound of the girls' footsteps on the stairway, Nell threw up her hands. 'Mary, whatever was I thinking? I shouldn't have said those things in front of the kids, especially Dolly. She takes in everything. Every single word. But I've not been thinking straight, have I? I blame all these planes fighting one another, and those bombs last Wednesday. What if the Germans decided not just to drop the odd bomb but to really start on us, the ordinary people, like they did when Martin was fighting out in Spain?'

'They wouldn't do that again, Nell.' Mary took the towel off the hook under the sink and rubbed her face dry. 'People wouldn't put up with it.'

'I'm not so sure. Look what they're doing over on the Continent, and what they did to our boys at Dunkirk. Everyone's saying they might invade any day. Everyone.'

'Well, I'm not. That's just the scaremongers talking. You want to be like me and ignore that sort of talk. It's defeatist, that's what it is. Unpatriotic.'

'But say they did invade, what would we do

then? Think about it, Mary, they've only got to cross the Channel and they'd be here, right on our doorsteps. What would happen to my babies then, eh? How would I look after them?'

'Nell, you worry too much.' Mary took off her apron, patted her hair into place and then hooked her handbag over her arm. 'Believe me, it *will* all be over in no time. I know you can only just remember the Great War, but they'd never let the likes of that happen again. Never.'

'I wish I could be as certain as you, Mary, but I keep getting this nasty feeling that this is all going to get ever so much worse before it gets better.'

''Course it won't.' Mary put her hand on her daughter-in-law's shoulder. 'I know what you need – you need to go and see Sylvie; she always cheers you up. Go on, go and have an hour or so with her – everything's under control here.'

She looked at the clock again. 'I'll keep the kids with me at the shop – they'll love that, they can help out with little jobs – and you go and have a few laughs. And before you say anything, I'll leave them spuds in cold water for tomorrow and we can treat ourselves to fish and chips from Siddy's tonight. The kids'll love that and all. Go on, pop over to the Hope for an hour or so. It'll do you the world of good. And you can bring back a couple of bottles of pale ale for

47

Joe and Martin. Put a smile on their faces and all.'

'But—'

'I'm not listening, Nell. You go and get your bag and we can walk down the stairs together.'

Nell smiled fondly at her mother-in-law. 'What, so you can make sure I'm going over Sylvie's?'

'You can read me like a book, girl. Just like a flipping book.'

Chapter 3

Freddie Jarrett flicked the butt end of his roll up into a high arc. It flipped over and over and then fell sparking into the gutter, but Freddie didn't notice, all his attention fixed elsewhere. 'What's wrong with you, Li? I rushed over to you from work and you've hardly said a word to me all afternoon. I still don't understand what you're so worried about. It's been six months now. You know no one over here in Bow is going to know or recognise us.' He tried a smile. 'Unless you've got a secret auntie living over this way who's going to trap us?'

Li Mei, her face contorted with the effort of not crying, gripped his hand. 'Don't laugh at me, Freddie,' she said in her throaty cockney accent. 'But I keep seeing things.' She looked around her, as if scared that someone might overhear what she was saying. 'Things in fours. Look, you can see for yourself. There are four boys running along over there. And four pigeons pecking in the road.'

'Seeing things in fours? What're you on about now?'

'Shhh, not so loud.'

'Why not?'

She leaned closer to him. 'Four means bad luck. Really bad luck. It means that bad things are going to happen. So we have to be careful, make sure they don't happen to us.'

'You daft little thing.' He put his arm around her shoulders and pulled her close. 'I don't know, Li, you Chinese and your superstitions.'

'I'm not Chinese. I'm a Londoner, like you.'

'Try telling that to our families.'

'I wish I could, but you know how people are with foreigners, because of the war – any foreigners – I've even seen them spitting at them in the street. And we both know what they say about *Chinese* girls who go with English boys. Our families would stop us as soon as they found out. We both know that.' She pulled a face. 'No, mine would probably kill me.'

'I suppose so.'

'Worse, they might even send me to China.'

That was something that had never occurred to Freddie. 'Not while your grandparents need you, surely?'

'How can I be sure what they'd do? It's all such a mess.'

'Don't say that, Li.'

'And, I keep telling you, I wish you'd call me by my proper name. I've told you, Freddie –

Mei, that's my name. Calling me Li is like me calling you Jarrett.'

'I think Li sounds nice. Sweet. Just like you. And you can call me whatever you like, so long as you're here to call me something.'

He pulled her even closer to him.

'Don't, Freddie. People will see us.'

'Good. Let 'em. Let everyone see us. I'm fed up with all this hole and corner rubbish, hiding away all the time.'

'Freddie, don't! You know we can't.'

As they came to the gates of Victoria Park, in a struggle of hugs and playful slaps, Freddie stopped walking and wrapped both his arms around her. He tried to kiss her but she wouldn't let him.

'Not again, Li. Why not this time?'

'Because.'

'But you smell so lovely, and your skin is all soft. How can it be wrong?' His voice was low, breathy. 'Come on, Li, let's go down by the canal. It's such a beautiful day, and we can be alone there.'

'No, Freddie, you know I can't.'

'Li . . .'

'No. I promised my grandparents I'd be back in time to help them. You know how busy Saturdays are. They think I went out for a walk with Linda, and if her mum decides to come round for noodles for their tea, I'll be found out and then I won't be able to come out again for weeks. Maybe even months if my grandmother has her way. Maybe never again.'

Freddie sighed and let her go. 'I don't know how much longer I can stand it if it's always going to be like this. I don't know if I want to go on like this any more.'

'*Freddie.*'

'No, Li. I thought when your mum and dad went back to China it'd get easier. But if anything, it's got worse. And now we've had to leave Poplar because of that sodding bomb and move right over to Wapping, I'm beginning to wonder why I bother.'

'Don't say that, Freddie, please. Don't! I promise you, I'll get away tomorrow and we can . . .'

'We can what?'

'You know.'

Freddie's mouth went dry. 'You mean, you'll let me?'

Mei nodded. 'If you still want to.'

'If I still want to? Are you messing around with me?'

'No, I'm not. If bad things are going to happen then why should we worry? We might as well be happy while we can.'

'Yeah.' He couldn't think what else to say. He

was only sixteen and seeing girls – in that way – was all new to him, especially girls as beautiful as Li Mei, and now she'd only just gone and said she was going to let him . . . Blimey.

'I have to get back home now, Freddie.'

He could barely speak; it was like Christmas, Easter, hopping in the country, and his birthday had all come at once. He swallowed hard. 'I'll walk you to the bottom of Burdett Road. Then I've got to get off and meet a feller. But tomorrow I'll be there – whenever and wherever you want me.'

They walked along hand-in-hand – pulling apart when someone came along – neither of them saying a word as the bright afternoon sunshine warmed them through to their very bones. But the scarlet colour in Mei's cheeks was nothing to do with the heat of the sun – she had flushed red from her thoughts about what she had promised Freddie Jarrett she would let him do to her the very next day. The thing she had promised herself she would never ever do until the day she was married.

What had she done? Why had she said that to him? She knew why: because today everything was in fours and bombs were falling from the sky and the world was probably coming to an end, that was why.

As he made his way to the park, Alfie Tanner, Bella's older brother, was hot too. But, like Li Mei, it wasn't the sun that was making him feel so warm. Alfie was panicking. He'd come here to see a man he'd met the night before in a pub on the Isle of Dogs. A pub where *people like us*, as the man had put it, went to meet each other. A man who was old enough to be his dad, and who had completely bedazzled young Alfie Tanner.

He swiped his damp forehead with his shirt sleeve. Alfie was going to meet a man who had stroked his cheek and whispered in his ear and made him feel nauseous with a mixture of shame and desire. The man had promised him that it would all be perfect. He'd said he was going to tell his wife that he had to go out on 'a bit of business' and then he and Alfie could spend all of Saturday afternoon together in the park, in a secret place in the shrubberies that he knew. A place where *people like us* could meet. Now all Alfie had to do was walk past this young couple – a Chinese girl and an English boy – who were coming towards him. He felt more like fainting than walking.

The couple looked so happy: him grinning, her blushing. Why couldn't he be like that, carefree, not worrying about who saw that he was in love?

Love?

Who was he kidding? He'd never even done it before, and now he was meeting a man – a married man – and he could go to prison if anyone saw them together. And if anyone actually saw them doing . . .

Doing what?

Was he out of his mind? Was he really going to go ahead with this?

Alfie tried not to look at the young couple as they drew closer, but it was hard not to. He felt so jealous of them. What sort of world was it where ships were being blown out of the oceans, bombs being dropped on houses, and kids being sent away from their families, but where you couldn't spend a bit of time with someone you wanted to be with? It wasn't as if they were going to do it in full view of everyone. Why should anyone care what they were up to anyway? He really didn't know why, he only knew they would.

As he passed the young couple he turned round to give them a final look. Now they were holding hands.

And now he was kissing her.

Lucky bastards. It was probably hard for them – what with her being a foreigner – but at least what they were doing wasn't against the law. Why shouldn't Alfie be allowed to do that too? If he was ever blessed enough to meet someone who didn't think he was some kind of a freak.

Alfie Tanner wasn't the only young man watching as Freddie Jarrett suddenly stopped and took a surprised Li Mei in his arms again – right there in broad daylight, bold as you like, for anyone to see. But unlike Alfie, who was looking at them openly over his shoulder, this young man was watching them in secret. He had ducked into the park without either of them seeing him, and now he was skulking behind the massive gothic drinking fountain, looking for all the world like an overgrown child taking part in a gangly game of hide and seek. Though his intentions were anything but playful.

Like Alfie, he too felt jealous of the couple – so obviously in love and not caring about flaunting the fact – but he found their behaviour disgusting. What was a girl like her doing with an English boy? Did she have no pride? He wouldn't let this go on. He couldn't. He'd put a stop to it – whatever it took. Li Mei must not be allowed to behave like that. She was going to be his. That was the way it should be.

Li Mei, cheeks still pink, walked into the passageway of the little terrace house in

Pennyfields, a street in East London's China-town that was occupied by some English, but mainly Chinese, families. The street door stood wide open, as did the sash window in the front room that overlooked the street. Mei's grand-mother stood there to one side of the window, stirring big pots of food on a gas stove. On the other side of the window her grandfather stood at a scrubbed pine table that was piled high with wooden boxes of vegetables, a big brown china mixing bowl full of noodles, and two tin plates – one holding shredded chicken and the other a heap of tiny, dried pinky-brown shrimps. Mei's grandfather was busy chopping summer greens with a big, oblong-bladed knife, with all the easy skill of a man who had once been a ship's chef for more years than he could now remember.

'Hello, Grandfather, Grandmother.' Li Mei spoke to her grandparents in Cantonese. 'It's such a lovely afternoon. Let us hope a lot of people come for food today.'

Her grandmother smiled, her leathery face wrinkling into the deep lines that time and hard work had inscribed there. 'How could they resist, with my cooking and your sweet ways?'

Grandmother . . .' Mei covered her smile of delight with her hand and then slipped an apron over her head as she went through to the back scullery to wash her hands, wondering if her grandmother really could read her thoughts as she had always claimed she could whenever Mei had been naughty as a child.

She could only hope not.

Mei closed her eyes. But what if she could?

As the clock of nearby St Ann's struck four, the first customer arrived.

The Englishwoman – tightly knotted turban fighting her permed curls – stood outside on the pavement and called through the open window to Li Mei. 'Hello, love. All right, are you? Tell your gran I want some of that special Chow Mein she does, will you? And make it enough for the six of us. And ask her if she's got some of that sauce she does, you know, the hot stuff. My Bert loves it. Here, darling, here's my dish.'

She handed a deep roasting pan through to Li Mei, and a clean tea cloth. 'And a bit of extra chicken wouldn't go amiss if she's got any to spare. I know he's a greedy bugger, but I love having my Bert home for a couple of days and I want to treat him.'

Mei smiled and got on with explaining the order to her grandparents. This was looking good. Their first customer at four o'clock. A nice early start. Li Mei could only hope that it would carry on that way, because then, by the time the church clock struck nine, all the vegetables, chicken and shrimps would have been passed through the window to the customers eager for their regular Saturday night treat, and Li Mei would be scrubbing clean the stove top while her grandparents sat and rested, job done. Her grandfather would be reading the six-week-old Chinese newspaper that someone had brought him from the docks that morning, and her grandmother would be drinking cup after cup of her bitter tea. Mei could only trust that her grandmother wouldn't also be doing any reading of her own kind – mind reading, that is – because Mei had decided that tomorrow really was going to be the day she would let Freddie Jarrett do what he wanted.

She took a deep breath, contemplating her decision. When she went out for her Sunday afternoon stroll with Freddie, her life would be changed forever. And it was all the fault of those bad omens she had seen; they had made her feel she had nothing to lose. She could only pray she had not misread them, and that they were nothing to do with Freddie casting her aside once she had let him . . .

She couldn't even let the words form in her head – not with her grandmother in the same room.

'I said: *I want some noodles.*' Mei jumped as the young man raised his voice. He was standing outside on the pavement, glaring at her through the open window.

'I'm sorry, I was miles away.' She smiled as she realised he was familiar to her. 'I know you. You're Peter, aren't you? You used to live over in Narrow Street.'

'That's me.'

'I remember. Your father came over with mine. But he married a local girl.' She shook her head. 'I haven't seen you for such a long time. How are you? What have you been doing?'

'I've been away, stoking. On the ships.'

'That's hard work.'

He shrugged. 'It was okay, I didn't mind. Got injured though. And now I'm back for a while.'

Mei smiled again, glad to have remembered happy times when her parents had still been in London with her, before they had gone home to take over her father's family business. 'Noodles, you said. For how many?'

'Only for me. Unlike you, I don't have anyone to share them with.'

Mei's smile dissolved. 'How about your parents, Peter? Has something happened to them?'

'Dead. 'Flu. While I was away.'

She bowed her head. 'I didn't know.'

'No reason why you should, they'd moved away over to Plaistow. Thought they were bettering themselves, moving away from here.'

'I'm so sorry.'

'It doesn't matter. Why should it? Their marriage was wrong anyway. They should never have been together.'

'How can you say that? That's what ignorant people say, the kind who know no better.'

It was as if he hadn't heard her. 'I was there earlier but you didn't know, did you? In the park. I was watching the two of you, and I heard him calling you Li. What are you doing with an idiot like him?'

Mei looked over her shoulder at her grandmother. 'Please, keep your voice down.'

Peter frowned, considering for a moment, then thrust his hand through the window and grabbed her by the wrist. 'Why should I keep my voice down? Have you got something to hide? Something you're ashamed of?' He squeezed her arm so hard she wanted to cry out, but knew she couldn't. 'Shall I start speaking in Cantonese, so that they can understand me?'

Mei swallowed hard. 'Let me go, Peter, and I'll get your noodles. I'll get whatever you want. Or shall I call my grandfather to deal with you?'

'That old man? What could he do?'

'Peter, *let me go*.'

Slowly, he released his grip. 'You've got away with it – up until now. But you watch yourself,

Mei, because I'll be watching you and you won't even know it.'

She stared at him, wondering what she had done to deserve this. All she wanted to do was to be with the boy she loved. Was this her punishment for what she had promised Freddie? All those things she had seen in fours – she knew that bad things were going to happen to her.

Freddie Jarrett rapped his knuckles on the door of the Hope and Anchor – a pub on the Whitechapel Road – with all the confidence of a young man with the world at his beck and call.

Bernie Woods, a great bald bear of a man – in size as well as demeanour – seated at his usual table in the far corner of the saloon bar, lifted his head 'Get that, will you, Sylv?'

'Yes, sir,' said his wife, rolling her eyes and snapping him a sarcastic salute. 'Hang on a minute, Nell. I wouldn't mind, but it'll only be for him.' She looked at the clock over the bar. 'We're not opening for a good half-hour yet, so it won't even be them young doctors chancing their arms for an early one.'

Sylvia, standing on tiptoe, reached up and pulled back the bolts at the top and then the bottom of the door. 'Well, give me a bloody coconut, I was right.' The petite redhead hollered surprisingly loudly to her much older, much larger husband, 'Bern, it's for you. Shall I let him in or should I give him the bum's rush?'

'What do you think?' he growled back at her.

'In you come.' Sylvia stepped back to let the caller pass then peered out into the street before bolting the door shut again. 'I don't want any of them doctors from over the road thinking they can slip in before opening time. Right liberty takers they are at the best of times. Right cocky little sods.'

Freddie bowled across the room towards Bernie's table, passing Nell who was sitting up at the counter sipping lemonade. She put her glass down on the polished mahogany bar and frowned. She'd only seen him a couple of times, but it *was* him, wasn't it? Yes. She was sure of it.

'Freddie? Freddie Jarrett? Is that you?'

He froze to the spot. Bloody hell. What were the odds of her being here? He'd come over Whitechapel way looking for work precisely because there was no one round there who knew him, and had fallen on his feet with Bernie Woods, doing his street running for him. He'd only been working here for a few bloody weeks. This was all he needed, her putting her nose in when he was trying to get himself well in with his new boss and show how trustworthy, reliable and discreet a worker he was. That was what Bernie had said he wanted – for any worker of his to be 'discreet'. Freddie couldn't help but wonder how much this woman knew about Bernie's business affairs. He had no choice, he'd just have to brazen it out.

'Sorry, I think you're confusing me with someone else. I don't know you.'

'Yes, you do. It's me, Nell . . . Nell Lovell from the Buildings. You moved in across the landing, into my old flat. Well, the Harrises' old flat. You're Grace's brother, Kitty's boy.'

Sylvia glowered at her husband. 'Well, fancy that, Bern. This young feller-me-lad's a neighbour of our Nelly's. That's nice, don't you think?'

Bernie hauled himself to his feet. 'I think we should go upstairs to the flat, Fred.' He pushed open the door behind the counter. 'We've got a bit of business to discuss if you don't mind, ladies.'

'Don't you go making a mess in my kitchen, Bernie Woods.'

'As if I'd do that, my little sugar plum.' He winked at Freddie. 'And anyway, we're going into the front room.'

Bernie, still puffing from climbing the stairs that led to the flat above the pub, eased himself into an armchair by the window that overlooked Whitechapel Road. Freddie Jarrett, still unsure of his status, remained standing.

'You've been a dependable little grafter these past weeks, Fred,' said Bernie, rubbing his aching thighs. 'I've been pleased with you. Very pleased. But in my line of business I have to be discreet. It's the number one rule in this game, Fred – discretion.'

'Mr Woods, I swear on my life, no one will know what I'm doing. No one. I had no idea that that woman knew you and Mrs Woods.'

'Know her? The girl used to live here with us. She's my Sylv's best mate. Before the war her father-in-law, Joe Lovell, used to work here and all.'

'I promise, no one but the punters will know what I'm doing. No one.'

'So, what story you gonna spin Nell then, to account for what you're up to when you're out collecting the bets for me?'

'I'm running errands and doing odd jobs for you, Mr Woods. What with you losing your regular staff to the forces and that.'

'You're a quick liar, I'll give you that. Can you keep it up?'

'Easy. I swear on my life.'

Bernie looked at the fresh-faced kid, reading in his expression how much he wanted this chance, and knowing he had him exactly where he wanted him.

'Fair enough, Fred, but we'll have to see how it goes. Now, where's this morning's takings? I was expecting you earlier.'

'Sorry, Bernie.'

'Don't let me have to tell you again.'

'You won't.'

Downstairs, Nell and Sylvia were at the bottom of the stairs straining to hear what was going on; they weren't having much luck.

'What do you think they're up to?' whispered Nell.

'I'm not sure, but you can lay money on it that if that old man of mine's involved, it'll be something dodgy. The betting, I wouldn't wonder.'

'His sister said he had a good job, so he'll have money for a bet.'

'You don't think Bernie'd be interested in him if he didn't!'

'Shhh, hold on, Sylv, I can hear them moving around.'

Sylvia and Nell hurried over to the bar and climbed back on to their stools. Nell casually patted her bouncy blonde curls into place and picked up her lemonade.

Sylvia, equally nonchalantly, lit a cigarette.

Bernie came back into the bar followed by Freddie.

Sylvia flashed her teeth. 'Hello, boys, everything all right?'

'Couldn't be better, my little angel. Young Freddie here's agreed to take a permanent position with us. He'll be doing odd jobs about the place and a bit of running around for me. It'll be right handy having him working here.'

Now Nell was puzzled. She was sure that Grace had said her brother had a job on the railways. How was he going to work for Bernie as well? Maybe the girl had got a knock on the head when they'd been bombed out. She certainly carried on as if there was something wrong with her – once she opened that mouth of hers there was no stopping her. Yet she was shy at the same time. A strange kind of a kid.

Bernie clapped Freddie on the shoulder. 'Come down the cellar with me, lad, and I'll show you how to change a barrel.'

Change a barrel? Now it was Freddie who had to do his best to conceal his confusion at this new turn of events. No one had mentioned barrels before, and he didn't much like the sound of it. Bar work was the last thing he wanted. He wanted to be down the Lane collecting bets off the stall holders and their customers. He enjoyed that – they all listened to him and laughed at his jokes as if he was a grown man, like they were beholden to him. And they were, if they wanted a bet.

At the bottom of the cellar steps, Bernie sat down on a crate of empty light ale bottles and winked. 'Just to add to the cover story, Fred. You know how nosy women are. Fancy a fag?'

'Quick, while they're down in the cellar.' Sylvia climbed down off her stool and went behind the bar. She took a key out of the till and opened a locked cupboard under the counter. She took out three packets of cigarettes and handed them across to Nell. 'Here, take these for Mary.'

'Thanks, Sylv. Her and Joe have been eking theirs out; they're so short in all the shops.' Nell raised her eyebrows. 'But obviously not here in the Hope they're not.'

Sylvia winked. 'Don't ask. You know Bernie and his contacts.'

'They'll both be really grateful, thanks.'

Sylvia relocked the cupboard and went back round to the other side of the counter. 'We don't half miss Joe working here. This new boy, this Fred, he seems all right, but how can you trust a stranger when you've got money and spirits around the place? Seems a bit unkind but that's one of the reasons I've taken to locking the cigarettes away.'

'He'll be all right.' Nell sounded more confident than she felt. The Jarretts were turning out to be more than a bit of a mystery.

'Do you know what I'd love, Nell? If it was like it used to be and you came back and lived here, because I don't half miss you. There's plenty of room for you and Martin and the kids.'

Bernie, with Freddie close behind, appeared through the cellar door at that minute. He was waggling his eyebrows. 'I heard that, Sylv, and I agree with you, my little beauty. And you should have said how the boys from over in the hospital miss our little Nelly and all. You used to light this place up like a Roman candle on Bonfire Night.'

'Bernie! I am a married woman.'

'Still a beautiful-looking one though, girl.' He looked up at the clock. 'Coming up to a quarter to five.' He eased his massive frame back round behind the counter and began pulling himself a pint. 'Time to have a little bit of a straightener to get me ready and in the mood for the first customers.'

'While you're there, Bern, turn off that bloody George Formby, will you? I can't stand him and his bleedin' ukulele. Why can't they just have some decent crooners on the wireless for a change?'

'I'm sure I don't know, my little petal.'

'You daft old sod.'

As the wireless clicked off, Nell slipped down from her stool. 'I'd better be on my way.'

'No, don't rush off, Nell.' Sylvia took her hand. 'Stay and have a drop more lemonade. It's sweltering out there.'

Chapter 4

As Mary turned into the street and caught her first glimpse of the corner shop, she stopped dead in her tracks; something was definitely not right. She drew in a long, deep breath, held her hat in place and began running. Sarah Meckel was standing outside on the pavement with a drum of scouring powder in one hand and a wet cloth in the other. Her arms were dangling by her sides and her head was bowed. The woman looked utterly crushed.

'Sarah? Why aren't you upstairs with David? What's going on? Whatever's wrong here?'

Sarah lifted her head; her gaze was directed at Mary, but it was as if she wasn't actually looking at her. 'Don't worry, Dolly and Vicky are in the shop. Florrie's in there with them.'

'I meant, what's wrong with you?'

Sarah let out a shuddering sigh as she flapped the cloth at the shop front. 'They've done it again, Mary. They've written more of their disgusting slogans. All over the windows this time. While that little Saturday girl was standing right there at the counter setting out the cheese and stuff. They couldn't have cared less. But she was so scared she didn't know what to do. There were no customers, no one to help her, so she just stood there, watching them while they did it. She waited for them to finish, then, when they'd gone, she called up the stairs to me and ran off. Didn't even wait for her wages. But I'm not blaming her. Why should she have to put up with such things?'

Mary looked at the remains of the white-washed phrases. 'What's wrong with them, Sarah? Who'd even think such filth, let alone write it?'

'I don't know, and I don't know what else I can do. I've put up signs saying we're not German but Jewish, and our accent is from Russia. And I wrote that other one, saying that we've lived here since before the last war, and that David lost his health fighting for this country. That he's a good, brave man. But still they won't believe me. Still they carry on.'

'Aw, Sarah.' Mary didn't know what else to say. She took her friend in her arms, thinking back to those terrible days when even Joe – Mary's loving, gentle, kind husband – had been swayed by the Blackshirts. They had been dark, dark days for so many reasons.

And now this.

'There was one on the door this morning, first

thing, when I opened up. It said we should be taken into detention, and one of the ones I've just scrubbed off said we should be marched away and shot. *Shot*. Why would they hate us so much?'

'Sweetheart, I am so sorry. I had no idea when me and Nell came in for the shopping earlier. I'd never have gone back home and left you if you'd said something.'

'What was there to say? Why upset you as well? There's Mr Churchill telling us all that this is our finest hour, but he doesn't have to put up with this rubbish, does he? They're treating us as if we're the enemy. If only they'd think about what they're doing, and who they're doing it to, Mary. There's me doing my best to be fair and keep everybody round here fed. And as for my David, if only they'd take the time to ask and to think, they'd realise exactly what that man sacrificed in the trenches for this country.'

Sarah let the cloth and scouring powder fall from her hands on to the pavement. 'This summer has been the worst of my life, Mary. Even worse than when David came home so ill after the last time – at least then I thought he'd get better, that there was hope. But when that raid happened last Wednesday, it was almost more than he could take – the sound of the bombs dropping, the anti-aircraft guns, the flashes and the noises. He was terrified. Shaking. I couldn't console him. I'm really afraid that he'll lose his mind completely if this goes on for much longer.'

'Let's go inside and I'll make you a cup of tea.'

'Let me pull myself together first, and finish scrubbing off this last bit. I don't want the girls seeing me upset. Especially Dolly. I can't help but remember when Mosley's beasts had a go at us and that little girl had to witness her own mother being attacked by them.' She smiled through her tears. 'Do you remember how brave Florrie was that day?'

'How could I ever forget, Sarah? Now, you go inside.' Mary bent down and picked up the cloth and the scouring powder. 'I'll clean this off. You go in and look after yourself.'

'I'll wait out here with you, if you don't mind, Mary.'

''Course I don't. You do whatever you feel's right. Now let's get this muck cleaned off.' She shook her head in distaste as she read the foul words. 'I wouldn't mind, but the little bastards – excuse my French, Sarah – can't even bloody spell properly.'

Mary scrubbed the last of the whitewash off the window and waited until Sarah had blown her nose and wiped her eyes before leading the way into the shop.

'Hello, Florrie,' said Mary, smiling broadly for the sake of the children. 'Did you get yourself something nice, girls?'

Dolly and Vicky were sitting on the two wooden customers' chairs by the counter. They each held a blue-rimmed white enamel cup and there was a plate of biscuits on Dolly's lap.

Florrie, still in her dressing gown despite it being late afternoon, was standing by the girls, leaning against the counter, drinking a cup of tea.

Dolly nodded. 'Auntie Sarah gave us milk and these orange wafers. They're lovely. But she wouldn't take my tuppence.'

'Sarah, you shouldn't.'

'Why not? I had that whole tin of them left out the back. What's the point in saving things when we don't know what's going to happen tomorrow?'

'I suppose so, but what with how tight stuff's getting, you shouldn't be so generous all the time.'

Sarah didn't reply. Instead she began wiping the already immaculately clean counter with a dry cloth from her apron pocket.

'Sarah? Sarah, are you all right, darling?'

Florrie walked over to her and gently stroked

her cheek as she spoke to Mary. 'Will you have a talk with her? Because, I'm telling you, she's worrying me. I've not seen her so down in a long time. Tell you what, I'll make you both a cup of tea, and then I'll get myself upstairs and get ready for work, and you two can have a nice talk about things. You will talk to her, won't you, Mary?'

'Of course I will.'

'Can we have another biscuit, Auntie Sarah?'

'You and Vicky can eat the lot, Dolly.' Sarah took her handkerchief out of the sleeve of her blouse and blew her nose again. 'You girls make sure you enjoy yourselves whenever you have the chance. You remember that. Always.'

Dolly nodded gravely. 'I will, thank you, Auntie Sarah.'

She nudged her little sister, and whispered something to her out of the corner of her mouth.

'Thank you, Auntie Sarah,' said Vicky.

'God willing you'll be safe out there once it gets dark, Florrie. That blackout's a real menace.'

'Don't you worry about me, Sarah. Anyway it won't be dark for hours yet, and that's why you should be upstairs with David.' Florrie was standing there resplendent – in full make up, saucy straw hat tipped over one eye – in the doorway that led up to the rooms above the shop. 'And me, I've got no God to answer to, have I? I mean, why would He bother with the likes of me?'

'Don't say that, Florrie, you're a good woman.'

'Blimey, Sarah, I wish you'd tell that to the local Old Bill. Perhaps then they'd let me get on with my business and stop moving me on all the time.'

Laughing and waving her arms, Florrie leapt at Dolly and Vicky, and tickled them until they squealed with pleasure. 'Me, I can't wait for the sun to go down. And as for the blackout, it's made my job the easiest it's ever been.' Florrie winked at Mary, her heavily mascara-coated lashes touching her thickly powdered and rouged cheeks. 'Plenty of lonely servicemen *and* it means I don't have to see their ugly mugs while I'm doing the business. Winner all round, if you ask me.'

Mary smiled indulgently. 'You're a girl you are, Florrie. See you later, love.'

'Please God,' said Sarah.

Florrie smoothed her skirt down over her hips and straightened her shoulders as if preparing for battle. ''Bye, Mary,' she said, wiggling over to the door. She stopped then and jabbed one thumb over her shoulder towards Sarah. 'And please try and talk some sense into her, will you?

Tell her it's only a few idiots who can't even let her see who they are because they're such a bunch of cowards that they have to wait until that dopey Saturday girl's serving. Maybe persuade her to go away for a bit, so they can both have a rest.'

'Good idea. I'll do my best, love. Now you take care.'

'You can lay money on it.' She waggled her fingers in a little wave. 'TTFN, everyone.'

Sarah looked confused.

Dolly giggled. 'You know, Auntie Sarah – TTFN. Ta-ta for now – it's off the wireless.'

Sarah shrugged and shook her head very slowly. 'No, Dolly, I didn't know, but then most things are a mystery to me these days. I don't seem to understand much at all.'

Dolly and Vicky, having finished their milk and wafers, turned their attention to polishing the glass-topped lids of the biscuit tins that were lined up along the front of the counter. Once they had stored every variety from chocolate wholemeal to fig rolls, but although they now contained little more than plain or broken varieties, Sarah still kept them on display on the principle that in a world that seemed to be spinning off its axis, the less that changed the better. She and Mary took the children's places on the customers' chairs and sipped at cups of tea – their third – which helped fill the gaps when conversation flagged. What could either of them say about this crazy world? Mary had wanted to close the shop, but Sarah had insisted that they had to stay open so they could serve any women coming home from work. It was only right, she had said, in her usual controlled yet kind way.

Her cup drained, Mary couldn't put it off any longer, so she tried another tack. As she spoke, she kept her voice low so the girls couldn't hear what she was saying. 'Now I'm here, Sarah, and all that's cleaned off the windows, why don't you go up to be with David? I can take over.'

'No, thank you, Mary. I'd rather stay down here, if you don't mind. When I put my head around the bedroom door earlier he was getting some sleep at last. I really don't want to disturb him. God will understand why I'm down here. But as for me, like I said, I don't seem to be able to understand anything at all these days. And I don't know if I'll ever understand anything ever again. Why are people so full of hate? The slogans are there every single day now – and they're getting more daring all the time. What contempt for us. What hatred they have festering in their souls.'

'They're only words, Sarah.'

'I know, but it's not only their vile words that are troubling me. It's these continual dog fights going on overhead. The noise of the planes and the guns . . . it's making David more nervous than ever, after everything he went through in the trenches. Mary, I don't think he can put up with it any more. He stays there in bed with the covers pulled up over him, even in this boiling hot weather. He's hiding away in that room like a frightened child, having nightmares and calling out.'

'So how about getting away for a bit, like Florrie suggested?'

'She's been saying that for a while now. And she's right, it would make sense to get him out of London, Mary, or I don't know what will happen to him. That's why it's such a relief when he eventually manages to drop off for an hour or so. Florrie does her best to help, but she needs her own rest after working all night.

'And that's something else that worries me. When I took her in, I never approved of what she did for a living, and I still don't – how could I? But that girl sacrificed her fiancé in the Great War and she deserves our respect for being able to go on at all. Lots of women gave up on life when they were left alone. But before all this started, when she used to go down the docks to do her business, the girls all kept an eye out for one another. Now, with the blackout, they've got no chance. There could be madmen out there. Murderers. I would love to take her away from all this, but I know she wouldn't go.'

'So you've really been thinking about leaving then, Sarah?'

She covered her eyes with her hands and nodded. 'Yes, for a while now. Trouble is, I'll have to leave Florrie here, Mary. She's determined she won't go with us, so I've got no choice, have I? Much as I've grown fond of her, and as much as she's done for me over the years, David has to be my priority. I've got to get him away from all this. Away from the noise and the hatred. I want to be able to make him feel safe again. I owe it to him, Mary, after everything that man's been through.'

She had never heard her friend say so much before. 'Where would you go?' she asked quietly.

Still Sarah covered her eyes. 'David's got a distant cousin, Ruth. She married Stanley, an English boy, and they settled down in Devon. I wrote to her last week and she said we'd be welcome, especially as she lost him, her husband Stan, at sea a few months back.'

'I'm sorry to hear that, Sarah.' Mary paused, thinking about the terrible mess people were making of the world and wondering how it would all end. If it could ever be normal again. 'What will you do about the shop?' she asked eventually.

Sarah dropped her hands from her eyes and looked steadily at her. 'I'm going to ask you a favour. You don't have to say yes, but please let me ask you at least.'

'Of course.'

'Mary, would you run this place for me, until all this is over and I can bring David home? I know it's a lot to ask of you, but I don't know what else to do.'

'Me? Run the shop? I wouldn't know where to begin.'

'Yes, you would, you've worked here long enough. You know how to do things. And any new rules, the Ministry explains it all and sends the paperwork over. You could take on some more help if you needed it. Anything. Please, Mary.'

'I'm ever so flattered you'd even think I could do it, Sarah, but—'

'Mary, listen to me, I wouldn't ask you if I didn't think you could cope, and it's important to me that Florrie's all right. I know you wouldn't make her life a misery. This is that girl's home, it has been for a long time, and I'd hate to think of her having to look for somewhere else to stay. To be honest with you,

Mary, if it wasn't for her I've almost got to the point where I wouldn't really care what happened to this place. But I can't bear the thought of having Florrie upset as well.'

The shop door stood wide open to let in whatever breeze there was, but whoever had just come in made sure they gave the door a good rattle so that the bell above it jangled loudly.

It was Ada Tanner. She stood there, taking in the scene through sharp, darting eyes. 'You two look cosy. Nothing better to do than sitting around drinking tea while them two kids act as your skivvies?'

'Afternoon, Ada,' replied Mary. 'Nothing wrong with enjoying a little chat with a friend, now is there?'

'*Friend?*' Ada spat out the word. 'Most women have more to do with their time than having chats with friends.' She sniffed loudly and waddled into the shop. 'I'd be getting ready for the rush if I was you, not sitting there on my backside, aw, no, not me. That wouldn't be my way at all. You see, me, I'd be thinking about all of them hard-working women doing their bit for the war effort who'll be finishing work soon and will be wanting to get in a bit of something for their families to have for their teas.'

'Finished, have you, Ada?' Mary asked.

Ada glared at her and sniffed.

'Because it's funny, you know, I thought you didn't approve of women working for the war effort,' Mary went on. 'Changed your mind, have you? Come over patriotic all of a sudden? You'll be having your Albert joining the Home Guard at this rate.' She grinned at Sarah. 'I can just picture him in his tin hat, pedalling off as fast as his legs can take him when the warning goes.'

Ada didn't bother to reply. She might have been married to her husband for more than forty years, but she was long past worrying about defending him – except when there was nothing else to moan about. 'And while we're at it, I thought I heard you saying something about that Florrie Talbot as I was coming in the shop. I saw the shameless old tart just now. Walking along with her nose in the air like she owns the flaming street. She'll be on her way down the docks as usual, looking for half-cut sailors who've got past being choosy who they go with. You mark my words, that's what she'll be up to. Pity she doesn't get herself an honest job like all those girls grafting in the factories. Working their fingers to the bone . . . while she just pulls down her drawers for any bloke what comes along.'

'Do you mind, Ada?' said Mary. 'There are children present.'

Ada sniffed disdainfully, and Mary turned to Dolly and Vicky.

'If you two have finished your milk, why don't you get off back to the Buildings and play with the other kids in the courtyard? I won't be long.'

'Thanks, Nan,' said Dolly, and signalled for Vicky to follow her.

'Dolly, you make sure you keep hold of Vicky's hand,' Mary called after them.

Sarah stood up. 'Is there anything I can help you with, Ada? I've had a delivery of pilchards come in if you want a tin?'

'I'll take a couple, and I was after a bit of soap and all. Some of us like to keep ourselves tidy, even if others can't be bothered.' She looked Mary up and down – ignoring the fact that she was as immaculate as ever – assessing her as if pricing her up for market. 'You can stick it on the slate for now.'

Mary blinked slowly, doing her best to control herself. 'You get yourself back to the Buildings, Ada. I'll bring your things with me when I come home later on.'

Ada waited to see if there would be any other reaction. When there was none, she stomped out of the shop. She stood on the pavement outside, wondering if the greengrocer's might prove a more productive source of gossip. No, sod it, she'd go home. She deserved a rest, a woman of her age.

'How on earth does that poor Albert put up with her, Sarah?'

Ada poked her head back in the shop. 'What was that?'

'Nothing, Ada.'

She sniffed suspiciously. 'I suppose there's plenty who'd believe you. Aw, and you can leave them tins and the soap on the doorstep,' she said to Mary. 'I'm going to have a little lie down when I get home and don't want to be disturbed. I only hope them kids aren't making too much noise down in the courtyard.'

Sarah watched in amazement as Ada shuffled off home, then let out a sigh and clapped her hands – just the once – in wonder. 'A couple of tins of pilchards and a bar of soap? She's got some neck, that one. She had a bar of Lifebuoy from me only last week. I know what she's up to, she's hoarding things. Mary, I'm telling you, people never fail to shock me.

'Do you know, a woman turned up here early this morning, before those hooligans came back, and the Saturday girl called me down – for about the tenth time. This woman, she'd pulled up in a taxi, if you don't mind. Beautiful clothes she had, and hair done up like a film star's – she frightened the life out of the little girl; the kid was shaking. Never seen anyone like that in her life. Well, this woman, she asked me what I had to sell her. Held out a wad of pound notes and said she would pay me good money for whatever I could let her have. Anything, she said she'd take. Anything. Bold as brass.

'I said I didn't recognise her and asked what she was doing coming shopping round this way, and – you won't credit this – she said she spends her time going from shop to shop all over London, to see what she can get. Proud of it, she was, like she was doing something clever.'

Sarah pointed at the goods on her shelves. 'That woman – believe me, she was no lady – thought she was entitled to take food out of the mouths of my friends and neighbours, and all because she had money in her purse.'

She tapped the side of her hand against her throat. 'I've had it up to here with people like that, Mary. Right up to here. And that's another reason why I need to get David away, so he isn't affected by the likes of that woman getting me down. I have to try and stay cheerful for his sake, even though I feel like crying my eyes out half the time. So please, Mary, say you'll look after the shop for me. I'll make sure it's all fair and above board, and you can take on whatever staff you think you need – if you can get them, of course.' She paused. 'Please.'

'Sarah, I'd love to help you, but I really don't think I'm up to it.'

'Mary, if not for me, then for David.'

What could she say to that?

Chapter 5

'I was in bed, you know, having a little rest.' Ada's eyes followed the shopping basket as Bella put it down on the kitchen table. 'A woman of my age needs her rest.'

Bella ignored her grandmother's complaints – she knew that there was no point in doing otherwise. 'There you are, Nan, a nice parcel of saveloys, faggots and pease pudding from the market for yours and Granddad's tea. They'll probably be cold by now so you might want to steam them for a bit in a colander, but Mum said I was to tell you that everything was nice and fresh this afternoon.'

'She's all right sending messages for me, pity she don't come round here to see us herself.' Ada took the paper parcel from the basket and sniffed it suspiciously. 'What's she supposed to be up to this time that was so important she couldn't cook something herself, let alone actually come round and see me?'

'She is a bit busy, Nan. You know how it is, she's always got so much to do, looking after us and that.' Bella considered for a moment then added, 'And our Alfie, he had to go out and all. He's a right fidget he is – always on the go. You never know what he's up to.'

She saw the thunderous expression on her grandmother's face. Had she said too much?

'I didn't ask about him, and I don't much care either. He can sort himself out. It was your mother I asked after.' Ada half-filled a saucepan from the kettle, unwrapped the food and put it into a green enamel colander.

'Granddad in, is he?' asked Bella, handing her grandmother a tin plate from the shelf over the sink so she could cover the colander before putting it in the saucepan. 'Having a rest too, is he?'

Ada lit the front ring on the gas stove and set the food to steam. 'No. He's down talking to Jimmy Brown. They'll be going on about their pigeons as usual. The pair of them still haven't got over having to get rid of their racers. Your grandfather don't stop whining on and on about how the bloody government made their decision about who could keep their birds for flaming war work and who couldn't. "Rotten politicians," he says. "Idiots, the lot of them." That's all you hear out of him. And I don't say so to him, of course, but I can't say I blame him. Tell me, what was so wrong with your grandfather's pigeons that he had to get shot of them? That's what I want to know. How could they have done anyone any harm, up there in their loft on the roof? What did they think they were? Nazis in pigeon suits waiting to attack us in our beds, eh? You tell me that.'

Bella, well used to her grandmother's rants, didn't want to encourage her with an answer – however weird the question. 'Shall I go over and give Granddad a call, Nan? Tell him his tea's nearly ready?'

'You might as well do something useful with yourself for once, and you can take this rubbish out with you and all.' Ada flicked a dimpled hand at the greaseproof paper on the table. 'And you can shove it down the chute while you're at it. I don't want it hanging around here, making a mess for me to have to clear up later. I've got more than enough to be getting on without that taking all my time up.'

Bella screwed the wrapping into a tight ball. 'Anything else, Nan?'

She handed Bella an old china cup with no handle. 'You can see if that German's got any mustard pickles for my savs.'

Now she'd really lost Bella. 'What German's that, Nan?'

'Her, round in the corner shop. That Sarah Meckel or whatever fancy foreign name she calls herself.' Ada opened her purse and handed

Bella half a crown. 'And make sure you bring the change back and all. And you'd better make sure you remind her she was going to send me a couple of tins of pilchards and a bar of soap round. I don't trust that woman. She'll have promised them to me – aw, yes – but then she'll go and sell them to whoever offers her more money. And me, an old woman who wouldn't harm a fly – what chance have I got, eh? So remind her – I want them pilchards and I want that soap. And I want them on the slate. I'm not paying good money until I see them with me own eyes.'

'Yes, Nan.'

'And when you go home, you can tell your mother that it wouldn't do her any harm to come round here once in a while. Tell her she seems to have got out of the habit since that son of mine went overseas.'

'Dad couldn't help being sent away, Nan.'

'No, but he should have kept a firmer hand on that mother of yours before he was, and then perhaps she'd behave herself like a proper daughter-in-law should. Taking care of me, that's what she should be doing.'

'Yes, Nan.'

Ada folded her meaty arms across her barrel of a middle. 'Well? What are you standing there for, gawping like you're catching flies? We knew how to wire in when I was a girl. We didn't hang around like a fart at a funeral. So go on, sling your hook, go down and see your grandfather and tell him his tea's ready, and then go and get me my mustard pickles. And don't forget to take that rubbish out with you to the chute either.'

As Bella stepped out on to the landing, she heard Ada call after her, 'And the soap and pilchards, mind.'

Bella was pulling open the rubbish chute just as Grace Jarrett was coming out of number 55 – exactly who Bella had hoped to see when she'd volunteered to come over to Turnbury Buildings for her mum. Grace was holding little Bobby in her arms.

'All right, Grace?' Bella shoved the wrapping paper inside and slammed the chute door shut.

'Yeah, I'm taking Bobby out for a bit of fresh air before Mum gets home for her tea. It's been so warm in the flat he's been grizzling all afternoon and I want to settle him down. Mum gets so tired working all day, she deserves a bit of peace when she gets in.'

'You can walk with me, if you want. I've got to go over the road to Mr Brown's place first to tell Granddad that his tea's nearly ready, but then—'

'Who's Mr Brown?'

'Granddad's pigeon-racing mate. He lives over in the old terrace. And then I've got to go round to the shop for my nan. That'll be a nice walk for the baby. He'll be out like a light before you know it.'

'That's nice of you, Bella, but I won't, thanks all the same. You'd better go ahead if your granddad's tea's nearly ready. I'll be ages walking down the stairs holding the baby.'

'Why? You got a bad leg or something?'

'No, nothing like that. It sounds daft but I get scared I'm going to fall. Especially carrying this little one.' Grace wrinkled her nose in embarrassment. 'I wind up going down slower than a toddler, holding on so tight to them banisters like they were going to start jiggling around and moving like one of those special staircases you hear about.'

'Do you get fed up having to mind him all the time?'

'Not really.'

'Tell you what, I'm used to the stairs, I'll carry your little brother down for you, and then we can have a good old natter on the way.' Bella smiled encouragingly – here was just the opportunity she'd been hoping for. 'And you can tell me all about that *big* brother of yours. He's a right nice-looking feller, your Freddie. Got a girlfriend, has he? I've bumped into him a few times on the landing and the stairs and that, and I keep trying to get a chance to say hello properly to him, but he's always rushing off to work or somewhere. What hours does he do then? Long ones, I know that.'

Grace didn't like the way this was going. Freddie was definitely not on her list of topics for a nice afternoon chat. Since her dad hadn't been around, who knew what Freddie got up to? No good was her guess from the secretive way he'd been behaving lately and the money he seemed to have to spend. Her mum had tried to rein him in, but it was a waste of breath, and now she was working she didn't have the time anyway. It was all she could do to keep things going the way they were, without putting more on her plate.

'I'll tell you what,' Grace said, unlooping a string threaded with keys from around her neck, 'you go down to the sheds, Bella, and get Bobby's pushchair out for me. Leave it there and go over and see your granddad, and by then I'll be down and I'll see you over by the terrace. All right?'

And by then I'll have had the chance to change the subject well away from what my big brother's getting up to.

*

Albert Tanner ruffled Bella's hair. 'Hello, young 'un, what sort of a mood's your nan in this afternoon then?'

Bella turned down her mouth. 'Watch yourself, is all I can say, Granddad.'

'I'd better get me old tin helmet out then. It saved me plenty of times in the last lot.' Albert laughed, taking off the flat cap he was wearing despite the heat. The sleeves of his collarless white shirt were rolled up to his elbows and he had a white scarf tied round his neck. 'And who's this new face coming over to join us?'

'This is Grace Jarrett and her little brother Bobby. You know, they moved in across the landing a few days back. Nan must have told you about them.'

'She probably did, darlin'. Your nan tells me loads of things, but I have to say I don't listen to the half of what she goes on about. If I did, I figure my head'd explode. She rabbits more than that bleed'n Lord Haw Haw.' He leaned forward, still lithe, and chucked Bobby under the chin. 'Hello there, little feller.'

Bobby replied with a grin that apart from two bottom teeth was mostly pink, dribbly gums. He gurgled happily.

'We'd better be off, Granddad.' Bella held up the chipped cup. 'Nan wants some mustard pickle for her saveloys.'

'So, your big brother, Grace – Freddie. You never did say – courting, is he?'

Grace didn't know what to say, but at least Bella wasn't asking about Freddie's job. Who knew what he'd been up to since they didn't have their dad around to control him?

'I'm not sure to be honest, Bella,' she said – not telling a complete lie. 'You know what boys are like. They don't have much to say for themselves. Well, not to their sisters they don't. It's probably different when they're chatting to their mates.'

Bella came over all dreamy, staring at a vision that only she could see, somewhere in the middle distance. 'I reckon he is seeing someone, a good-looking bloke like him. All that dark wavy hair and that lovely clear skin. He'll have plenty of girls after him, will your Freddie.'

They turned the corner back into the street that was dominated by the five floors of Turnbury Buildings. Bobby was now sprawled in his pushchair, dozing contentedly in the warm afternoon sun.

'I love this weather,' said Bella, closing her eyes and lifting her face to the sky. 'Shame Mum didn't want to go down hopping this year. It would have been smashing down there.' She opened her eyes and turned to Grace. 'Do you go?'

'We used to, but we can't, not now Mum's working.' She glanced away so Bella couldn't see her face. 'Everything's different now, for all of us.'

'Let's have a go at pushing that.' Bella handed Grace the mustard pickle that Mary Lovell had ladled into the cracked cup from the big earthenware jar that stood at one end of the shop counter, and the single tin of pilchards she had assured them was all she had for Ada, and took a firm grip of the pushchair.

'I've decided I'm going to have loads of kids when I get married,' said Bella, enjoying herself steering the baby along in his pushchair. 'Five at least. No, make that six, that'd be better. Three girls and three boys. That'd be nice that would. A good even number, so there'd be no jealousy.'

'Six? Why would you want so many?'

'So I won't have to go out to work, of course. It'd kill me if I had to work as hard as your mum. Mind you, mine's only got me and Alfie at home and she doesn't seem to be showing any sign of finding a job. Too busy spending time with her next-door.'

'Who?'

'Our neighbour. Mum's always in there. Or off out somewhere. It's like they're a pair of kids again since my dad and next-door's husband's been away.'

'Don't you mind?'

The corners of Bella's mouth drooped as she thought about it. 'Why should I, if she can get away with it? I know she seems happier now than when he was around. I miss him, mind, and I know Nan does. He was the only one who could ever make her laugh.'

Bella bumped the pushchair clumsily down the kerb, making Grace flinch, but Bobby slept on.

'Wonder your mum doesn't go out more, Grace. She must find it ever so hard with you three to look after, working all day then having to start all over again when she gets home. If I was her, I'd be down the pub or out at the pictures.'

Grace said nothing.

'How about you? Do you miss your dad while he's away at sea?'

Grace stopped walking and the cupful of mustard pickles dropped from her hand to the pavement. The yellow liquid and the glistening green and white vegetables spread across the pavement around her feet, like the blood and entrails of a big squashed bug.

'What the hell are you doing?' screeched Bella. 'I only asked you if you missed your flipping dad. Now Nan's gonna kill me stone dead when I tell her you've dropped her pickles. It's bad enough we could only get her the one tin of flaming fish and no bloody soap, now she'll really go potty. I can't believe you just did that. Have you gone mad?'

Still Grace said nothing; she just pointed up at the sky.

'*Bloody hell*,' yelled Bella then, even louder, '*Run, Grace, run!*'

Chapter 6

The workroom in a sidestreet off Brick Lane was a big, high-ceilinged, noisy space, with one whole wall made almost entirely of glass so that it let in plenty of light. There were two rows of industrial sewing machines running down the centre of the room that, when they were all being used together, made it almost impossible for anyone not used to the volume to hear what even the person sitting next to them was saying. And because the machinists – all female – were paid at piecework rates, the machines ran continuously. Even a brief pause meant money was lost. After a while the workers became accustomed to the racket and learned how to pitch their voices just so. Eventually they learned a primitive form of lip reading to communicate with their colleagues.

Yet despite their keenness to earn as much as possible, it was still a relief when the shriek of the buzzer signalled that they should stop for their afternoon tea break. It was late today because there had been an urgent order of battle jackets to put through and the factory manager had insisted that they finish that first. He was playing not only on the promise that they would all be taking home nice fat pay packets if they did the extra work but also on their patriotism, conjuring up visions of the needs of 'our boys' stuck out at the front, desperate for supplies. He wasn't sure which argument had worked best, but they'd all got stuck in, and now the order was complete. They were all more than ready for their break.

The machinists flicked switches off within seconds of one another, leaving only the faintest humming sound coming from the cooling machinery that seemed to vibrate in the hot still air.

There was much stretching of arms above heads and murmurs of 'Thank Gawd for that' throughout the room.

'Come on, girl,' said Joyce, the woman sitting next to Kitty Jarrett. 'Let's go and get ourselves a cuppa. Don't know about you, but I could bloody do with one. The fluff off that cloth's got right down my throat and now my chest feels like it's been sandpapered.'

'Just right for undercoating and a nice gloss finish then,' laughed one of the other women.

After queuing at the glass-fronted counter – the days of the tea trolley had long gone since the workers here were now given their midday meal and even their breakfast if they came in for the early shift – everyone took their cup of tea and slice of cake and found a seat at one of the long refectory tables.

Kitty eased herself along the bench seat and was soon joined by Joyce.

'They might work us like horses, Kit, but do you know, I love it here.' She picked up her cake and examined it as if it was a precious jewel. 'I've always liked having a bit of something sugary, and now they're cutting back on it in the shops, this is a real treat.' She took a bite of the iced sponge, being careful not to lose a single crumb. 'When I sit down to my dinner in here, I thank goodness, Kit – every single day – that they're looking after us workers, knowing I'm going to have my pudding and a drop of custard afterwards.'

'Yeah, we're all doing well for now, but for how much longer?' said a woman sitting across the table from Joyce. 'I've heard that they're gonna put a stop to all this extra grub for works canteens.'

'No,' said Joyce. 'Whoever told you that, they're having you on. We're too important to upset, we are. We're the War Effort, girl.' With that she opened her mouth wide and shoved in the rest of her cake.

Kitty wasn't used to the commotion and banter of the factory yet – particularly the racket in the canteen where all the women seemed to feel free to speak about things she had been brought up to think of as unmentionable – so she sat there quietly, sipping her tea and nibbling at her slice of cake. It seemed such a waste, her eating it. She didn't feel all that hungry and she knew young Bobby would love it. Especially the icing; she could just picture him licking it off the top of the sponge and getting it all round his little mouth.

She lowered her head – she was sure no one was looking at her, because they were all too busy gossiping and stuffing their faces – and carefully slipped the cake into her clean hankie which she popped into her handbag.

'Oi! I saw that, beautiful.'

Kitty froze. Someone had seen her. And, worst of all, it was Harry, the factory floor supervisor. He was a tall balding bloke in his fifties who, since the majority of the more eligible men had been called up, had decided that meant he had been catapulted into the role of Casanova – there to lap up the goodies of his very own, very eager harem. He was deceiving himself, of course, but was more than happy in his self-delusion.

He leaned further forward, not even

bothering to conceal the fact that he was staring at Kitty's shapely figure.

'Taking it home for the old man, are you?' He blinked slowly and smacked his lips lasciviously. 'I know how you girls like to look after us men with a bit of something sweet.'

'I'm sorry, I didn't know I wasn't allowed.' Kitty's voice came out as a hoarse whisper. 'I'll put it back.'

'Good job I'm around to keep an eye on my girls, eh?' Harry stood up and took a bow while the other machinists cat-called and whistled at him. Then he walked towards Kitty, still sitting next to Joyce, and squeezed himself in between them on the bench.

'You take it home with you, darling. Take another slice, if you like. Go on, go back to the counter and help yourself. Say I said so.' He leaned in closer to her, but didn't lower his voice. 'Take it as one of the perks of working with Handsome Harry.'

The backchat and taunts rose in a crescendo of ribaldry.

Kitty, despite her dark brown hair, had skin so pale it was almost translucent. It signalled her emotions as clearly as a set of semaphore flags; she was now blushing the colour of a beetroot.

'Don't take any notice of that lot.' Harry nudged her and winked. 'You'll soon get used to them. They're always jealous of the young pretty ones who work here.'

Kitty dropped her chin. It was a long time since someone had called her pretty; she was still quite young, she agreed with that, even though she sometimes felt as ancient as that old girl Ada Tanner who lived across the landing in the Buildings. But pretty?

'Oi, you, lover boy,' shouted one of the women. 'You do know our little Kitty's a married woman, don't you? You don't want to go upsetting her or you'll have her old man round here after you.'

'She never is,' said Harry with mock surprise. 'She can't be married. She can't be no more than sixteen, seventeen, tops.'

'I've got a sixteen-year-old son at home,' Kitty said quietly – thinking back, as she so often did, to how different things had been when Freddie had been born.

'Well, I wish you'd give my old woman some lessons, Kit, 'cos you're looking bloody good on it, darling.' Harry sighed theatrically and put up his hands in surrender. 'But if it's true, and you have got an old man, then as sad as it makes me, I must step away. Husband in the forces, is he? Or is he in a reserved occupation, still at home, all nice and cosy with the little lady?'

Kitty said nothing, just studied her lap.

'Must have been horrible, being bombed out,' a heavily made up woman with an elaborately tied turban called across to Kitty. *'Especially with your old man away.'* She emphasised her point, looking slyly at Harry. 'And dirty old men like you must be in their element, with all us girls at a loose end. All with itches that ain't being scratched.'

Harry clasped his hands over his heart and lifted his chin in the air, the picture of a romantic lover. 'You don't understand, it's knowing that I'm coming in to see my lovely girls that makes it worthwhile me getting up of a morning.' Then he broke into a grin and rubbed his thighs. 'No, I can't tell a lie, it's better than that. It's knowing I'm going to get the odd flash of leg what makes my life worth living. Come over here and give us a smacker. Show me how much you love me.'

'Cheeky sod.' The woman patted her turban and looked Harry up and down. 'Anyway, you couldn't afford me. Money I'm earning here, and no old man indoors to feed – the bleed'n army can do that – I've got plenty in my purse, and it's made me a bit more fussy over who I spend my time with these days.'

One of the other women slurped the last of her tea, stood up and leaned against the wall. She lit a cigarette, raised her head and blew a column of smoke straight up into the air. 'This machining might be all very well for some, but my sister-in-law's started doing engineering work. She's making, I dunno, bits of tanks or something. What I do know is she had to pay one pound two and six for the training course over in South London, but now she's done that, she's earning a bloody fortune and there are some right good-looking fellers in her factory and all. Great big hunks of men, she said they are, solid muscle every one of them.' The woman folded her arms around herself. 'Can't you just imagine, all that rippling flesh sweating in this hot weather?'

She poked out her tongue at Harry. 'Not like the specimens we have to put up with in here. Plus they don't have to do Saturday afternoons.' She wagged her finger at him. 'And I've heard that that scent factory over in Stratford has been turned into a munitions place. Munitions is good money and all, you know. I wouldn't mind having a go at that. I'm not sure what it involves, but I've always been good with my hands.' She winked saucily at Harry. 'My old man can vouch for it, and I reckon they'd appreciate that sort of a skill in a munitions factory, don't you?'

Harry, not impressed that he might have rivals for the affections of *his girls*, puffed out his chest. 'I don't know what you're moaning about, Beryl, you can earn plenty here if you put in the effort. And while we're at it, there's a lot of women being made to do full-day Sunday shifts so you can't complain about having to do the odd Saturday afternoon now and again.'

'I don't mind doing the extra hours,' said Joyce, the woman who'd been sitting next to Kitty. 'In fact, I look forward to it 'cos it gets me away from that lot indoors. Honestly, why I didn't leave them evacuated down in Sussex, I do not know. I only wish they'd sort out the schools once and for all; this messing about is driving me mad. At least if they'd be definite about when and where they had to go, I'd know where the little buggers were at least half of the time. They're as good as running wild, my boys. They really need to get back into a routine or, at this rate, I won't be surprised if I have the coppers on my doorstep, telling me they've been nicked.'

Harry didn't take any notice of Joyce's concerns about her children. He was more concerned about losing 'his girls' to the lure of the munitions factories. It was getting more and more difficult to get good workers, what with all the new opportunities springing up all over the place, and even harder to get them to stay. He wouldn't have cared less, but the trouble was, the number of machinists he had in the workforce affected his bonuses: they worked hard, he got paid well; they slacked, and he got bugger all extra in his pay packet.

'I reckon you lot should count your blessings for working here,' he said, all his bravado now giving way to petulance.

Beryl, the woman who'd said she fancied her chances in engineering, burst out laughing. 'Will you look at the face on him?' She blew Harry a noisy kiss. 'I wouldn't leave you, Harry. And if I was being truthful, I'd have to tell you, I've never been flaming happier than I am now. As a matter of fact, I'd say that—'

'Shhh!' The woman opposite Kitty jumped to her feet and gestured to everyone to keep quiet.

They kept on talking.

'Listen,' the woman urged them. 'What's that noise?'

As one, the women – and Harry – rose to their feet and scrambled off the benches. They stood for a moment, listening in total silence, and then they rushed out of the canteen and back into the workroom to look through the big plate-glass window.

What the hell was going on out there?

Chapter 7

Joe Lovell slowed the lorry to a halt a few feet before they reached the exit from the dock. 'Do you reckon that little feller needs a drop of water before we head off back to the coal yard, Tom? It's flaming hot out there today. More like July than September.'

Tommy picked up his brown and white terrier from where he was sitting between his feet. He touched his nose to the dog's snout. 'What do you think, Bradman? Fancy a drink, do you, mate?'

He held the dog up in front of him. The Jack Russell's pink tongue and his stub of a tail both wagged, but not in his usual good-tempered appreciation of any attention from his young master – the dog was clearly disturbed, distracted by something only he was aware of.

'Yes, please, Granddad, if we've got time. He's panting like anything, and he's been acting all funny for the past half-hour. I hope he's not ill. He's never even sneezed before and I wouldn't know what to do if he got poorly.'

Tommy buried his face in the little dog's fur.

'You feeling all right, are you, Bradman? Too hot for you, is it, boy? Is that what's wrong?'

'Don't upset yourself, Tom. You're right, it'll be the heat getting to him, that's all. It's making me feel funny, and how he must feel with all that fur on him . . .' Joe stuck out his tongue and panted in a fair imitation of the dog. 'I'd be doing that and all. So come on, let's give him that drink, shall we? I mean, we can't see the little feller suffering.'

Joe pulled on the handbrake and jumped down out of the cab. Bradman jumped out after him. Tommy passed Joe a crazed china saucer and a beer bottle with a stone screwtop from the footwell then leaped down to join them on the cobbles.

Bradman was just finishing his second helping of water from the beer bottle when someone shouted over to them.

'Nearly done for the day, have you, Dad? Off soon, are you?' It was Martin, Nell's husband and Joe and Mary Lovell's son.

Tommy sprinted over to him with Bradman running at his heels, even more frantic than usual to keep up with him. 'Hello, Dad.'

Martin still glowed with pleasure every time Tommy called him that – Tommy and Dolly might not have been his natural children but he loved them every bit as much as he loved Vicky, his own daughter. The two older kids had been through so much when they were younger, he was only glad that he could give them a decent life at last. A life that had absolutely nothing to do with the animal who'd fathered them, Stephen Flanagan – him or his disgusting twins. He'd reached the point these days when he rarely even thought about how Stephen had 'drowned' or about what had happened to those two older kids of his. Good riddance was Martin's attitude. He had nothing to be ashamed of; he'd done the right thing back then and nothing would ever persuade him otherwise.

Martin pushed the mop of thick, straight dark hair off Tommy's forehead – so different from his sister Dolly's and his mum's blonde curls – and pinched his cheek.

'Hello, son. You and Granddad getting off home now, are you?'

Joe joined them, shaking his head. 'No, Mart, me and Tom thought we'd do one more load before we creep off for the night. With all these ships, the coal stores run out in no time.'

Martin nodded approvingly. 'You're a right pair of grafters, you two. Makes me really proud to be able to say you're my family.'

Tommy bent down and patted his dog. 'Bradman works hard as well, Dad. He guards that lorry with his life. Even though he's feeling a bit funny today.' He turned to Joe. 'But that's the heat, isn't it, Granddad? And we all still have to do our bit, don't we? It's what keeps us free.'

'Exactly right, Tommy. Good boy.'

'Good for the both of you.' Martin grinned at Tommy. 'No, good for the three of you.' He took the watch from his waistcoat pocket. 'Let's see, what is it now? Coming up to twenty to five . . . I'll see you all later then. I'll be home about seven, I reckon. I don't think there'll be another cargo tonight.'

'All right, son.' Joe turned back towards the coal lorry. 'I'll let Nell know if we get home first.'

Martin walked off, waving cheerily without looking back at them. 'Thanks, Dad,' he called. 'See you.'

As Joe steered the truck out through the dock gate he spotted Florrie Talbot standing outside on the pavement. Joe waved in acknowledgement to the bored-looking policeman on duty at the gate and received a brief, not very interested, nod from the officer in reply. The man was clearly far more interested in hiding the cigarette he was smoking than in dock security, which suited Florrie just fine as he very pointedly failed to move her on or even show that he had noticed her.

Joe was far more open – he couldn't help but

stare at her. Florrie's thick make up looked so strange in the bright sunshine, as did her perky little black straw hat with its clutch of bright red cherries that bobbed about over her left ear. The fewer your clothes and the less stuff on your face the better in weather like this, was Joe's opinion. The newspapers that very morning had said that the temperature had soared right up into the nineties, and they had even printed photographs of people lounging around in deckchairs on the beach. It was as if the whole idea of the country being at war was some kind of a bad joke or maybe a mistake – like this scorching weather. How could it be almost autumn?

Joe slowed down to a halt. 'All right, Flo?'

'Let's see.' Florrie looked thoughtful and put a finger to her chin. 'If it wasn't so bloody hot. If I had a couple of grand stuffed in the teapot I keep on the mantelpiece instead of a couple of bob. And if I was a few years younger . . .' She nodded. 'Yeah, then I reckon I'd be just about all right. How about you, Joe? How are you going, mate? You're working so many hours these days, I hardly see you.'

He laughed and gave her a thumb's up. 'I'm doing all right, my love. No complaints from me at all.'

'I saw Mary earlier, in the shop. She was there

with the girls. What lovely kids they are. And so pretty, just like their mum.'

'They're that all right, Flo.'

'You and Mary must be right proud of your granddaughters.'

''Course we are. And of our grandson.' He grinned at Tommy who was doing his best to keep an increasingly frenzied Bradman under some sort of control, but wasn't managing to do a very good job of it.

'We'll have to love you and leave you, Flo, this little dog's getting himself in a right old tizz. Now you be careful, right, girl?'

'I'm never anything else, darling.' She blew Tommy a kiss. 'See you later, boys. And take care of that dog of yours. Stick him under the cold tap when you get in.'

Joe pulled away with another wave and a friendly smile as a weather-beaten man in his forties, sporting a wiry ginger beard, sauntered out through the dock gate behind the truck.

'Florrie Talbot,' he roared. 'Well, if you're not the best sight for sore eyes I could ever have wished for. Here I am, a man who's been away at sea with nothing but a crew of hairy-arsed, smelly-footed seamen for company, and look at you, my best girl. No, I tell a lie, my *very* best girl. But I don't suppose you'd have any ideas for a cure for what ails me, would you, my little darling? After all those weeks away, my legs are proper wobbly and between you and me, I could do with a touch of something or other to put me back on the straight and narrow.'

Florrie looked him up and down, slowly batting her eyelashes. 'Do you know what, gorgeous, I know exactly what you need to get your land legs back – if that really is all that ails you. Because you do know what a particular type of girl I am, don't you, Charlie? I know you sailors, and I definitely do not want to go catching no dose of – you know what off you.'

'Florrie, I've not been within a hundred yards of another woman since you waved me goodbye from this very river. How could I? You're the love of my life, and you have been these last . . . let's see, how many years must it be now?'

'Oi, hold on. I don't want none of that love stuff.' Florrie stopped him talking, raising her hand to his face and trying to blot out the memories of another one that she could usually keep in its secret place at the back of her mind, the face of the man she had loved and lost – the hero who had gone to war but had never returned. The face of the only man she had ever truly loved.

She pulled herself together. Charlie was her first customer of the day, after all. 'And as for counting the years – I can do without that and all.'

'I wouldn't dream of saying how many years, Flo, because I might be a crusty old sailor but I am still a gentleman.'

'Gentleman? You're a lying old seadog, that's what you are, Chas, but I forgive you. How could I not when you've still got that twinkle in your eye? Now, where's that parrot you promised me?'

Charlie threw up his hands in mock distress. 'And there was me looking everywhere for a monkey to fetch home for you. Good job I never found one, eh? That would have been a right disappointment, wouldn't it? They can't even talk, you know.'

Florrie wagged her finger at him. 'You are such a rotten liar, Charlie.'

'Don't tell me off, Flo. You know how much I love you, girl.'

'Here we go again.' She put her hands on her hips, staring unashamedly at his groin and considering for a moment. 'You love me, do you?'

'You know I do. With all my heart.'

'Like I said, you are a rotten, lying old hound, but come on, I can see you're in a bit of a hurry, and I reckon I've got a little treat in store for you.' She linked her arm through his. 'And I just know you'll want to show me your full appreciation.'

'I always appreciate you, Florrie. You're like a strong knot in a bad storm.'

She raised her eyebrows. 'Glad to hear it, Charlie. There's not a girl alive who wouldn't want to be told she's like a knot! Now, walk back through the gate, all nice and calm, and don't let that dock copper, the great six-foot streak of tripe, see us.' She snuggled in to him and whispered: 'If we slip back in there, there's a cosy little place I found that no one's been using.'

'How come?' Charlie looked dubious. 'It's not falling down or been bombed or anything, has it?'

'No, it's as safe as houses. It's only empty because it's not had the windows bricked up yet.'

Florrie, with her finger to her lips and holding on tightly to her seaman as if he might float away on the next tide, dodged silently through the gate and past the police officer. She needn't have worried about being so cautious, he was far more interested in lighting yet another cigarette than in the security of what he was supposed to be guarding. Getting a supply of tobacco was obviously not a problem – for him, at least.

*

With Charlie the sailor boy now hardly able to contain himself – it had been a very long and lonely voyage – they made their way towards the squat, brick-built dock office that Florrie was pointing out with a silent lift of her chin.

She looked over her shoulder, checking that no one was spying on them, and turned the door knob, grimacing as it squeaked like a frightened mouse.

'In we go, sweetheart,' she said, her voice barely audible. 'And be careful you don't trip over anything, I left the blackout blinds down last time I was in here.'

'Florrie, what are you telling me, girl? Don't break my heart, because there was me, thinking I was the only man in your life.'

'Get in there, you silly great bugger.'

'You silver-tongued little beauty, you, come here!'

He grabbed Florrie around the waist, knocking her hat clean off her head.

'Granddad?'

'Yes, Tom.'

'Bradman ain't half acting funny still.'

The little terrier was whining and scrabbling at the floor of the lorry's cab as if trying to burrow his way out through the footwell.

'I know we've only just got going, but can we

stop again for a minute? He must feel really bad. Look at him. He's not right. I've never seen him acting like this.'

''Course we can stop.'

Tommy opened the door and climbed down, expecting Bradman to follow him, but instead the dog squeezed his way under the seat and started whimpering as if something was terrifying him.

Tommy was now almost in tears. 'What do you think's wrong with him, Granddad? Has he gone barmy or something? They said in the papers we should have dogs put down when the war started, didn't they? But why should he start doing this now? What do you think, Granddad? Will he be all right?'

'I honestly don't know what's up with him, Tom.'

Tommy felt sick – his granddad usually knew everything, so if he didn't know what was wrong with Bradman then who would?

The vet, that's who. They'd take him to the vet.

'I know, Granddad, we'll take him to the—'

The last of Tommy's words were lost as a siren started wailing, driving the little dog even closer to hysteria.

Tommy looked over his shoulder in the direction of the alarm.

He gasped, for a moment unable to speak, then he found his voice. 'Granddad, look.' Tommy was pointing up at the sky. 'That's what must have got him all overexcited.'

Joe reached across the cab to try and grab him. 'Get in the lorry, Tom. *Now. Move!*'

Tommy scrambled back inside, slicing his kneecap on the step. He had just closed the cab door when the first blast struck. All he felt was a whoosh of air and a sickening lurch in his stomach as the lorry jolted forward, and the darkness engulfed him.

Chapter 8

Florrie lifted the corner of the blackout curtain.

'Sod me.'

The wide, beautifully clear blue sky was pierced by planes, dots of silver glistening in the bright afternoon sun. She watched, not saying a word as the dots grew bigger and bigger, with smaller dots following on behind them.

The sailor was looking over her shoulder. 'There's hundreds of the buggers. Hundreds of them.'

The droning planes flew towards the docks – V-shaped formations of bombers escorted by what looked like double their number of fighters.

As the first V reached its target, the bombers peeled off into a line and then formed a circle, dropping their deadly loads one after another.

'Shit!' The impact of the first explosions made the abandoned dock office shudder, throwing Florrie backwards and knocking the sailor clean off his feet.

'Is it safe in here, d'you reckon?' Her elbow hurt and she knew without feeling them that she'd torn her stockings. *Bugger*. They were new as well.

'We'll soon find out,' said the sailor, hauling himself to his feet.

Florrie was back at the window, scared but fascinated by the relentless surge of yet more V formations coming in to replace the ones that had already discharged their bombs. 'Look at them! Just bloody look at them, will you? Evil bastards.'

'I think you'd be better off getting away from that window, don't you, Flo? It's not been taped up and that glass could hurt you.'

'Bastards,' was all Florrie could come up with by way of a reply.

'Bastards,' agreed the sailor, but she couldn't hear him over the noise of the building as it came crashing down around them.

Joe touched his forehead; there was no blood but he had a lump the size of a hen's egg where he'd smacked forward into the windshield. He tried to keep his breathing shallow to stop the pain in his ribs as he turned to see to Tommy.

The boy was slumped sideways, oblivious of Bradman yelping frantically at his feet.

'Jesus! Are you okay, Tom?' Joe stretched across to sit him upright, but before he could reach him, the passenger door was yanked open. It was Martin.

'Tom? Tommy? Is he all right, Dad?' Martin touched Tommy gently on the side of his face. 'Come on, Tom, wake up, son. Please.'

'I think he's only stunned.'

'*Blimey O'Reilly*.' Martin ducked as yet another volley of explosives fell from the sky. 'We'll have to get him somewhere safer than this.'

'How about over in one of the warehouses?'

'No, there's stuff in there that's gonna go up like fire crackers if this carries on. Can't you smell all the burning?'

Joe stuck his head out of the lorry window and took a deep, slow breath. 'That's gas, and . . .' he sniffed again '. . . burnt sugar, and, aw, I don't know – stuff. Burning paint or something.' He started coughing, his eyes watering.

'Let's get this window wound up,' he said, squinting down at the ground, puzzled by what looked like small balls of flame flashing past the front wheel of the truck. Then he recoiled. 'Aw, sod me.'

'What is it, Dad?'

'It's the rats – they're pouring out of the buildings and they're only on fire.'

'We've got to get Tommy away from here, but

we'll never make it to the shelter with this lot going on all around us.' Martin looked frantically about him.

'I know, Dad, help me get him over to the ARP post by the gates. That'll be safest. That place has more sand round it than Brighton Beach.'

Another blast. Joe ducked. 'Brighton's not got any sand.'

'No, and we've got no choice, Dad. Just hurry up, will you? I'll carry Tom and you get the dog.'

Martin scooped Tommy up in his arms, sending Bradman into an even wilder frenzy. 'Stick your jacket over him, will you? Calm him down.'

Martin looked up at the sky; they were still coming: unrelenting, pitiless – and terrifying.

'Now!'

Martin and Joe started running, dodging and weaving as molten metal and bits of brick and wood splintered around them. More fires were starting to take hold, despite the efforts of the fire crews who were desperately hosing down the warehouse walls. Getting across the few yards between the truck and the dock seemed to take longer than negotiating the entire running track that wound around Victoria Park.

Tommy's eyes flickered open. 'Dad? What's happening?'

'Thank God you're all right,' said Martin and Joe in unison as if they'd been rehearsing.

'What do you think you're up to? You can't come in here.' The warden in the dock's ARP post grabbed protectively at the door that Martin had just kicked open. He could only use one hand as he was holding a cup of tea in the other. 'There's rules, you know.'

'Rules? Do us a favour, mate, my boy's hurt and the whole bloody place is going up out here.'

'Well, you can't bring that dog in.'

'Oh, no?' Joe shoved past the man, put Bradman, who was now almost out of control with panic, on the floor and dragged the comfortable-looking armchair as far from the door as he could. 'Put Tommy on there, son. Then I'll drive back to the Buildings to check on Mary, Nell and the girls.'

Martin looked up at the sky through the doorway and then pulled the door firmly shut. 'I don't think you'll be driving anywhere for a while yet, Dad.'

'But I've got to—'

'They'll be all right; they'll either have gone down to the cellar in the shop or they'll be in the laundry.'

'I feel so helpless.'

'Look, there's plenty to do here.' Martin glared at the warden, who still had the cup of tea in his hand. 'For all of us.'

'Dad, I can help.' Tommy was sitting up, rubbing his head. 'I can take messages for people; let everyone know what's going on, and who's needed where – like them boy scouts do that they showed us at the flicks.'

The warden drained his tea cup and made a loud smacking noise with his lips. Then he wiped his mouth with the back of his hand.

'Is that all you're gonna do? Stand there enjoying your tea? This kid's more willing and brave than you'll ever be,' sneered Joe. 'You're a good boy, Tom, but you need to recover first. You took quite a wallop on the head. You can run messages next time, eh?'

'Granddad's right. You stay here till you feel better, Tom, and we'll go and see what's got to be done outside.'

Martin opened the door again. The heat almost blasted him off his feet.

'Jesus Christ!'

'They'll be no blaspheming in my post,' said the warden indignantly, trying to recover the moral high ground.

'Fuck off,' said Joe.

*

Grace and Bella sat on a camp bed down in the basement laundry of Turnbury Buildings, with Bobby's pushchair parked between them.

'I've never heard anything like this.' Grace's eyes were wide with fear. 'Not even when we got bombed out. Listen to it, it's just not stopping.'

The laundry, despite being underground and part of a solid, brick-built structure, shook as if it were made of nothing more than matchwood.

'Say we hadn't made it back over here before they started dropping the bombs?'

'Don't.' Grace clutched hold of the pushchair handle. 'And I don't know how he's still asleep.'

'Wish I was,' said Bella. 'And I bet Granddad wishes my nan was and all.'

Ada and Albert were across the other side of the laundry, sitting on the kitchen chairs that Albert had been instructed to fetch from upstairs. Bella couldn't hear what her grandmother was saying but she took an educated guess that she was blaming her husband for the bombs.

'I'm glad they're both down here though. Because then I know they're all right. I only hope my mum is as well.'

Another massive explosion made Grace screw up her eyes, and grip the pushchair even tighter. *Please don't let anything happen to my family*, she said to herself over and over again.

'And that Alfie's all right as well, of course. Not that Nan'd care if he wasn't.'

Grace opened her eyes. 'What?'

'Alfie. My brother.' Bella cupped her hand over Grace's ear and whispered to her. 'Nan doesn't like him because he's a nancy boy.'

Grace pulled away. 'How do you mean?'

Another loud crash, but Grace only half noticed it.

'You know – a pansy.'

'Aw, right.' Grace didn't sound very sure of herself. 'So, he's a pansy, is he?'

'If you ask me I'd say he is, and it'd explain a lot of things about him. But he's hardly going to tell anyone outright, now is he? I mean, who wants to go to prison just because they like to . . . you know.'

'No, I don't really.'

'You don't know much about anything at all, do you, Grace?'

Grace, inheritor of her mother's pale colouring, blushed scarlet. 'Mum says it's best that way, that it keeps you safe when you don't know too much. It helps keep you out of trouble.'

Bella nudged her and laughed, all bravado against the bombs whistling and thumping down around them. 'Hark at you – Little Miss Innocent.'

A flutter of plaster, almost pretty, like a dry snowfall, fell from the ceiling.

Bella grabbed Grace. *'Bloody hell.'*

Grace didn't react to the crumbling ceiling; all she could concentrate on were the words spoken deliberately loudly by a woman sitting over next to Ada.

'You know what I don't understand,' the woman was saying, 'is how people keep having more and more little ones when they know there's a war on.' She gestured towards Grace with her knitting. 'You'd think a woman of her mother's age would know better, wouldn't you? It was different in my day; we knew how to keep ourselves to ourselves.' The woman was sitting in a deckchair that she'd set up next to Ada's kitchen chair, calmly carrying on with her knitting as if nothing was happening.

'Is that why you had nine kids then, Lil?' asked Ada, always ready for a row. Even if she was the only one in the room she'd find something to moan about.

'There wasn't a war on when I had mine.'

Bella rolled her eyes. 'Hark at that old cow. Listening to this lot drives me mad at times, Grace. You know, I never thought I'd say it but I'll be glad if they tell me I've got to be one of these mobile women. Funny though, I've never even thought of myself as a woman before, let alone a mobile one. I'm only bloody sixteen. But never mind, at least it'll mean I can get away from all their complaining and going on about stuff all the time. And it'll be a laugh. Here, I tell you what'd be really good – if we got sent somewhere together. That'd be great, wouldn't it? Wouldn't do any harm to ask, would it? I'll bet there's plenty of places that need more than one person.'

Bella was getting into the swing of her daydream now. 'Here, where do you think they'd send us? Somewhere safe, I hope. Maybe to a nice farm with lots of big strong men and little fluffy animals – I'd cuddle the lot of them. I'd love that. Can you imagine? We could have a right old time together.'

'I won't be going anywhere,' said Grace quietly.

'Why? You got secret war work, have you, Grace? You a spy or something?

'Not exactly.' She reached out to Bobby and stroked the sleeping child's head. 'But with Mum at the factory, I've got to stay here to help her.'

Lil, seemingly having either forgiven or forgotten Ada's criticism about the size of her family, worked at retrieving a dropped stitch in the complicated looking garment she was working on. 'I was due over in Forest Gate a good hour ago. I'd lay money that that posh tart I do for over there is going off her head. Saturday night and no help? She'll be raving. I'm telling you, she doesn't know how to do a hand's turn, that one. All of them, they'll all be wondering where their tea is. But, trust me, they won't be worried we're having seven bells bombed out of us over here. Not them selfish bleeders. All they care about is themselves.'

A loud crash had her turning up the volume, but didn't distract her from her knitting – or her bad-tempered rant. 'Not that she'd ever ask, but I bet she thinks I've got a *treasure* of my own to do all the flaming housework for me and my lot, all my cleaning and making all our meals and that. 'Cos that's what she calls me – *her treasure* – the silly condescending tart. She'll be in for a shock all right if I go and get myself a job in the munitions factory. That'll teach her. See how she manages then.'

'You? In a munitions factory?' Ada sounded appalled at such a notion. 'You're too bloody old for that kind of work.'

'Am I? You wait and see. They'll start drafting more and more youngsters into the forces and that, and then they'll have no choice will they? They'll have to take on older ones to do war work, even old girls as worn out as you, Ada.'

Such a thought had never occurred to Ada

before. War work? At her age? Surely not. She blinked, for once genuinely lost for words.

It was the sailor rather than Florrie who screamed.

'Here, do us a favour,' she said, sprawled out on her back across the rough concrete floor of the abandoned dock office. 'It's bad enough having bloody bombs chucked at us – I don't want to go deaf and all.'

'Sorry, Flo, I was a bit taken aback.'

'Never mind, Charlie, just calm yourself down. Now, are all your bits moving all right?'

'Far as I can tell. How about you?'

'Let's see.' Florrie took a deep breath and sat upright. She brushed a thick layer of brick dust off her dress, and felt around for her cherry-adorned hat. 'I've lost me titfer, but I don't think anything's broken.'

The sailor scrabbled forward on his knees, feeling his way in the pitch darkness. He took Florrie in his arms and planted a kiss on the side of her head, missing her lips completely. 'I tell you what, Flo, if we survive this, girl, I'm going to marry you.'

'You've been saying that every time you've landed here for years, you lying old goat.'

'Help. Help us.' A voice came from somewhere close by. 'Please.'

Florrie squinted into the dark. 'Who the hell's that?'

'It's me, Florrie, Maudie Waites.' Another massive crash brought down another shower of bricks. 'I was in here with a feller, and he don't seem to be breathing right.'

'It's no good, we're going to have to get down to that cellar.' Mary waited for one of the pauses in the awful racket that was going on outside the shop and crawled out from under the counter. 'Come on kids, Sarah, hurry! Right now.'

Dolly, hanging on to little Vicky's hand, followed Mary without a word. She wasn't one to argue at the best times but now she was rendered speechless by fear.

'You take the girls down, Mary. I've got to go up to David.'

'But—'

The terrible noises overhead started again.

'Go on, take them.'

'That's it, down we go.' Mary found matches in her apron pocket, lit the gas lamp at the top of the stairs that served the shop's cellar, and led the way down.

At the bottom, she lit another lamp. Usually the girls would have been thrilled to have been allowed to go down into the Aladdin's cave of a store room, with its ceiling-to-floor shelves stacked with interesting-looking cans and packets, but today even the bright wrappers couldn't distract them from the madness of what was going on up above.

Mary settled them down on cardboard cartons: Dolly on one full of Smedley's tinned peas and Vicky on one of Camp coffee.

'Right, what shall we sing?'

Before Vicky could yell 'Teddy Bears' Picnic' – as she invariably did when a sing-song was suggested – a series of rapid explosions, barely muffled by the stock-lined cellar walls, had the girls screaming and clinging to one another as if they were on a life raft that was about to sink.

'All right, don't worry, Nanny Mary's here.'

Mary picked up Vicky and took her place on the box, then pulled both girls to her, folding them in her arms. Somehow she had to get Sarah and David down to the cellar. But how?

Kitty, blood trickling down her cheek from the glass that had rained down out of the huge window-frame into the workroom – despite the lattice of sticking tape that the ARP warden had insisted would save them from such accidents – stood staring out of the yawning gap in the direction of Wapping.

'The whole place is on fire,' she said, her voice flat with despair.

'That's where you live, isn't it, Kit?' said Joyce, who was sitting on the floor picking bits of glass out of the sleeve of her overall.

Before Kitty could answer, Harry had her by the hand. 'Get away from there, Kitty, and get yourself down on the floor. It's not safe.'

Joyce looked put out. 'What makes her so special?'

'Shut up, Joyce, the girl's husband's away.'

'So's mine,' muttered a plain-looking woman huddled next to Joyce, 'but I don't see Harry fussing over me. Her with all her blushes. Truth is, she's a flirt. You take my word for it – it's always the quiet ones. She's no better than a trollop, you mark my words.'

Mei crouched with her grandparents under the table in the front room. Her grandmother's eyes were closed as she muttered some incantation Mei couldn't have understood even if she had been paying attention. All she could wonder was whether this was some sort of punishment for what she had promised Freddie. If it was, then it wasn't fair – her grandparents hadn't done anything wrong, so why should they be made to suffer? Perhaps that was part of her punishment, that she had to see them going through this. Why had she ever given such a promise to Freddie?

In the cellar of the Hope, Sylvia was clinging on to both of Nell's arms. She might have been almost a foot shorter than her friend, but she could be very determined.

'No, Nell, I'm telling you, I am not going to let you out of here. Not until this is over. You know Mary will be looking after the kids, so what's the point of you going out there and getting yourself killed, leaving them without a mother?'

'I think it's time we cracked open a bottle,' said Bernie. 'Me and you'll go up and get some glasses and a bottle of Scotch, eh, Fred?'

Sylvia screwed up her face in wonder. 'Bernie, are you insane?'

'Don't worry, Sylv, we'll be one minute. And that noise isn't that close by anyway. It sounds like it's over by the docks to me.'

Nell burst into loud, agonised tears.

'Well done, genius,' hissed Sylvia.

'Sorry, Nell. I didn't mean to upset you. Tell you what, though, I'll bet them planes'll be moving over this way soon.'

Sylvia threw up her hands. 'For Christ's sake, Bernie, go upstairs and get whatever it is you want . . . and then do us all a favour, will you? Start thinking before you open that big fat gob of yours.'

*

Upstairs in the bar, Freddie was getting nervous. Bernie seemed in no hurry to get the glasses, acting as if he couldn't even hear the commotion that was going on outside.

Bernie pulled a glass of beer, and held it out to Freddie. 'Fancy one?'

'No, you're all right, Bern.' He wasn't about to stand there supping a pint. 'Shall I get the glasses?'

Bernie took a leisurely mouthful of his drink, and then wiped the froth from his mouth with his handkerchief. 'You've been doing well collecting the bets, Fred.' Another painfully slow mouthful. 'How do you fancy a bit more responsibility?'

Freddie looked over towards the door. How strong was that thing? Would it hold up against a direct hit, or even a heavy blast?

'Well?'

'Well, what? Sorry, I didn't hear what you said.'

'Do you fancy a bit more responsibility?'

'I don't know. I suppose so. What sort of responsibility?'

'It'd involve driving – and before you say anything, I'll teach you in no time. Nothing to it.'

'But there's no petrol.'

'There is for deliveries, son.'

'What sort of deliveries?'

Bernie winked. 'Let's just say deliveries of things that have become a bit hard to come by. But that's for us to know.'

'I'm not sure.' Things were moving faster than Freddie could keep up with. He hadn't meant to get himself quite so involved in all this. The gambling was one thing – he could melt into the crowds around Wentworth Street the moment he had any hint of police attention. But since he'd been working for Bernie, he'd heard so many rumours about him that he felt he should be slightly more cautious than he'd been at the beginning. 'It's not something I feel I could jump into.'

''Course not. You take your time and think about it. But remember, some people might knock the blackmarket, but me, I see it differently. I see it as providing a service – getting hold of stuff that people need, stuff they'd have to go without if I wasn't getting hold of it for them. Stuff that cheers them up during these hard times.'

'Bernie!' Sylvia's disembodied voice screeched up from the cellar. 'Will you get down here?'

He turned to Freddie and rolled his eyes. 'Women, eh, Fred?'

Freddie wasn't sure how to respond.

Bernie didn't seem to notice. He finished his

pint and took a bottle of Scotch from the shelf behind the bar. 'Well, what are you standing there for? Grab some glasses and shift yourself. There's bombs going off out there, you know.'

Chapter 9

The loud, steady wail of the all clear had the dock's ARP warden sighing with relief. 'Thank goodness for that.' He looked at his watch. 'Would you believe it? Going on six o'clock. A full hour and a quarter they've been bashing us.' Gingerly, he opened the door. *'Bloody hell, will you look out there?'*

Joe looked over the man's shoulder. 'Hell's the right word for it.'

Thick smoke and flames billowed and roared from almost every building; the fire crews on land and on the river were aiming their hoses in all directions, desperately trying to get some sort of control over the madness that surrounded them. The heat was so intense that even the paint on the fire boats had started blistering. It was almost unbearable.

There was no other way to describe the scene but hellish – the dock itself was on fire, and, so it seemed, were all the others along both sides of the Thames, and there were casualties everywhere.

The three hundred and forty-eight German

bombers with their escort of six hundred and seventeen fighters had done the deadly job they had come to do.

Martin slipped between Joe and the warden. 'Dad, if your lorry's all right, get our Tommy away from this, will you? He doesn't look well.'

Tommy, hearing his name, but still groggy from his head injury, tried pulling himself up from the armchair. 'How do you think West Ham are doing, Dad? I bet that kid from the ground floor that they'd muller Tottenham today.'

'Don't you worry yourself about that, Tom, you just rest yourself. You took a right wallop.'

Tommy cocked his head groggily. 'What's all that noise out there? What's happening?'

Joe bent down next to him. 'I don't want you to be scared, Tom, but there's been some bombers flying over and they've started a lot of fires out there in the dock.'

The boy rose precariously to his feet, rubbing his head. 'Aw, yeah, I remember. But you don't have to worry about me, Granddad. I told you, I can be like a boy scout. I'll borrow the warden's bike and take messages round to everyone.'

'You're a good lad, Tom.' Joe patted him on the shoulder. 'But I don't think so, not this time.'

Martin turned to the warden. 'That pitcher of water, pass it over here.'

'Why? And say I need a cup of tea to calm my nerves?'

'I said, give it here. And you better had – if you know what's good for you.'

Grudgingly, the warden handed him the big enamel jug that held his water supply.

'Stand still, Tom,' said Martin, 'I'm going to pour this over you.'

'What?'

'You'll be glad I did, believe me.'

The cellar of the Hope was too deep for them to hear the all clear, but it soon became obvious, when the building stopped juddering, that the onslaught had finished.

Nell stood up. 'That's it, I'm off. I've got to make sure everyone back home's all right.' She slung her handbag on her arm and swigged back the last of her whisky – it wasn't something she'd ever even tasted before and it stung her throat and her eyes, but she thought she'd better prepare herself for what she was about to see when she went upstairs and out on to the street.

'Hold up, Nell.' Sylvia beat her to the bottom step. 'I'll get my jacket and come with you.'

'Are you girls sure about this? Why don't you give it another half-hour, just to make sure?'

'I can read you like a flipping book, Bernie Woods. You're thinking that you'll have to open up by yourself if I go off with Nell. And you're worrying how busy we're going to be, because the customers'll be queuing up at the door after all this palaver.'

'As if that even occurred to me, my precious little jewel. I'm worried about you going outside, that's all. Give it an hour, make sure it's safe.' But Bernie should have saved his breath.

'Don't be so stupid. Nelly's got to get back to the kids and make sure everyone's all right, and I am not letting her go alone.'

Freddie made sure that he too drained his glass. Like Nell he'd never tasted whisky before either so he was hardly going to miss the opportunity – nor was he going to miss the chance to impress his boss, after he'd had a proper chance to think about what was meant by taking on more responsibility. And, if he was honest, he was worried about his mum and Grace and little Bobby – he had to see for himself that they were all right. 'If it's okay with you, Bernie, I'll go with them. I can make sure they're safe, and check on my mum and that.'

Sylvia did her best to hide her grin. 'Aw, ain't that nice, Bern, young Freddie here wanting to be all gallant and escort us girls and check on his family?'

Bernie frowned. He had no chance of winning

this one. If Sylv was leaving with Nell then he wanted Fred to stay and help him, but now Sylv had gone all soppy. And what the hell was Fred up to anyway? The lad hadn't struck him as the sort who would worry about others. People could still surprise Bernie, even after everything he'd seen in his life. He'd just have to make the best of a bad situation and earn a few extra points from Sylvie. 'Good lad, Fred. Thanks. You make sure you look after my girls, and I hope your family's all well.'

Li Mei, her muscles aching, crawled painfully out from under the table. She felt as if she'd been shut away in a drawer for the past hour.

'Grandfather, Grandmother, I have to go out. I need to see if Linda is safe.'

Her grandmother whispered to Mei's grandfather in low, forbidding tones about the cruelties of the Japanese during the last war.

'You are right,' he said, 'she must stay here with us until we are sure it is not dangerous for her. There could be soldiers out there.'

'But, Grandfather, what soldiers?' All Mei wanted to do was to find Freddie, to see him with her own eyes, to reassure herself that nothing was wrong, that nothing had hurt him, that bad things weren't being sent to punish them because of what she had promised him he could do. And what if he *had* been hurt? What would she do then?

She couldn't stand even to think about it, knowing that it would be her fault for promising him that forbidden thing. She should have taken notice of the omens and obeyed them.

'You heard the planes, Mei, and the bombs dropping. Now you do as you are told.'

'Please?'

'No, Mei. You will stay here with us.'

'But the all clear . . .'

'No. I will hear no more from you. Now make your grandmother some tea – you can see how upset she is.'

Slowly, the man rolled off Alfie who was lying face down in the bottom of one of the trench shelters that had been dug on ARP orders in Victoria Park.

'I'd been looking forward to getting close to you, Alf,' he said, leaning awkwardly to one side so that he could fish the packet of Players out of his jacket pocket, 'but this is ridiculous. Cigarette?'

'How can you be so calm?' Alfie was still shaking, his nerve endings vibrating as fiercely as the ground had been only a few moments earlier.

'Why not be calm? What happens, happens. We can't stop it. So what's the point in fretting about what we can't change?'

'I'm not fretting, it's—' Alfie couldn't hold himself together any longer. He buried his face in his hands and wept, not really sure what he was most scared of – the bombs or his feelings for this man.

'Go on, Dad, hurry up and get that thing moving. Get Tommy safe and make sure all our girls are OK.'

Joe nodded stiffly. 'Are you sure you won't come with us, son?'

'I can't. There's too much to do here.'

'Look after yourself then.'

Martin ducked and covered his head with his arms as another shower of bricks fell from the buckled side of one of the warehouses. 'Get going.'

'Be careful, Dad,' shouted Tommy as Joe pulled away as fast as he could.

Joe gripped the steering wheel as the truck bucked and reared like a nervous pony as he negotiated the potholes and debris littering the roads, while Tommy clutched Bradman to his soaking wet chest, whispering and shushing to reassure the little dog. The smoke was so thick that Joe had to put on his headlights – it was like the middle of the night.

'We'll go to the shop first, Tom, because that's on our way back, and that's where I reckon your nan's gonna be, and the girls.'

'How about Mum?'

'Don't you worry about your mum. She'll be safe and sound down in the laundry, having Ada Tanner driving her barmy.'

Joe could have cheered as – at last – they rounded the corner and saw that the shop was still standing. The smoke wasn't so thick here and they'd already been able to see Turnbury Buildings in the distance, rising high above the surrounding houses, and knew that they hadn't been damaged.

He parked by what had been the kerb, but was now a mess of crushed paving stones.

'Tom, I want you to listen to me. Don't be afraid, but I want you and Bradman to stay here while I go in and see what's what. Promise me you'll do as I ask?'

'Can't I come with you? Say you need help . . .'

Joe shook his head. 'Not this time, Tom. You just do as I say. That was a proper crack you got on that noggin of yours.'

*

It was a long time since Joe had been anywhere near a church – Martin's christening, if he remembered right, or maybe someone's wedding – but as he kicked open the shop door he was murmuring a prayer with all the fervour of a devout worshipper.

'Mary?'

There was no one there.

Apart from the now broken door hinges, the shop looked exactly as it did when Sarah and Mary locked up of a night. All tidy and no lights on. But there was no sign of Mary.

He felt like an intruder as he went over to the door behind the counter and called up the stairs to the flat, 'Sarah? Are you up there? Are you all right, girl?'

'Is that you, Joe? It's me, Mary.'

'Yes, love, it's me. Where are you?'

'We're down here in the cellar.'

She was alive. Thank God for that.

'Stay where you are, I'm coming down. Is anyone hurt?'

'Just come down, Joe. Now.'

He could tell that something was wrong. 'What's going on, Mary?' The gaslight was still on, and Joe was only halfway down the steps when he could see for himself what it was. Mary was cuddling Dolly and Vicky to her, and the girls were staring – wide-eyed and tearful – at an almost frenzied David who was being restrained by a desperate-looking Sarah.

'Mary, take Dolly and Vicky upstairs. Tommy's out in the truck. He's had a bit of knock on the head, but he's okay. And I'll help Sarah and David back up to the flat.' He conjured up a smile. 'That suit everyone?'

Martin, sleeves rolled up, shirt sticking to his back with sweat, climbed over the rubble with a pickaxe in his hand. The heat from the blazing warehouses was too fierce for him to get close so he was working around the perimeter, seeing what he could do to help the rescue and demolition squads. Even away from the main fires, it was still almost unbearable.

'Sorry, fellers, I'm gonna have to take a quick break.'

'About time and all, the way you've been grafting,' called one of the senior firemen. 'And the rest of you, you're all going to have to take turns having a few minutes' break or you'll be no use to anyone.'

Martin puffed out his cheeks and dragged himself behind one of the high surrounding walls, where there was what looked to be a small lean-to office block. Most of its roof had caved in, but he could still lean against the front wall. He sniffed for any hint of leaking gas – none that he could detect – and lit himself a cigarette. Wearily, he let his head drop back against the rough brick. Even at this distance from the fires the wall felt warm to the touch.

He flicked his match on to the ground and drew a deep drag of smoke down into his lungs.

What was that?

He turned and pressed his ear against the wall.

There it was again.

Someone was calling for help, and he recognised the voice.

'Florrie? Florrie, is that you?'

'Martin?'

He looked at the state of the roof. Shit! She must have gone in there with that bloke she'd been with. 'Yeah, it's me, Florrie. Don't worry, I'll get help. We'll have you out of there in no time. But don't make any more loud noises or you'll have that lot coming down on top of you.'

'Be as quick as you can, Martin. My mate Maudie's in here and all, and her friend . . . he don't seem too well.'

Mary sat in the cab next to Joe, while Tommy, Dolly, Vicky and Bradman rode in the back of the truck on the mound of empty coal sacks.

'Thanks for helping Sarah get David back upstairs, Joe.'

'Poor sod.'

'I know. He terrified the girls, but Gawd alone knows what that poor man saw during the last lot. No matter what Sarah said or did, it was like he was somewhere else once the bombing started. Somewhere so horrible you couldn't begin to imagine it.'

'Doesn't even bear thinking about, Mary. Brave man like him reduced to a jabbering mess . . . shocking, that's what it is, really . . . Flipping heck!'

'Hold on kids,' Joe called over his shoulder. He pulled hard on the handbrake and stared through the windshield.

Part of the old terrace opposite Turnbury Buildings had taken a direct hit. Over half the houses had been damaged in some way, and people were busy collecting whatever they could of their belongings, but the one on the end – the one that had been the home of the Jennings family – had taken the worst of it. It looked like a doll's house with its front opened up for everyone to peep inside. Yet all the furniture in the bedrooms was still standing neatly in place as if nothing had happened. A mirror over the downstairs fireplace was still intact and a clock was left standing on the mantelpiece. But the curtains were flapping through what once had been the windows, and the wallpaper looked as if someone had torn it neatly from the walls using a knife and ruler to measure it into equal strips. The rest of the ground floor was nothing more than a heap of rubble.

Joe scratched his head. It didn't make sense, but then nothing made any sense today.

Rescue squad workers were carefully picking their way through the bricks and timbers, putting any reusable materials to one side for repairing and shoring up what was left of the terrace.

Mrs Jennings was standing staring at the ruins of her home. She was holding a bird cage with what looked like a little bundle of yellow feathers lying on its sandy floor, and she had a baby's pushchair by her side, but there was no sign of her husband or her three children.

Mary was the first to speak. 'This doesn't look good, Joe. I'll get the kids indoors.'

He took a deep breath. 'I'll stay down here and see what I can do to help.' He lowered his voice. 'And have a good look at young Tom's head, won't you, love?'

Mary nodded and, without a word, Dolly, Vicky and Tommy – carrying a still trembling Bradman – followed her through the archway that led into the front courtyard of the Buildings.

She stopped, looked over her shoulder at the terrace and swiped her eyes with the back of her hand. 'Take care, Joe.'

Following the instructions of the warden in charge, Joe set to work helping the other men dig through what had once been the Jennings' scullery.

His shovel hit something that made a metallic, hollow sound. He cleared away the loose bits of brick and saw a freestanding kitchen unit – a green and cream Maidsaver – that had fallen on its side. He had found a piece of timber and was levering it out of the debris, not caring about the splintered wood that was working its way into his palms, when he saw the first sign of what he'd been dreading – a child's shoe, the little buckle still neatly fastened.

'Over here,' he called, barely able to get the words out.

It took less than ten minutes for the rescue squad to find the Jennings' three children.

'I'll get something to cover them with until the ambulance arrives,' said Joe. 'I've got a tarpaulin in the back of the truck.'

As he climbed on to the back of the coal lorry, he heard the scream. Mrs Jennings had dropped the birdcage and was on her knees weeping over her dead children, wiping the dried blood from their lifeless little faces.

Gently, Joe put his hand on the woman's shoulder. 'Come on, girl, stand up. You'll hurt yourself kneeling on all them bricks.'

She looked up at him with an agonised expression on her face. 'Why did I bring them back here, Joe?'

He didn't know how to reply. 'Is Frank at work? I'll go and get him for you.'

She crumpled into a heap – a burst balloon with all the air let out – not caring, or maybe not even knowing, that she had cut her face on a shard of broken glass from one of the windows. 'He was there, in the scullery with the kids . . . he was getting their shoes on for them so we could all go over to shelter down in the laundry.'

Joe knelt down beside her and held her, letting her cry.

'Anyone got any cups we can use?' It was Siddy, the owner of the local fish and chip shop; he was pushing a handcart covered with a big blue and white tablecloth. 'I've cut a load of corned beef sandwiches for everyone, and there's an urn full of hot tea here. But all my cups got smashed in the blast. Bleedin' nuisance! I don't know where I'm going to get any new . . .' It was then that he saw Mrs Jennings. 'Still, there's worse things that can happen than losing a few cups, eh?' he murmured.

'I think we should be getting on our way,' said Harry. 'The all clear's been over long enough. They won't be coming back again tonight, and there's nothing we can do here until they patch up that window. And I shouldn't think that's going to be much of a priority, not with all the damage out there – and that's just what we can see. Christ knows what it's like with all them fires burning down by the river.'

'Right. Time I got home,' said Kitty, patting at her hair and sending up a little cloud of plaster dust, which she didn't even notice. She was too flustered by the realisation that she'd been sitting on the floor so close to Harry. Whatever had she been thinking of? She knew only too well what could happen when you let someone get too friendly with you. It could end up leading you into all sorts of trouble.

She searched around for her handbag. 'I've got to get back to check on the kids. Will you look at the time? It's nearly seven o'clock. Freddie and Grace'll be wondering where I've got to. And little Bobby must be terrified by all the noise. I hope they're safe. Say they're not? Aw, dear!'

Kitty spotted her bag, snatched it off the floor and fled.

It wasn't easy, but she managed to get home in less than an hour despite the chaos of smashed buildings, blazing fires, diversions around burst gas and water pipes, and officials issuing conflicting orders on just about every other street corner about where people should or should not go. She knew how she had felt when that bloody stray bomb had destroyed their home – but that had been nothing compared to this, and no one had been hurt. How could anyone survive this? She had to get back to her children.

But, even as she ran, she truly wasn't sure whether she was hurrying home to see that her children were safe, or running away from the unsettling feelings that Harry had awakened in her. Because she couldn't deny it, she missed having a man beside her – and not just because she now had to shoulder all the responsibility for her family. There were other things she missed about Dan not being around any more.

Kitty's hand flew to her mouth. She'd seen terrible damage as she'd been making her way through the streets, but she hadn't really believed that any of it would have affected her own family. For some reason she'd got it in her head that they'd be safe because they'd already been bombed once before. How could she have been so stupid?

Two men were sliding a blanket-covered stretcher into the back of an ambulance. A woman was kneeling on the pavement nearby, weeping uncontrollably. The man from across the landing – Joe Lovell, she thought he was called – was holding on to her.

She saw Freddie who was helping to pull rubble out of the back of one of the houses. So at least he was all right, thank God. But where were Grace and Bobby?

Please don't let them be in that ambulance.

'Fred! Freddie! Where're Grace and Bobby?'

He straightened up, stretching his tired muscles. 'They're all right, Mum, they were still down in the laundry when I got back. I made sure that Nell from our landing got home safe, and then I went straight down there and checked on them. I was worried about you, though.'

'You're a good boy, Freddie.'

Good? Freddie felt himself colour. He'd heard that twice today. If only she knew. 'But they'll have gone back upstairs now, and—' The rest of his words were drowned out by the unmistakable rise and fall wailing of the air raid warning.

'Surely not again,' shouted one of the rescue workers, slamming down his pickaxe.

'Get yourselves down in the laundry under the Buildings, all of you,' yelled someone else. 'Over there.'

People started running towards the court-yard.

The woman kneeling on the pavement by the ambulance hauled herself to her feet and she shook her fist at the sky. 'You animals! You bloody animals! You took my babies, my three precious babies. And my Frank. My poor, poor Frank . . .'

The ambulance crew who had joined the rush for shelter had left the vehicle's doors open, and the frantic woman started to climb inside.

Joe grabbed her by the hand. 'Mrs Jennings, you've got to come with me, love. I'm going to take you down to the laundry.'

She pulled away from him. 'What does it matter what happens to me now? What have I got left to live for? Nothing, that's what, nothing at all.'

'I'm sorry, but you've got no say in it, darling, because I'm not leaving you here.' Joe picked her up and slung her over his shoulder as if she weighed no more than one of his sacks of coal.

*

When Joe sat the wild-eyed woman down on one of the camp beds next to his wife and Mary cuddled her as if she were a lost child, not even Ada had a nasty remark to make.

A massive crash shook the building above them.

'Bloody hell,' said Sylvia to Nell, stroking Vicky's red-brown curls. 'I hope that great daft sod of a husband of mine has got himself back down the pub cellar. He don't even know he has to blow his nose if he's not got me there to tell him to.'

'He'll be all right, Sylv.'

'I do hope so, Nell. I really do. I know Bernie's got his ways, but I couldn't begin to imagine life without him.'

Chapter 10

'Hello, lovely, come to admire our beautiful bodies, have you? Or did you come down to offer us a nice cup of tea?' The pug-faced workman put down his spade and shrugged his shoulders, working his aching joints.

He had almost finished digging out the footings for one of the new brick surface shelters that were being built to service the remaining inhabitants of the old terrace and those residents of Turnbury Buildings who didn't fancy risking the basement laundry. It might have been far too late for all those families who had lost their homes and loved ones on that terrible first day of the Blitz, but the authorities thought that a 'morale booster' so close to the docks would be a good thing – for the locals and to use as propaganda in the London papers. The authorities hadn't reckoned with Ada Tanner.

'That'll be a waste of time, you putting that up. I've heard all about them. They don't work, you know. The roof'll blow right off, just like the lid of a saucepan that's boiling over. Useless. It's all right for them with gardens. They can have them Anderson shelters put in, all nice and snug, thank you very much. But us? Who cares about us? Don't make me laugh. No bugger cares, that's who. Why do we always have to put up with all the rubbish, eh? You tell me that.'

The workman's colleagues all burst out laughing. 'That went well, Cyril. But then, you always did have a special way with the women, didn't you, mate? Wonder they've never signed you up for the films. You'd have them queuing up round the block with that mug of yours. Ripping off their drawers they'd be.'

'Do us a favour,' snapped Cyril.

'Favour? It's her what wants a favour doing. Go on, give her a kiss, you'll be well in there.'

Ada watched for a further week and a half as the men slowly constructed the shelter, the daily conversation following its usual line of Ada asking sarcastic questions, and poor Cyril – the man she had selected as the unfortunate focus of her rants – being required to supply answers. Hard as he tried, nothing he said could save him from the mocking laughter of his workmates. Ada never laughed, she took it all very seriously. They were building a surface shelter – for her benefit – but that wouldn't have pleased her had it been furnished entirely by Waring &

Gillow, with matching carpet and curtains and hot tea on tap.

'Oi, Cyril,' one of them would call as she arrived each morning. 'Your bit of skirt's here.'

Today Ada settled herself on the low wall that ran along the front of the terrace and kept watch. She'd brought herself a sandwich wrapped in greaseproof paper, and a flask of tea. Supervising was tiring work.

'Forty people?' she sneered, completely out of the blue. 'Forty? And just the one chemical khasi? What're you mob trying to do – kill us all off before Hitler gets the chance? And don't even start me on the rats it's going to attract up from the river. And how exactly are we supposed to keep warm? Tell me that, eh?'

'Don't worry, girl. Cyril'll give you a cuddle, won't you, mate?'

'Piss off,' said Cyril, pretending he was giving his full attention to pointing the bricks. Why him? He had enough aggravation at home from his old woman. Why couldn't he be working somewhere peaceful, like Occupied France?

The day the shelter was completed, Ada could barely contain herself, waiting for the air raid warning to go. The moment the siren went she had her bag – complete with blanket, sandwiches, flask and a torch – and Albert in tow, carrying two deckchairs, all ready for the off.

She was already composing her letter of complaint as the new shelter's walls rattled and shook around them. And she wasn't the only one who didn't think much of the alarmingly flimsy construction; as soon as the all clear went, her neighbours from the terrace and the Buildings all packed up and cleared off as quickly as they could. They either went back home to their beds – with a bit of luck they might get a few hours' sleep before morning – or else made their way down to the basement laundry, knowing that exhausted as they were, sleep would not come easily. Life had become such a tedious and at the same time terrifying merry-go-round of hard work, fear and continual fatigue, that it was sometimes difficult to know what to do for the best. At least the people living in and around Turnbury Buildings still had the laundry.

The only one who stuck with the surface shelter was Florrie. She looked about her as the others hurried away. 'I don't know what's the matter with that lot, refusing to come in here, it's safe as houses.' She chatted away to herself, as she often did when she was waiting for customers, and then she took off her hat and stretched out on one of the wooden benches that lined the walls, resting her head in her hands. 'Me? I'm not complaining. I think it's bloody wonderful in here, especially since the dock office got knocked down and now this bad weather's started.' She gave a little sigh. 'Shame we didn't have somewhere like this before that happened, and then perhaps that bloke Maudie was with wouldn't have copped it when the roof collapsed – poor sod.'

Twenty-five minutes later, Florrie had smoothed down her skirt and was giving her latest customer a none-too-friendly shove towards the door. 'Look, you can't stay here all night. I've got other gentlemen to see.'

'But the all clear's not sounded yet.'

'Go on, you've had more than your money's worth. Now get off with you, you big brave soldier.'

'Cow!'

'You and all, mate. Now bugger off, before you give me the hump and I go round and tell your old woman what you've been up to.'

'What d'you mean?'

'It might be pitch dark, but I know you, Lou Thompson, as well as I know my own arse – so go on, *bugger off*.'

Florrie opened the door and Lou, with much

cursing and muttering about being over-charged and under-valued as a regular – there was no point now trying to disguise the fact that Florrie knew him – stomped off into the night. She stood in the doorway looking up at the sky. Snow was falling gently; beams from the searchlights were criss-crossing one another, making patterns against the night, and the red glow of burning buildings dotted the otherwise pitch-dark horizon like rubies. It felt strange to find it so beautiful, but that's what it was – beautiful. She could hear the drone of planes and the sounds of the ack-ack guns, but she wasn't scared. Some things scared her, but not this.

She saw the flare of a match; a man was waiting outside.

'Hello, darling, sorry for the delay. Been waiting long, have you?'

'What, for you? Hardly.'

'Please yourself,' she said, 'and I hope the warden catches you next time you strike a match in the street.' She slammed the shelter door shut and lit the Tilly lamp that dangled from the hook by the lavatory compartment. Then she sat on a bench and used the guttering flame to light herself a cigarette.

Perhaps the snow was keeping everyone indoors. That or the bombs.

Outside the man leaned against the wall of the shelter, apparently unconcerned by the raid going on around him.

'Is that you, Rick?' Florrie heard a young male voice ask.

'Who else do you think it is?'

'How did you know I was going to be here?'

'I followed you.'

'Why?'

'The way you behaved earlier in the pub, telling me you couldn't see me tonight, made me think you'd gone and got yourself another bloke.'

''Course I've not. You know I'd never do anything like that to you, Rick. You know how I feel about you.'

'So why are you here then, Alf?'

'I came over to see my nan, check if she's all right. It's been a while.'

'Rather see her than me, would you?'

'No. 'Course not. I told you – it's been a while.'

'Then why suddenly tonight, when you'd already arranged to spend the evening with me?'

'It's hard to explain.'

'I thought you said you loved me?'

'You know I do.'

'Show me then.' Rick began unbuttoning his fly. 'Get down on your knees.'

'I can't do that here.'

'Why not?'

'Because I can't. They're my nan's flats. Right there. And it's snowing.'

'I knew you were lying. Who is he?'

'Rick, I swear—'

By now Florrie had her ear pressed against the door. This was better than the wireless.

'If you don't show me you love me, I'm going to turn round and walk away and you'll never see me again.'

'But, Rick, please, I can't. Not here.'

'I'm giving you one last chance.'

'Don't do this to me, Rick. I'm begging you.'

Florrie was getting cross by now. Very cross. Why wasn't the younger-sounding one standing up for himself? If she rolled over and gave in like that, started begging every time someone had a go at her, she'd be dead by now.

The talking had stopped, but she could hear the unmistakable sounds of a fight.

Florrie took a deep breath – why her? – and pulled open the door.

She could see the silhouette of someone bent double and another man striding off into the blackout and the dangers of the raid.

'Get in here, quick, before you get us both blown up.'

Florrie took the injured man by the arm and dragged him into the shelter.

'What's your name?'

'Alfie.' He still sounded winded.

'Has he hurt you much?'

He shook his head. But Rick *had* hurt him, more than Alfie would have believed possible. He couldn't help himself. His shoulders shook, his chest heaved, and he broke down in tears.

'I did want to stay with him, I told him I did when we were in the pub, and I wasn't lying. But then I kept thinking about my nan. Guilt, I suppose, because I was feeling – I don't know – so happy, so excited, though I knew she wouldn't approve. So I decided, there and then – right out of the blue – that I should try to see her, try and make friends. Especially now I know I'm going to get my call up papers soon. All I wanted was to see her, tell her how much she means to me . . .' He paused, trying to find the words. 'Even if she turned her back on me, at least she'd know the truth.'

He wiped his nose with his cuff, leaving a streak of blood and snot across his top lip. 'And this is what happens.'

'Here, let me.' Florrie took a handkerchief out of her bag and dabbed at the blood.

'It's not fair. All I want is someone to love me. My dad's away, my mum couldn't care less about anyone, my sister's got her own life and my nan despises me.'

Florrie rolled up the bloody hankie and stuffed it in her coat pocket. 'I know a lot of people from round this way, Alf. So who's your nan?'

'Ada Tanner.'

Florrie's eyebrows shot up. 'I can see your problem, kid. She can be a tough old bird.'

'You don't have to tell me.'

'Look, sweetheart, if you ever want to have a chat to someone or go out for a drink – just as a friend – then leave a note for me in the corner shop. It's good to be able to talk to someone, to get things off your chest.'

She held out her hand, ready to shake his. 'Florrie Talbot's the name.'

Before Alfie had a chance to respond, the door to the shelter opened. 'Didn't know you were busy, Flo,' a man called over. 'I thought I saw a bloke leaving a couple of minutes ago.'

Florrie frowned and then nodded, understanding what he meant – he must have seen this young feller's friend go. 'Sorry, darling,' she said to him. 'Come back in about a quarter of an hour, eh? I'll be ready for you then. And get that door shut, will you, before the warden sees the light.'

As the man closed the door, Alfie screwed up

his face in disgust and looked her up and down. 'You're nothing but a tart. Get away from me!'

'Look here, sonny, you might think I'm the lowest of the low, but do you know what people think of your type?'

Alfie turned away so she couldn't see his face. 'I'm sorry, I'm upset. I shouldn't have said that. I had no right.'

'No, you didn't, and I'm losing money here while you're coming over all Lord Muck on me. I'll have you know I met a bloke once in the Oporto and he was a foreign prince. We spent the whole evening in that pub together. Right lovely manners he had. So if I was good enough for him to speak to, then I'm sure I'm good enough for the likes of you.'

'I said I'm sorry.' Alfie dropped down on to the bench. 'It's all . . . I don't know . . . getting too much for me to cope with.'

He burst into tears again and Florrie, with a resigned sigh, sat down next to him and wrapped her arms around him, pulling his head on to her shoulder, hoping that his nose had stopped bleeding and that it wouldn't spoil her coat. 'It's all getting too much for a lot of people, darling, but we can't go round upsetting everyone else when we feel like it. It's not kind.'

*

172

As Florrie comforted the weeping lad, Martin and Nell were standing on the roof of Turnbury Buildings with tin helmets on their heads, stirrup pumps in hand, and rows of buckets filled with water or sand ready to quench any fire that broke out. They were unaware of the drama going on in the street shelter five floors below them, and even if they had known about it they had other things to occupy them.

'Martin, will you please stop going on about it?'

'No, Nell, I won't. There are enough men in these Buildings to take their turn at fire-watching. You've got no need to be doing this. No need at all. You should be down in the laundry, safe with Mum and the kids.'

'This is the last time I'm going to say this – hang on.' Nell darted over to the edge of the roof and neatly flicked away an incendiary bomb with her foot, sending it clattering harmlessly on to the cobbles of the street below.

'There. Practice makes perfect, they say, and I can do this job almost with my eyes closed. And it's only fair, really. Because of having the kids, I don't have to work the hours most people are having to put in. And because of having the kids, I don't want this roof catching light! Honestly, Martin, I can easily get by with a bit less sleep. Think what everyone else is doing.

There's Mary running the shop now that Sarah and David are down in Devon – please God they're both OK, 'cos I'm not sure I like the sound of that relative of David's very much. Then there's Joe, driving the coal lorry all day and the ambulance most nights – he must be worn out. And I can't imagine what sort of things he's seeing. It's bad enough hearing on the wireless and reading in the papers about how people are suffering, without having to witness it with your own eyes, night in, night out.'

'You're making *me* feel bad now, like I should be doing more.'

'What? Down the docks most days, rescue squad work when you're not there, and fire-watching a couple of nights a week? It's terrible being married to such a lazy man, Martin. Really terrible.'

Nell pushed back her helmet and kissed him gently. 'I love you, Martin. And I love the kids. And that's why I still don't know what to do for the best about evacuating them. These raids don't feel like they're ever going to stop, and after what happened down in the terrace with that poor Jennings family, how can we justify keeping them with us?'

'You've not heard the latest news then?'

'What news? I hear and read so much these days.'

'This wasn't on the wireless. I heard it from one of the other dockers, who heard it off his brother-in-law. It's shocking. The Nazis, they torpedoed this ship . . .'

'That's nothing new.'

'No, but this one – the *City of Benares* it was called – had kids on it who were being evacuated, and a lot of them died. Can you imagine how their families must feel, thinking they were sending them away to somewhere safe and then that happening? You'd never forgive yourself, would you, knowing they'd died all on their own? Little kids. No, Nell, I think we're right to stay together. We'll just have to be prepared.'

'What, like you are now?'

'Eh?'

'Look behind you.'

As Martin spun round, Nell poured a bucket of sand over the fizzing incendiary that had landed right behind him.

'See, bit of luck I was up here, eh?'

She was trying to sound light-hearted, but inside she felt as if she was turning to stone. How on earth could those poor bereaved parents ever cope with life again, knowing they'd sent their own children to their deaths? And it wasn't only British parents and their children. She couldn't help but wonder what was happening to ordinary families over in Germany, too.

Li Mei woke with a jolt. Her back ached from where she'd been lying on the hard platform of the tube station, and the smell of the makeshift lavatory – a bucket behind a sacking curtain – made her want to heave. She looked at the clock. Half-past six. They'd been out all night. They'd only come down here to sit out the raid after they'd been to the pictures. The film – *Waterloo Bridge* – had really upset her and she'd cried on and off for nearly an hour. Then she must have fallen asleep.

'Freddie, wake up. I've got to go. My grandparents will be going mad.' She stood up unsteadily, doing her best not to step on the people surrounding her as they packed up their bedding and gathered their possessions together ready for the daily trek home and to work.

Freddie put a hand out to her and she helped him up. 'Let me have a minute, Li, to pull myself together. Then we can get going.'

'No. People will see us.'

'It'll still be dark out there.'

'Please, Freddie. I'm going to have to lie to my grandparents as it is, don't make things even harder for me.'

'When will I see you again?' His voice was

urgent. With everything that had been happening since that terrible Saturday back in September, when it felt as if the whole of the East End had caught fire, he and Mei still had not done what she had promised him they would, and the frustration was driving him mad. He loved her so much. And now, having spent the whole night with her, without being able so much as to touch her beautiful skin – it was killing him.

Mei looked anxiously at the clock again. 'I don't know. Later today?'

'Where?'

'How about that cafe on the Whitechapel Road that you go to – that's open on Sundays, isn't it? And I can say I've gone over to the market with Linda. They'll believe that.' *And I can see through the window if Peter has followed me*, she thought. 'Now I really do have to go, Freddie.'

'What time?'

'Eleven? Midday?'

'Eleven.'

'See you then.'

Freddie watched Li Mei until she disappeared into the throng climbing the stairs up to the street above.

As she went out into the dark, cold wintery morning she was surrounded by people, and should have felt protected by the crowd, but Mei had the strange feeling that everyone was watching her – just her, picking her out from the rest. She knew how suspicious people were nowadays of anyone who looked or sounded even slightly foreign; there were stories about violent attacks just because someone had an odd-sounding name. But it was probably just tiredness making her imagine that things were worse than they were – that and the trouble she knew she'd be in if she arrived home without getting her story straight.

She kept close to the others, the sound of their footsteps muffled by the snow that had fallen. Not many of them were speaking, most of them too fatigued after three long months of nightly raids.

Gradually, the crowd began to thin out as people turned off into sidestreets or gave up their trudging and waited at bus stops for the early-morning service to begin.

Mei was moving as quickly as the slippery pavement would allow – she had to get home soon or her grandparents would never let her out of the house again. As she walked more quickly she had the uncomfortable feeling that someone was keeping in step with her.

No, don't be silly, she was just spooking herself.

Mei stopped suddenly and looked over her shoulder.

'Peter?'

'*I saw you*. I stayed awake all night just watching. He was so close to you, it was disgusting! I wanted to pull him away from you and punch him till he couldn't breathe, beat him until he couldn't stand . . .'

'What are you talking about? You're mad!'

'It's not me who's mad, it's you. What do you think you're doing, going with an English boy?'

'What's it got to do with you?'

'You should be with *me*. If you don't tell him to keep away from you, I'll tell your family that you're seeing him.' He stroked her face, making her flinch.

'Don't you dare touch me!'

'You let him kiss you. How can you let him do that? It's not right.'

'I don't understand you – your own mother was English.'

'And do you remember what people used to say about her?'

'No.'

'Then I'll tell you, shall I? They called her a whore – to her face. English and Chinese people all said the same, to her and about her.' Peter was staring into the distance now, his fists clenched. 'And me . . . they called me a mongrel. A bloody mongrel.'

Mei saw her chance. She backed away from him and started running, slipping and sliding in the snow.

She didn't have a chance. He caught her easily, dragged her down a narrow side alley and slammed her against the wall.

She could feel his damp breath on her face as he loomed over her.

'Now kiss me like you kiss him.'

He grabbed her hair and pulled her head back, covering her mouth with his.

Mei felt sick but she couldn't let him think he could just get away with it. She had to do something.

She bit his lip, hard, until she could taste the rusty blood on her tongue.

He reared away from her, holding his hand to his mouth. 'You've done it now. If you don't stop seeing him, I mean it, I'll kill you both.'

'You really are mad.'

'No, I'm doing this for you, Mei. Can't you see that? You'd be better off dead than being with him anyway. So, I'm warning you – break up with him or you're both dead.' He took a long-bladed knife from inside his overcoat. 'Both of you. Do you understand?'

Mei nodded.

Despite the early hour, when Mei turned into Pennyfields she could see her grandparents standing at the street door, looking up and down the road.

Her grandmother – still dressed in what she had been wearing when Mei had said goodbye to her the day before – came hurrying towards her. 'Granddaughter, where have you been? We thought you had been killed by the bombs.'

'We went to the pictures, and the warning sounded so we went to the underground station to shelter.' Mei very carefully avoided saying who exactly *we* were. 'I fell asleep. I am so sorry that I worried you. As soon as I woke up, I ran home.'

Her grandmother looked so old, so frightened. 'Mei, your grandfather and I thought we had lost you. If anything happened to you, I think we would die. That's why you stay here with us and why we don't let you go to work in the laundries. We all know what that can mean for Chinese girls. Men think they are fallen women. They treat them as if they do not value themselves as the precious jewels we know they are.'

Mei lowered her head. 'I need to get washed, Grandmother. And you look like you need to sleep. I am sorry that I worried you.'

Only a few hours later, full of guilt at the web of lies she had spun for her grandparents before they went upstairs to try and get some rest after their sleepless night, Mei was heading towards the cafe on the Whitechapel Road where Freddie was waiting for her.

'But you can't mean it. What's got into to you? A few hours ago everything was fine between us.'

'No, it wasn't, not really. We both know that. I'm sorry, Freddie, really sorry, but I can't do this to my grandparents. I can't keep lying to them.'

Li Mei felt so disloyal, but at least it wasn't a total lie she was telling him: Chinese families did expect their children to do as they were told, and that included marrying into other Chinese families.

'They're old, Freddie. They can't take the strain of worrying about me all the time.'

'Are you ashamed of me, because of the work I do?'

'I don't know what you do. You've never told me. I think there are lots of things you don't tell me.'

'Like what?'

'Like what your parents would think about you seeing a foreign girl.'

Freddie shrugged. 'Truth is, Li, I don't know.

I've not wanted to risk putting up any more barriers between us.'

'I sometimes wonder if you only ever want one thing from me.'

'How can you say that? You know how I feel about you. And to prove it, I'll wait. I'll wait as long as you want me to.'

She had to be brave, she had to do this for all of them – for her grandmother, her grandfather and for Freddie – she had no idea what Peter was capable of, and she wouldn't take the risk of finding out.

'It's over, Freddie.'

'No, don't say that.'

'I'm sorry.'

He stood up, scraping his chair back across the floor. 'Okay.' He threw half a crown on the counter and walked out into the street, hiding himself and his tears among the crowd of market-goers as he pushed past on his way to the Hope. Right, Li didn't want him any more, he had better get used to it.

If only he had waited a few moments longer he would have seen that Mei too was broken-hearted.

'Hello, Bernie.'

'Morning, Fred. This is a nice surprise. Wasn't expecting you this morning.'

'Thought I'd pop over. See how things are going.'

'Good boy, Fred. We had a lock in during the raid yesterday and the barrels want changing. And you're just the feller for the job.'

With a nod to Sylvia, who was polishing glasses behind the bar, Freddie followed Bernie towards the cellar steps.

'You all right, love?' she asked. 'Only you look like you've lost a shilling and found a ha'penny.'

'I don't suppose I am feeling too good, really, Sylvia. Tired, I think, like everyone else.'

'You don't have to tell me about being tired, Fred. My great daft lump of a husband's not got a clue about going to bed at a normal time. Now, I mean it, you're looking peaky, so don't let him work you too hard.'

Down in the cellar, Freddie took off his overcoat and jacket, rolled up his sleeves and got stuck into changing the barrels.

'I've decided I'll do that extra work you were talking about – delivering the merchandise – if you still want me to, Bern?'

'Aw, yeah, why the change of mind?'

'I've thought about it, and I've not got anything else to do with my time till they decide they're going to call me up.'

'Well, that's something you don't have to worry yourself about, kiddo.'

'How do you mean?'

'About being called up. It won't happen.'

'Do you know something I don't?'

'No, but being called up, you can put that right out of your mind. I'll sort it all out for you when the time comes.' Bernie winked. 'There's doctors' letters can be had if you know who to go to. And as business is booming –' he made a show of touching wood '– it's all hands needed on deck these days, and yours are about the only ones available. Well, the only hands I'd trust amongst the thieving hounds and rogues around here who've already made sure they'll not be called up.'

Such a bare-faced case of the pot calling the kettle black would, at any other time, have had Freddie stifling snorts of derisive laughter, but all he could think about now was that his beautiful Li didn't want him any more. He didn't think he'd ever find anything funny again.

Chapter 11

Sarah Meckel sat in the dingy back parlour of the Devon cottage that belonged to David's cousin Ruth; the lamps hadn't been lit yet even though it was already getting dark. Still, at least it meant that Sarah didn't have to look at the depressingly faded wallpaper with its overblown cabbage roses and their once white background that was now fly-blown and foxed by damp. It bore little resemblance to the place that Sarah had imagined she was bringing her beloved husband to – when was it? – two, nearly three, months ago now. Despite thinking that her only concern would be David's condition after the long journey down from London, it was the state of the cottage that had really thrown her. She could only be grateful that her husband was in no state to notice where she'd brought him.

She understood – of course she did – that Ruth was still in mourning, but the neglect and dirt here appalled her. Stan had only been dead since the spring, surely it couldn't have got like this so quickly? Sarah had done her best to clean up but it was a struggle to make even a slight impression on what must have been years of accumulated dirt, grease and neglect.

'I don't know how you can bear having him near you, making all that fuss all the time. All them funny noises – it's not natural. I always thought that having to have some snotty-nosed cockney kids billeted on me, like some have around here, would be bad, but *him* – he makes me shudder. I'd have been better off with kids.'

It was only the third thing Ruth had said to Sarah all day – the first had been her regular complaint that the row David made every night when he had his nightmares was making it hard for her to sleep. The second was that she thought Sarah should use *something from the doctor* to shut her husband up. Sarah had protested that the elderly local doctor had been unsympathetic; all he could offer was the suggestion that David should pull himself together and a bottle of sleeping tablets strong enough to knock him out.

Ruth hadn't been impressed when Sarah had expressed her reservations about giving David drugs, and her constant complaints and harsh unbending manner were making it increasingly clear that she wasn't so keen on them being here – not now she realised exactly how ill her cousin was.

'He scares me . . . all that babbling and

hollering all the time. *I* couldn't put up with him.'

'I still love him.'

'I loved Stan once. Fat lot of good that did me.' Ruth, a thin yet strong woman with grey hair, weather-beaten skin and gnarled, crêpey hands, got up from her armchair and went over to the heavily carved mahogany credenza. The massive piece of furniture overpowered the low-ceilinged room, making the claustrophobic space even darker.

'Fancy a sweet sherry?' said Ruth, opening one of the credenza doors with a wince-inducing squeak of its unoiled hinges.

'I think it's a bit early for me, thanks all the same.'

'Time doesn't mean much to me,' sighed Ruth. 'Not now.'

She took the bottle out of the cupboard and held it up. 'Well?'

'Go on then. Thank you.' Sarah couldn't blame her for her attitude, she supposed, having a relative she barely knew – plus his wife – landed on her.

'And take one up to him while you're at it. It might knock him out for a while and then we can have our supper in peace.'

Sarah bit her tongue – reminding herself that they should be grateful for this woman's hospitality – and took the two little more than thimble-sized glasses from Ruth, carrying them up the narrow, dog-leg stairway to the bedroom she shared with her husband.

As she eased open the door, David began thrashing around in the bed.

'Don't worry, my darling, it's only me.'

No answer other than an incoherent whimpering. Another nightmare. If only she could help him escape from this constant torment.

The chill in the unheated room added to the already unpleasant feeling of damp and smell of mould that had been there even in the autumn when they first arrived. Now it was winter it had become almost unbearable.

Sarah put down the two tiny glasses on the floor by the bed and went over to fetch David's overcoat and her astrakhan top coat from the wardrobe – there was hardly anything else in there. They had had to travel light, with just the one small suitcase – it was all she could carry, what with having to look after David on the long train journey.

Gently, she draped the overcoat over the bed and tucked it in around him. Then she hooked her coat over the curtain wire to block out the wind creeping its way in through the cracked window-frame. She picked up the two glasses of sherry and, with a silent shudder, gulped each one down in a single mouthful.

Sarah shut the door behind her as quietly as she could and went down to the sloping-roofed kitchen where she rinsed the two little glasses under the single cold tap in the deep stone sink that dominated the far end of the room. A pot of lokshen soup was reheating on the dull, matt black range. This was the third day that they would be having the soup, and Sarah could only wish she had been firmer with Ruth and insisted on roasting the chicken as she'd wanted to. She wouldn't have wasted any of it, she would have used the leftovers to make the soup – and there would have been rather less of the stuff for them to have to wade through.

She gave it a desultory stir. It didn't smell too bad, it was just that Sarah wished she could have made something that might have tempted David's ever-dwindling appetite. He was eating such a small amount lately that he was wasting away before her eyes. He did little more than sip the odd cup of black tea and sleep, and even then he never seemed to get any rest because of the visions of goodness only knew what that tormented his every waking and sleeping moment.

Still, when she thought about the alternative

for them, being back in London with all those raids, she knew they should be grateful to Ruth.

Sarah rinsed the wooden spoon under the tap and rested it across the top of the pot, bracing herself to go back into the parlour and sit in silence with Ruth until it was time to eat.

No, she couldn't do it. Cold as it was, she decided to go outside and get some fresh air.

She made her way along what had become the familiar route of the rough path that led down to the orchard. A few weeks ago she would have been crying – coming out here so no one could hear her – as she stumbled along over rocks and roots, thinking about her darling David, of the wonderful, strong and confident man she had married when she had been little more than a girl. But she didn't cry any more; she had wept so much it was as if she had run out of tears.

Dusk had descended quickly but she hardly noticed the cold as the dark evening air surrounded her. At first it had chilled her very bones as she remembered how in London the dark had felt warmer, cosier, more familiar, even with the blackout. Here the dark had felt strange – worryingly so – but it was no longer frightening as it once had been. If David had been well they might actually have enjoyed standing here amongst the bare fruit trees, looking up at the stars twinkling in the sky in a way she had never seen before. And they'd have laughed as they tried to guess which animals were making those extraordinary sounds. She thought about Mary's grandchildren, and how they would have loved running wild in the fields that surrounded the cottage, and what fun they would have had, planning expeditions to the high cliffs that led down to the beach.

Or maybe they'd have hated the place as much as she had come to. Apart from her love for David, her hatred for it was just about the only emotion left alive in her.

She leaned back against the rough bark of an apple tree, thinking about her friends back in Wapping, wishing she was with them – perhaps they could help her feel again – but knowing, deep in her heart, that David couldn't survive going back there. Not yet. Maybe never. If it weren't for the letters that Mary sent her, London and their old life there would already have faded from Sarah's mind like a dream.

She drew her fingers down her cheeks, thinking.

Could David survive anywhere in the state he was in?

Could she?

*

'Come on, hurry up and have a look before it's too dark to see.' Martin was beckoning excitedly to Mary and Nell. 'Look, we've finished.'

Joe, toolbag by his feet, stood proudly with hands on hips, admiring his handiwork – a run of chicken and rabbit coops, standing in the lee of the sheds in the Buildings' courtyard. They had a sturdy brick and metal outer frame over them – a miniature air raid shelter – with strong padlocks on the doors to keep out both animal and human predators.

'I'll be fetching the animals home from that feller in the ambulance station tomorrow night, but you mustn't let the kids start giving them names. We've got to start breeding them up to get a decent stock going, then we can start sharing them with the neighbours. We'll have a right little farm going here soon.'

Mary laughed. 'You've done a really good job, you two, but once the kids start feeding and settling down the animals before the blackout, they're bound to give them names. So you're going to have a bit of a job stopping them, I can tell you.'

'They'll be all right,' said Nell. 'They've got Bradman as a pet. But they mustn't let *him* get a whiff of this little lot.' She bent down and peered inside the run. 'You really have done a good job here, you know.'

''Course we have,' said Joe. 'We used my old father's tools, didn't we?'

Mary looked all dreamy. 'Fresh eggs whenever we want . . . I can't wait.'

'Wait till you see what else me and Dad have got planned. It's been our little secret for weeks.' Martin winked surreptitiously at Joe. 'A pig club, so everyone's got something nice to put on the table at Christmas. We thought you'd like that, Mum, 'cos we know pork's your favourite.'

Now Mary looked stunned. 'Wherever will we keep it?'

'There's that bit of wasteland at the end of the terrace, I suppose,' said Nell, sounding unconvinced. 'But it's a bit soon since that got bombed, it wouldn't seem right.'

'Well, you'll be pleased to know that me and Martin have got it all organised already. We've had them for a couple of months now, behind the canteen in the dock. They love it there, what with all the scraps.'

'They?'

'We've got three. And some of the other blokes have a couple between them and all. Great big sods they are.'

'Language, Martin.'

'Sorry, Mum. Large Blacks they're called.'

'Hark at Farmer Giles,' laughed Nell.

'Don't take the rise. So long as we're careful, there should be enough for everyone in the Buildings and the terrace. Even if it's only half a head to make a bit of brawn.'

'However did you sort all that out without us knowing?'

'One of the fellers in the dock knows someone. It was a bit complicated – all the paperwork and that – but what isn't nowadays?'

Nell was frowning. 'I know this doesn't sound very sensitive, what with you two having to work there everyday, but are they safe? I mean, *you* can go in the shelter.'

'And so can they.' Joe sounded like a nervous kid who'd just been caught with his jumper stuffed full of scrumped apples – he certainly couldn't meet his wife's gaze. 'We kind of . . . found some spare metal shelters in the dock, the coffin-looking ones, and sort of . . . adapted them. And before you say anything,' he added quickly, 'we did it with a nod from the ARP. Nobody likes being shut up in them things, it's like being put in solitary. But we've turned them on their sides, chopped out a bit then joined them together again and made them lovely for our porkers. One of us shoves them in there as soon as the warning goes so—'

Martin cut in then. 'Good job it's not long to Christmas though, Mum. They've got that fat, I don't know how much longer we can fit them in there.'

Mary suppressed a grin. 'You should be right chuffed with yourself, Joe, about how good you are with your hands. And we all need shelter, even animals.'

Nell put her hands over her ears. 'That was good timing, Mary. Listen to that row.'

As Mary spoke, the air raid siren had started warbling its terrifying yet infuriating wail.

Tommy's head appeared over the edge of their balcony on the fifth floor. 'Don't worry, Mum,' he hollered through cupped hands. 'I'll get Dolly and Vicky down to the basement.'

'Thanks, Tom,' Nell shouted back up to him, then shook her head at Mary. 'Can't they leave us alone? Take a Sunday off at least?'

She turned and trotted away towards the entrance to the Buildings. 'Move, you lot. Time we were getting inside,' she called over her shoulder.

'Not me, love,' Joe told her. 'I'm on ambulance duty tonight.'

Sylvia was in the cellar of the Hope, standing with folded arms, by the makeshift bar that Bernie and Freddie had cobbled together down there out of barrels and planks. The place was almost full – but Freddie was nowhere to be seen.

'How could you have sent that boy out in this?' she accused her husband.

'Stop worrying, Sylv, he knows what he's up to. And anyway, I never made him do it. He wanted to.'

'Sometimes, Bernie, I swear, I could batter you.'

'Stop leading off, girl, and see if these young chaps want a drink.'

'Drink? Drink?' Sylvia's voice was rising to dog-whistle level. 'They should be over the road in that hospital. You'd bloody corrupt a nun, you would, Bernie Woods.'

'I don't know what you mean, my little flower. I'm just doing my bit for morale, that's all. Think of it as me war work.'

Freddie had taken to driving as if born to it. Not only did he enjoy the freedom it gave him, the attention he attracted from young women as he sat up in the cab of the Bedford van was something he was planning to cash in on soon. There was quite a bit of room in the back . . .

Sod Li. If she didn't want to know, then she could get lost. He'd spent enough time moping about, kidding himself that she'd just turn up one day. He'd find himself someone who appreciated him. And in the meantime, he'd sit back and enjoy all the female interest and the independence of being a driver. Although even he had to admit that it was a bit hairy tonight – scary, if truth be told – but at least it made him feel young and alive.

He stuck out his chin, doing his best to convince himself. Who cared about Li?

He turned on to the Bethnal Green Road but immediately had to drop his speed as a fireman waved him down. The man seemed to be leading the crew that was struggling to contain a blaze dangerously close to the Bishopsgate goods yard.

'Hang on, son, you won't be able to get through there. There's an unexploded bomb up on Cambridge Heath Road. You'll have to find another route round the back. Or park up and get down the shelter, if you've got any sense.'

'Please, mate, let me through. I'm not going down that far. And I've got some really important stuff to deliver – for the rest centre in the school along there. Medical supplies and blankets.'

'You're a brave kid, I'll give you that.' The clattering of incendiaries as they fell on to the cobbles nearby had the fireman stepping neatly aside. 'Go on then, but be careful.'

'Thank you, I will.' Freddie flashed the man his most heroic smile and pulled away.

*

He could only drive at a crawl as he was worried that he'd miss the turning in the blackout, but he had good eyes and spotted it in plenty of time.

He pulled into the kerb, got out of the van and leaned into the doorway set back a little in an otherwise blank brick wall. He knocked discreetly, then a bit louder.

'About bloody time,' said the aproned man who eventually opened the door. He stepped outside on to the pavement and pulled it to behind him so that the light from the room behind didn't leak out. 'I could have got bloody blown up, waiting for you.'

Freddie stepped away from him. 'Well, don't bother thanking me for risking my life, will you? *I* could have got bloody blown up fetching it here. Tell you what, I'll take this stuff back so you can get down the shelter, shall I?'

'Stop fannying about, will you?' tutted the man. 'And let's get that gear indoors before the warden or a copper turns up.'

Freddie and he ferried a pile of boxes from the back of the van through the anonymous-looking door. Inside was a brightly lit, well-equipped commercial kitchen.

'Right,' said the customer. 'That's two crates of sugar, one of bacon, two pounds of butter, three of marge, and four bottles of Scotch. All correct.'

'Glad to be of help,' said Freddie sarcastically, still smarting from the man's rudeness after he had risked his life and liberty delivering these goods to him. 'But I think you'll find that's four pounds of butter and six bottles of Scotch.'

The man snorted – a very annoying pretence at a laugh. 'Sorry, must have been all that hanging about with bombs going off around me. It's confused me.'

'Yeah, that'll be it.' Freddie would have liked to have punched the monkey bastard right on his fat nose.

'What's with that tone of voice? Who do you think you are, you little arsehole?'

'Well, let's see, I'm the bloke who's delivering for Bernie Woods. And you, you're a cafe owner. I've just lied to a fireman that I'm delivering to a rest centre, I could have got nicked at any time during the journey over here for carrying blackmarket goods, and – aw, yeah – you need those goods. So, before you start getting flash with me, mate, I'd like to see how you'd open your cafe without my, let's say, *special* deliveries.'

The man shrugged. 'The bombs—'

'Yeah, I know, they make you confused. Now, where's Bernie's dough?'

'David? David?' Sarah sat on the edge of the bed, carrying a tray of soup and bread. Her husband was still sleeping, but he'd eaten nothing all day. 'Can you manage a little bit of lokshen, darling?'

She stared at his face in the flickering gaslight. His skin was almost transparent, making him look like an El Greco saint: gaunt, unshaven, and – she couldn't bear the thought of it – close to death.

She put the tray of food, untouched, on the floor, and blew out the flame.

Chapter 12

It was Sunday night and everyone who was packed into the laundry down in the basement of Turnbury Buildings was feeling completely exhausted. There were just too many things to do. Sorting out the blackout morning and night; doing whatever war work you'd been allocated; worrying about what the kids were up to if the schools were closed yet again or while they were staying with strangers somewhere miles away in the country; queuing for . . . well, anything that was going. Sometimes you'd get on the end of a queue without even knowing what was on offer, then find it had run out of whatever it was before you got anywhere near the front.

Then there was raking out the grate and setting the fire ready to light when you came back home of an evening; brushing and beating the rugs; sweeping, waxing and polishing the lino and furniture; cooking whatever you'd managed to buy that day; and then having to hump it all up and down the stairs. And that was without the washing and the ironing, cleaning the windows, changing the beds, mending, sewing and knitting, and the hundred and one other things it took to keep a home going. It might have been a bit easier if everyone could have got a decent night's sleep for a change, but as soon as the warning went, down they all tramped back into the laundry, knowing that they had to sit there – in the cold – wrapped up in layers of blankets and coats until the all clear sounded and they could go back to their beds for a few precious, snatched moments of sleep.

At least tonight they didn't have to worry about the freezing weather – the women who were kept busy doing their war work during the week were taking this opportunity to tackle their laundry, and the tall racks of the drying cabinets were giving off a steady if damp heat. So everyone was pleased with the arrangement. Everyone, that is, except Ada Tanner, who wouldn't have expressed delight if someone had presented her with a bouquet of roses and a box of chocolates all tied up with big red bows.

'Who'd have thought it would ever come to this?' she asked no one in particular as she stood surveying the room while simultaneously supervising her husband with a series of increasingly abrupt hand gestures. The poor man was doing his best to please his wife with his efforts to convert her deckchair into a camp bed of which she'd approve. He carried on despite knowing he'd been on to a loser from the very start.

'Come to what, Ada?' asked a fatigued-looking young woman who was mangling her way through a big zinc basinful of dripping wet bedding.

'Women doing their laundry of a Sunday night. Never heard the likes of it before. It's not right. Monday, that's the day for washing. The whole world's gone flaming bonkers.'

'Not all of us have the chance to do it during the week, Ada,' said the young woman. 'I'd love to have the chance to come down here of a Monday morning, but some of us have to go to work, you know.' She was annoyed with herself for even entering into a conversation with Ada Tanner, but it was too late now. She'd opened the gate, might as well plough on.

'There was brick dust all over my beds from the demolition they had to do along the street. So what do you want me to do? Leave it? Let the kids get dust on their chests? Is that what you'd like? Would that make you happy? There is a flaming war on, you know.'

Ada didn't deign to answer. Instead she turned her attention elsewhere. Stabbing a chubby finger at Lil, who was busily casting on yet another dodgy-looking piece of knitting, she leaned forward as if to share a secret, but didn't bother to lower her voice.

'Here, Lil, have you heard about her from number twenty-five? You know – the peroxide blonde who doesn't ever do her blouse up properly.'

'I know her,' said Lil, voice dripping disapproval. 'Looks like she's no better than she ought to be, that one. In fact, she wouldn't look out of place on a street corner in Whitechapel.'

'You're right there, and listen to the latest. She's only gone and joined the flipping Land Army.'

'No! She never has.'

'I'm telling you. And her with her chap away in the RAF and all. I don't know about you, but that don't seem right to me – or any other right-thinking person, if you asked them. It's like all this doing your laundry on a Sunday business. Terrible shenanigans! It's not right, none of it. The Nazis might as well have taken over, the way things are going in this place.'

Mary glanced briefly at Nell, rolling her eyes in worn out wonder. 'Explain to me, Ada – what's so wrong with that girl joining the Land Army? At least she's doing her bit to keep this country fed. And it's not as if she's got any kids to look after, now is it?'

'No. And she never will have at this rate,

running around all over the place like a single woman. Disgraceful, that's what it is. And what's her old man to think, eh? You tell me that. That man'll be shocked to his very core. He won't know what's going on.'

Mary flashed another despairing look at Nell. 'Not everyone's got your high-flown morals, Ada.'

But any sarcasm was lost on Ada Tanner. 'No, more's the pity. I've heard things, I have. Like how all these men whose wives and kids are away in the country are trying it on with the girls they're getting to work in the factories.' Ada looked steadily at Kitty Jarrett. 'Any men work in your place, do they?'

Kitty's face flushed red. Had someone said something about Harry the supervisor? He was so over-familiar with her these days, getting worse as the weeks went by; it was making her feel really uncomfortable, but he wouldn't take her seriously when she objected, just told her she should have more of a sense of humour. But say someone *had* noticed and said something, it'd be her the women in the Buildings were gossiping about next.

What should she say in reply to Ada? It'd look strange if she didn't say something, defend herself in some way.

What should she do?

She needn't have worried; Grace wasn't having anyone being rude to her mother. 'Why don't you leave my mum alone? Why don't you just leave everyone alone? You talk about other people and what they do, criticising them all the time, but I've heard things about *you* and what you get up to. You're hardly one to talk.'

Bella, who had come over to the Buildings earlier that day to see her grandparents and to give them a few slices of leftover mutton that Ada had scorned, could only silently pray for the all clear or else the curse of silence falling over them all before Grace really got herself into trouble. But no, she was not going to be shut up that easily – recklessly, she ploughed on.

'I heard you went down the WVS Centre on the Commercial Road and stood there in the queue like some poor old girl, so you could claim one of the parcels of emergency clothing for yourself. And everyone knows they're meant to be for bombed out families like mine, not greedy old women like you.'

An audible gasp went around the room. Had the girl lost her marbles?

Ada puffed herself up to her full, if inconsiderable height. 'If the Yanks are stupid enough to send the gear over here, then why shouldn't I have some of it?'

'Because I know that none of it even fits you,

and you're selling it down the market to the second-hand stall holders.'

By now, Bella had her head in her hands. She could only be grateful that Grace hadn't said where she had heard this, or she herself would be in so much trouble.

Kitty smiled thinly and walked over to her daughter. 'Let's forget it, shall we, Grace? Because we don't want to upset your friend's nan, now do we? And you know it's not nice discussing other people's private business.'

But it was as if a dam had burst, and Grace couldn't stop the flow.

'Why not? She gets away with stuff like that all the time. And do you know why? Well, I'll tell you. Because she's a bully and no one's got the guts to stand up to her. She won't even see her own grandson, did you know that? And do you know *why* she won't see him?'

The whole laundry fell silent. All eyes were on Ada.

One of the women coughed theatrically and tried to cause a distraction. 'Have you heard that they hit more hospitals again last night, Kit? They must be doing it deliberately, if you want my opinion. My sister-in-law, she works over Stepney Green way and she said that they hit four of them. In one night. Can you believe it? It's shocking, that's what it is. Shocking.

Targeting people who are weaker than them.'
She glanced at Ada. 'How can people act so low?'

Still Grace wouldn't let it drop. 'I said – do none of you know why she won't see him? Her own grandson?'

'Leave it, darling.' Mary touched her very softly on the arm; she could feel the tension quivering in the girl's body. 'Come on, Grace. Please. You and your mum come and sit over here with us, sweetheart. Come on, Kit.'

'No, Mrs Lovell, I won't leave it. She's got to be told. She's a wicked old woman who won't even talk to her own grandson. And I'll tell you why . . .'

Another collective gasp.

'What's wrong with you?' snapped Grace, now trembling and tearful as she surveyed them all. 'I suppose none of you lot have any secrets? All perfect, are you?'

Mary put her arm around Grace's shoulders and steered her forcibly over to where Kitty was sitting, ashen-faced, frozen to her chair. 'No one's perfect, sweetheart. No one.' She turned to Nell. 'Pour Grace some tea out of the flask, will you, love? And put a nice big spoon of sugar in it.'

The girl's head drooped. 'I'm sorry, Mrs Lovell.'

Mary looked over at Ada, making sure the old gossip could hear.

'You're not the one who should be sorry, Grace,' she said. 'You were only saying what a lot of people have thought for a very long time, but haven't been brave enough to say. Not to her face, anyway.'

Chapter 13

'Nell.' Martin stroked her cheek, gently waking her. 'It's six o'clock, love. I'm off to work. Joe's just gone through to get a bath, and then him and Tom are off as well. I've seen to the rabbits and chickens, so you don't have to worry about them till later.'

Nell rubbed her eyes and yawned, making little Vicky stir beside her. 'I don't know why we stay down here in the laundry of a night; no one gets any proper sleep.' She stretched her arms over her head. 'I'm stiff as a board.'

'You know why,' said Martin, pulling the blanket up over his mum and Dolly who were crammed into the camp bed next to Nell and Vicky's. 'We do it so the kids are safe.'

'I know. And we're luckier than most, eh?'

'I've been lucky since the day I set eyes on you, Nell.' He touched his lips to her forehead. 'I can't wait for us to be able to spend some time alone. It's been so long.'

She pulled his face towards hers, and kissed him tenderly on the mouth.

'My good Gawd! Will you look at them two?'

squawked Ada from her spot on the other side of the laundry by the drying racks. She was pointing at Nell and Martin in case anyone didn't realise who the latest objects of her censure were. 'We'll be having Florrie Talbot down here carrying on before you know it. Disgusting, that's what that behaviour is, and completely unnecessary.'

Her voice was as tuneful as a peal of cracked bells, and, apart from the youngest children, everyone else in the laundry was now awake.

With a shared smile, Martin and Nell, gave each other a little wave and Martin left to see what was in store for him at the docks after a another night of bombing.

Some of the barely awake campers who had spent the night in the laundry, including Kitty Jarrett, decided to go through to the baths to ease their aching limbs and warm their bones before going off to work, but all Mary Lovell could think of was having a hot drink.

She tied the cord of Dolly's dressing gown tightly and helped the sleepy child put on her slippers. 'How about we go upstairs and have a nice cup of tea and a few rounds of toast before I get off to the shop, Nell? I had a bath a couple of days ago, so a wash down at the sink'll do me this morning.'

'Sounds good to me, Mary, and the kids can

have a few hours in bed. There's no school for them till this afternoon.'

'At least there's *some* school for a change,' said Lil, fingers itching to get on with her knitting, but her whole body aching to get upstairs for a sleep. 'My kids are driving me round the flipping bend.'

Nell pulled on her coat over the sweater and slacks she and Mary had taken to wearing – actually for the sake of warmth and modesty when they were sleeping in public like this, but according to Ada because they were part of the freakish new breed of women who thought they were men, what with their jobs and their smoking.

Automatically, Nell checked that her N-shaped pearl and gold brooch was pinned safely to her lapel – the little jewel that had been her sole possession when she'd been thrown out of the Foundlings' Home. When she remembered those cold, misery-filled days, it was as if they had happened to someone else or in another life. She was so grateful to Martin that her own children had experienced such happiness and with such a good man.

She wrapped Vicky in the blanket that had been covering the two of them, and picked her up. 'Off we go, little one,' she said to her sleepy-eyed child.

They stepped out into the courtyard – Mary holding Dolly's hand, Nell carrying Vicky. 'So you're opening the shop this morning then, Mary?'

'Yeah, but that Lottie, the Saturday girl is coming in at ten. She wants to do more shifts so she doesn't get called up for war work. I'm not convinced she's up to it, though, she can be so dozy. And now it's only me and her until Sarah comes back, it's not going to be easy.'

'I've been thinking about that, Mary. I know how unreliable Lottie can be. So if we can sort out looking after the kids between us – maybe ask young Grace Jarrett to help out minding them for a few hours – I can do the other shifts if it doesn't work out with her.'

'That would be ideal, Nell. I bet Grace wouldn't mind earning a few bob, and both the girls like her. You do, don't you, kids?'

Vicky nodded.

'She's nice,' said Dolly. 'And she's really good at cards. I don't mind playing with Vicky, but she's not old enough to play properly.' Dolly laughed. 'And I know it wasn't right, but how about when Grace shouted at Mrs Tanner?'

Mary flashed a look at Nell, doing her best not to start laughing. 'Well, she only did that because she felt a bit tired, didn't she? You're nearly eleven now, Dolly, and you know full well we don't do that sort of thing. And we don't want your little sister learning bad habits. You know how she copies you.'

'Sorry, Nan.'

'That's all right, but just you remember.'

They were about to go up the stairs that led to the fifth floor when someone called from the courtyard: 'Mrs Lovell.'

Nell and Mary – both Mrs Lovells – looked round. It was the post girl with her sack of mail over her shoulder.

'It's for you, Mary,' she said, holding out an envelope as she walked towards them. 'This is a bit of luck, the only other post I've got for your block is on the third floor and lower. It'll save me having to go right up to the fifth.'

Nell stifled another yawn and shuddered as the wind whipped across the courtyard. 'It amazes me how you get round every morning,' she said admiringly. 'Clambering through all the damaged streets and over all them potholes and that. I don't know if I could do it.'

The post girl shrugged. 'I quite like it. It's a lovely feeling being useful. The money's good, too, and we'll be getting uniforms soon as well.'

'That'll be smashing. You'll be able to save your own clothes for best.'

'That's what I thought. And we're going to be

able to choose between skirts and trousers. I think I'll go for trousers.'

'Good idea in this weather,' said Nell, cuddling Vicky closer to her. 'Still, at least it's not snowing this morning.'

'It's still blooming cold. You'd better get those young ones indoors, and I'd better get on with my delivery, before we all freeze to the spot.' She strode off ahead of them and they heard her footsteps as she trotted up the stairs towards the third floor.

Mary was staring at the address embossed on the back of the envelope. 'Whatever are these people writing to me for?' she said. 'I know it says it's for me but what's it all about? Why would a firm of solicitors be contacting me?'

'Excuse me, Mrs Lovell.' It was Bella, Ada's granddaughter, who had been sheltering in the laundry with her grandparents. 'Can me and Grace get past, please? We're really cold, and we don't want Grace dropping Bobby.'

'What? Yeah.' Mary was still distracted by her letter. 'Of course.'

'Thank you.'

Bella and Grace started up the stairs, Bella pulling faces at little Bobby who was gurgling happily in Grace's arms.

'There's a dance on this Friday. Fancy going with us, Grace?'

'I don't think Mum would let me.'

'There's nothing to worry about. It's in the basement of that big department store over in Stratford. So it'll be safe, even if there's a raid on. They're going to have a proper band down there and everything. It sounds really good. They're charging you for drinks but getting in's going to be free for everyone. The council wants to cheer us up, what with all the bombing going on. Go on, Grace, come with me. Ask her, she might surprise you.'

'No, there's no point, I know she won't let me. She doesn't hold with that sort of thing.'

'Why?'

'She says that girls get into trouble too easily if they start going to dances and that.'

'Suit yourself.' Bella opened the door to number 56, her grandparents' flat. 'Is she as strict with Freddie?'

'Not really, no. Especially since he's been working. Mum says he's all grown up, and how proud she is of him now he's bringing in money as well. She doesn't really stop him doing things.'

'Good, then you can ask him if he fancies coming along, if you like. I'll be here at Nan's all day. She said I've got to clean right through for

217

her. I couldn't say no,' Bella added artfully. 'Not with you nearly dropping me in it like that. I was sure you were going to say it was me who told you all that stuff. I couldn't believe the look on Nan's face.'

Grace shrugged. 'I didn't mean any harm; it sort of just came out when she picked on my mum.'

'Never mind all that, Grace. If I know Nan she'll have already got her false teeth stuck into someone else by now. It doesn't take her long.'

'I shouldn't have mentioned your brother. That was wrong.'

'Well, you can make it up to me then, can't you? After you've asked Freddie about the dance, you can let me know what he says so I can get myself all prepared.'

'I'm not sure.'

'Why not?'

'He still treats me like I'm his little sister. You'd be better off asking him yourself.'

'No, Grace, you know I've tried to talk to him before. You ask him for me. If you do, I'll give you a bar of chocolate I've been saving.' Bella smiled winningly. 'I bet you and your little brother would love that. And like I say, you did nearly drop me in it with my nan. It'll be a way of saying sorry.'

Grace looked at Bobby and sighed. 'All right, if you like.'

Freddie had had alcohol on his breath when he had got home the night before, and, much to his mother's annoyance, he had refused to leave his bed when the warning siren had sounded. He might be growing up fast, and even paying his way, but she couldn't help worrying about him. He was her first-born after all.

As Grace let herself into number 55 she could hear her brother snoring loudly. If only Bella could hear that.

She carried Bobby through to her mother's bedroom and put him in his cot, giving him a knitted toy bear that had been sitting on Kitty's bed. He stuck its leg in his mouth and began gnawing happily.

Grace pulled down the blackout blind and closed the door quietly behind her. Then she took a deep breath and knocked on the door to Freddie's room.

'Fred? Fred? Are you awake?'

'What do you want?'

'I need to talk to you before Mum comes back up to get ready for work.'

'Come in then, but don't put the light on, I've got a headache.'

*

'What, you mean that girl who visits her nan and granddad across the landing?' Freddie was propped up against the headboard, his hair sticking up in unflattering tufts. He'd obviously had a disturbed night.

'That's her. Bella. She's all right. And I know she really likes you. She's ever so keen. Mind you, looking at the state of you, Freddie Jarrett, I can't see the attraction.' Grace sniffed the air. 'And you smell like the whiff you get when you walk past a pub door. It's horrible.'

'Go on then.'

'Go on what?'

'Tell her I'll go with her. I've not got anything better to do on Friday night. And close that door behind you, will you, Grace? I'm bloody knackered.'

'You look it.'

'Yeah, yeah. That's enough. You just go and see your little mate.'

Across the landing, over in number 57, Dolly and Vicky had finished their breakfast and had gone off to bed. Nell was making more toast and tea for Mary, who was sitting at the kitchen table staring at the letter she had at last taken out of its envelope.

'They want to see me, Nell. "As soon as possible" it says.'

'Where are they?'

Mary looked at the letter again, bewildered as to what this could possibly mean. 'It says that they've moved away from their usual City address – the one on the envelope – for the duration, and that they've got temporary offices out in Romford somewhere. It's over a haber-dasher's. Here.' She held it out to Nell. 'They've written it all down for me. Where it is and that.'

'Why don't you go and open the shop, wait for Lottie, and tell her she's going to do a full day? You said she was after more hours. Well, let her find out what it's like a bit sooner than she expected. Then we'll get the bus over there.'

'You'll go with me?'

'Of course I will.'

'But how about the kids?'

'Missing another afternoon of school won't make much difference.'

'I don't want them being any more disrupted than needs be, Nell. And when you think about it, I haven't got a clue what I'm going to be faced with when I get to Romford. It's bound to be something serious. I don't want them getting upset.'

Mary stood up and took a bite of toast and a swig of tea. 'I'd better get to the shop . . . and let's hope those hooligans don't turn up while Lottie's on her own. The stupid so-and-sos haven't even noticed that Sarah and David aren't living there at the minute.'

Nell gave Mary her handbag. 'Look, I can see how flustered this is making you. And that's why I'm going with you. No argument. We'd have had to have gone over to the Aldgate bus station to get the Greenline anyway, so we might as well drop the girls off at the Hope and pick it up in Whitechapel. Sylvia's always only too pleased to see them. You can use the phone box on your way to the shop and give her a call. Tell her we'll be over about half-past ten.'

Nell handed her the letter. 'Take that with you, and then you can phone the solicitors as well while you're at it. We don't want a wasted journey.'

Mary and Nell sat on one side of the big partners' desk facing Mr Bennington, a grey-haired man in a very old-fashioned suit. He had a pair of half-moon glasses balanced on the end of his nose, and looked so ancient, Mary could only presume that they'd brought the old boy out of retirement to replace a younger man who had been called up. All Nell could think of was that she wished he would just get on with it – this was becoming all too reminiscent of the occasions in her childhood when she'd sat across from the matron in the Foundlings'

Home, wondering what she was supposed to have done this time, and what her punishment was going to be. And he was talking in what might as well have been a foreign language.

'I'm sorry, Mr Bennington,' said Mary at last, her reluctance to interrupt such a posh, well-spoken person worn thin by the gobble-degook he'd been spouting. 'Would you mind explaining that in words I can recognise? Because you've got me really confused.'

He took a moment, straightened his pen rack and then extended a pale hand which had clearly never done so much as a single day's physical labour and indicated a stack of papers on the desk. 'The documents I have here in front of me are the Last Will and Testament of Sarah Meckel.'

'Sarah? Last Will and Testament?' Mary's hand flew to her mouth. '*No!*'

'If I may continue, Mrs Lovell?'

'I'm sorry, but I don't understand. You don't mean she's passed away, do you?'

'I'm afraid I do. This document was prepared by a solicitor in Teignmouth and legally wit-nessed. I also have a letter for you from Mrs Meckel, one from the local police, and another from Mr Meckel's cousin further explaining the circumstances. Oh, and a set of deeds, of course.'

He took off his glasses. 'The news I have for you is mixed, Mrs Lovell.'

Mary could feel her eyes filling up. 'Would you get it over with, please?'

'Of course. It seems there was some sort of an accident. Mrs Meckel and her husband had been drinking heavily . . .'

'But they didn't hardly drink. Either of them.'

'Mrs Lovell, may I continue?'

'Sorry,' said Nell, handing Mary a handkerchief. 'But Mrs Meckel was a very good friend of my mother-in-law's. And of mine.'

'Quite, but I am merely relaying what Mr Meckel's cousin told the police, and what is contained in this letter that was sent to me after they went through Mrs Meckel's effects.'

'I don't understand,' Mary's voice was flat. 'Why didn't Sarah just send me the letter like she always did?'

'If I may continue? Because of the alcohol they had consumed, and the sedative medication Mr Meckel had recently been prescribed for his nervous condition, they failed to notice that the gas lamp had blown out. The windows were old and had been stuffed with clothing to keep out drafts, as had the bedroom door. When Mr Meckel's cousin tried to wake them the next morning, she was unable to do so, and so she sent for the village policeman. I am afraid they both failed to regain consciousness.'

Mary slumped forward in her chair.

Nell sprang out of her own and knelt down at Mary's feet. 'Can Mrs Lovell have a glass of water, please?'

Mr Bennington looked at Mary disapprovingly; he wasn't a man who endorsed any show of emotion. 'I'll ask the girl to fetch one.'

Nell thought he might have offered them a cup of tea, knowing he was going to be passing on such bad news.

'So they've been buried already?' Mary, red-eyed and hardly able to take in what she was being told, took another sip of water.

'I understand that their religious custom requires a quick burial.'

'Who would have been there?'

'Mr Meckel's cousin, I believe. From her letter, it doesn't seem that there was anybody else.'

Mary started crying again. 'That's terrible. So lonely, and in a place they didn't hardly know. They should have been up here, with us, with friends – with people who cared about them.'

Mr Bennington took his watch from his waistcoat pocket. 'I do have another appointment at two. May I give you a bare outline of the details and then, if there are any questions afterwards, I'm sure I can deal with them at that point. If not, I'm afraid you'll have to come back at a later date, or we can communicate by letter if you prefer?'

Mary finished her water. 'It's all such a shock.'

'There are two instructions in the Will before it can be upheld. One is that a Miss Florrie Talbot be allowed to carry on living in the named premises—'

'The shop?'

'Yes, Mrs Lovell, the shop. And, secondly, that a monthly amount of monies – equal to one-twentieth of the shop's takings – be sent to Mr Meckel's cousin Ruth for the period of one year; after that time the same amount will instead be given to the aforementioned Miss Talbot. And, so long as these points are adhered to, the shop will then—'

'Will then what?' Mary blew her nose again.

'Pass into your legal ownership.'

Her hand dropped from her nose into her lap. *Bloody hell!*

'Quite.'

Mary sat on the Greenline bus, not noticing the snowy countryside as they made their way back from Romford, through Chadwell Heath and then onwards to the East End, nor even the other passengers who flashed glances at the two weeping women, wondering who they'd lost in this bloody awful war – a husband, child, brother? She held out the letter Sarah had written to her.

'She says David got so ill, Nell, that she thought he was dying. She doesn't say so, but I don't believe it was an accident. They weren't drinkers, and if the windows and door had been blocked, how could the gas have blown out? What's wrong with the coppers down there?'

'What good would it have done if they had found out it wasn't an accident, though? It would have made things worse, if anything.'

'You're right. I don't suppose Sarah would have wanted to have gone on without him anyway. And she knew there'd be no one down there to care for him if anything happened to her. From what she hinted about that cousin of David's over the months, and from the letter the cousin herself sent, she sounds a right hard-faced . . .'

Mary ran her finger along one line of the letter. 'The money for David's cousin, it's to pay her back for their funerals, Sarah says: "in case anything happens to us". It's not meant as a gift or anything. And I'll guarantee Sarah was already more than paying their way.' She waved the letter like a flag. 'She was miserable down there, Nell. Really miserable. That cousin was so mean to them. Sarah should never have gone away in the first place. She should have stayed up here with us.'

Nell dug around in her bag for another hankie. 'You know David couldn't have lasted up here, Mary.'

'He didn't last down there either, did he?'

They sat in silence for a while.

Eventually Mary blew her nose and sniffed, and Nell took her hand. 'I'll come with you to tell Florrie.'

Mary nodded. 'Thanks, Nell.' She stared unseeingly out of the window. 'I want her to know that she's always going to have a home, and just how much Sarah thought of us all.' Mary pressed her forehead against the cold glass. 'Generous as always, even now she's passed on. How can I own a shop? What'll Joe say?'

'I'm not sure, Mary. It's all come as such a shock, it's going to take some getting used to.'

Mary straightened up and leaned back in her seat. 'It was them little bleeders, you know, the ones who wrote terrible things all over the shop. They might as well have murdered Sarah and David with their own hands.'

'Let's not think about those idiots today, Mary. Tell you what, before we go to the shop, why don't we go to the Hope and ask Sylvia if she can keep the kids for the evening? I don't think they should be there when we talk to Florrie.'

'You're right.'

'Then we can raise a glass to our friends' memories and go and break the news to Flo.'

'Sarah was a good woman, Nell, and she loved that man with all her heart.'

'I know, Mary. I know.'

Chapter 14

While Nell and Mary were travelling back through Essex – going over possible ways of exactly how they were going to break the news to Florrie – a man they had never seen before was standing on their landing in Turnbury Buildings.

The man was staring at one of the doors. He checked the scrap of paper he was holding. Number 55 – that was the one. He tugged nervously at his earlobe. How was this going to work out? Would it just degenerate into yet another shouting match?

There was only one way to find out.

He knocked on the door. Once. Twice.

At the sound of someone knocking – everyone who lived there had a key or left their doors open – Ada appeared in the doorway of number 56, nosing as usual.

'Who's that?' she demanded, pointing at the stranger, but looking at Joe Lovell.

'Search me, Ada,' said Joe, letting himself and Tommy into number 57. 'We've only popped back for a sandwich and a cuppa tea before we start our next load.'

Ada, with her eye now firmly on the unfamiliar man standing outside number 55, kept on speaking to Joe. 'I saw Mary got a letter this morning. Important, was it?'

'I wouldn't know, Ada, I wasn't there, was I? But her and Sarah write regularly to one another, so maybe it was from Devon. Now, if you don't mind, me and Tommy are gasping. We've not stopped since first thing and the canteen's too busy looking after the firemen to worry about us.'

'Not so fast, you. There's more to this than you're letting on. Bad news, was it, the letter? 'Cos she looked right worried, I'm telling you. Face like yesterday, she had. You could tell she wasn't happy, so what—'

Ada swallowed her words as the door of number 55 opened and Grace stood there, her mouth opening and closing like a stranded cod's. This had the potential for some fine entertainment, Ada decided. They probably owed the bloke some money. He looked the shifty sort.

Now she couldn't take her eyes off Grace, who was obviously suffering.

Then the girl found her voice and came out with something that even Ada wouldn't have guessed if she'd been standing there all day: 'Dad? What are you doing here?'

Ada's head swivelled round like an over-weight owl's and she looked at the stranger. '*Dad*? That bloke's your dad?' she asked without a moment's hesitation.

The man barged into the flat past Grace, leaving Ada goggling.

'Oi! Hang on,' she shouted after him as he disappeared. 'Ain't you meant to be away at sea? Your boat got torpedoed, did it? Many hurt?'

Grace closed the door firmly in her face, leaving the elderly woman fuming – not so much from affront at being excluded in such a rude manner, as because she didn't know how long she'd have to wait before she got to the bottom of this one. If there was one thing she couldn't stand it was being kept out of her neighbours' business. In fact, it was often said by the inhabitants of the Buildings that she'd rather ding a full purse into the Thames than be kept in the dark about their comings and goings.

'The kitchen's down there,' said Grace, pointing towards the back of the flat.

As he made his way along the passage, Dan Jarrett looked at each closed door suspiciously. 'Where's your mother then?'

'She's at work.'

'Work? What work? How can she go to work when she has to look after you kids?'

'She does go out to work. She's a machinist.'

'I know things haven't been easy between us all—'

Grace mumbled something inaudible.

'Don't mess around, Grace. This isn't the time. I only want to talk to her.'

'I'm not messing around. Mum has got a job – in a factory. It's war work, making uniforms. In a place off Brick Lane.' She said it with a lift of her chin, acting far braver than she actually felt. 'That good enough?'

'Grace, don't let's be like this. What time's she due home?'

'An hour or so, maybe. I'm not sure.' Grace shrugged. This was like some kind of a bad dream. Why couldn't she have been out taking Bobby for a walk or something? Why wasn't Freddie here to back her up? 'It depends if they have to do any overtime.'

'Right.'

A soft murmuring came from the bedroom closest to the kitchen.

Dan Jarrett flinched. 'Is that . . . ?'

'Yes, Dad. It's Bobby.'

Dan bowed his head. 'He must be getting big.'

Florrie, Mary and Nell sat in Florrie's kitchen in the set of rooms above the corner shop that had once belonged to Sarah and David Meckel, but that now somehow belonged to Mary. It was still a bit much to take in.

She folded the letter that Sarah had written to her and put it back safely in its envelope; it was far more valuable to Mary than the shop could ever be. 'Such lovely words. I can hear Sarah saying them in my head as if she's in the room with us right now.'

Florrie sniffed loudly. 'It's all so sad.'

'Yeah, so sad. But that's the up and the down of it, Flo, what Sarah wanted: you stay here, and after a year you get a monthly allowance.'

'No, what she wanted, Mary, was for me to give up . . . you know, *working*. I wish I could have done it for her before she went, so she could have seen how much I cared about her.'

'You can still do it, Flo. There's plenty of work here. And we've always got on well together, haven't we?'

'I'm too long in the tooth to change now, Mary.'

'Don't say that,' pleaded Nell. 'You're a young woman still. Not that much older than me.'

Florrie sniffed miserably. 'Yeah, if you forget the year I had measles, we could almost be twins.' She shook her head. 'I'm forty bloody years old.'

'You don't look it.' Nell sounded more kind

than sincere.

Florrie poured them all another drop of port. 'I can't take it in, can you? Sarah was so lively, and full of decency, and always grafting so hard – running the shop, looking after David. And then having to put up with me—'

'Don't say that, Flo, she loved you.'

'And I loved her, Mary. She was the family I never had. So why didn't I go and fetch them back from staying with that rotten cousin of David's? You'd think that woman would have been over the moon, being related to a man who had been as brave as David was. It don't seem right, does it, her acting like that to him?'

'There's a lot of things that don't seem right in this world,' said Mary. 'But you mustn't blame yourself for anything, Florrie. We all know how much you cared for Sarah.' Mary drained her glass and stood up. 'Come on, Nell, we'd better get going. The warning'll probably be going soon. Why don't you come back to the Buildings with us tonight, Flo? I've got some cold meat and pickles we can take down the laundry with us. And you can come back here when I come to open up in the morning.'

'Do you know, I think I will, Mary. I don't much fancy being pleasant to a bunch of strangers. Not after all this. And it'd be kind of respectful to Sarah if I didn't go out tonight.'

As soon as Grace heard the key in the lock, she ran to the door to warn her mother.

'Mum, it's him . . . Dad. He's only here. In the kitchen.'

'What?'

'Honestly, Mum, I'm telling you, he's here.'

Kitty gathered her thoughts. So, Dan was back. Whatever it was that he wanted, she wasn't going to let him see she gave a single damn. Shoulders back. Head up.

'I'd better go and see what he wants then, hadn't I?'

She followed her daughter along the passage-way, but before they got to the kitchen she put a hand on Grace's shoulder and stopped her.

'No, Grace, this is for me and your dad to discuss. You go in and check on Bobby.'

'Dan.' Kitty prayed that her voice wouldn't wobble. 'Well, blow me down, this is a surprise. I didn't expect to see you again.'

'I've got a few days before my next trip, and I thought I'd go and look you up over in Poplar. See how things were going with you all. It was quite a shock when I saw the place smashed to the ground. It started me thinking.'

'Aw, did it? It was quite a shock for us and all,

having the bloody bombs dropped on us and losing our home. But no more of a shock than having you turn up here out of the blue.'

Dan's eyebrows creased. She'd got spirited in his absence. 'Where's Freddie?'

'Work.'

'No need to talk to me like that, Kit. I only wanted to know what was happening with him. What's happening with all of you. You get time to think about things when you're laying in your bunk of a night with the waves crashing against the side of the ship, not knowing if a U-boat's going to appear and end it all for you. It gets you thinking about your family.'

'Well, bloody good for you, Dan Jarrett. What do you want, Father and Husband of the Year awards?'

'Blimey, girl, if it's going to be like this, I might as well clear off now.'

'Go on then.'

'Please, don't be like this. I'm really trying here. I meant it, you know. When I saw the house had been bombed, I thought I'd lost you all for good.'

'You did that already, when you walked out on us, after you found out about . . .'

'Don't drag all that up again, Kit. I'm really trying here.'

'Pity you didn't try a bit harder when

you found out what had happened then, wasn't it?'

He stood up. 'Here we go.'

'What, running off again, are you? How many times do I have to tell you? It wasn't my fault. It happened. That's all.'

'Then whose fault was it? You're supposed to be the sodding mother here.'

In the room next to the kitchen, Grace put her hands over her ears. It was starting all over again. Why wouldn't they stop?

She bent over Bobby's cot. She was about to pick him up, but couldn't bring herself to do it. Instead, she put his little knitted bear safely in his sleeping embrace and then took her mother's coat out of the wardrobe. She let herself quietly out of the room and crept along the passage. Out on the landing, she took a moment to look back at the front door. She didn't want all this again – the rowing and the shouting and the accusations. It wasn't fair, not to any of them.

'Where are you off to in your mother's coat?' demanded Ada, who had fetched a kitchen chair out on to the landing to make her sentry duty more comfortable.

'Leave me alone, Mrs Tanner. Please, leave me alone.' Grace, usually so timid on the stairway, started off down the concrete steps at such a rip it was as if the whole of Hitler's army was after her.

'How could you have done it, Dan?' Kitty stared at the floor – she certainly couldn't look at him as she spoke. 'Saying you'd have nothing to do with him. How could you? Me, I had no choice. I had to get on with it. Carry on living. Get up every morning and make sure there was break-fast on the table for us all, and that the kids had some sort of a normal life.'

'That's the difference between the two of us then, Kit. See, I did have a choice.' Biding his time, Dan took out his cigarettes and offered the packet to Kitty. 'I could clear off to sea and forget about it all.'

She took one and sat down at the table oppo-site him. They took a moment lighting them. Then he let out a long, slow plume of smoke.

'Or I thought I could. But I was wrong. Kit, I realised I couldn't leave it like that. I hated being without you. And then when I thought you'd all been killed . . . that's when I realised how much I still loved you.'

Before Kitty could respond, the warning siren went. 'I am so sick and tired of this,' she sighed.

Dan wasn't sure if it was him or the bombs she was talking about, and thought it wisest not to ask. 'We'll be all right up here for a while, won't we? I need to explain why I acted the way I did – try and make up for how I behaved.'

Kitty picked up the bag she kept packed ready for what had become the nightly raids over the docks. 'You've not had a house collapsing around you, have you? You saw the damage over in Poplar. Our home in pieces, nothing left.' She stepped towards the kitchen door, her back turned to him. 'A bit like us, really.'

'Do you mean that?'

'I wasn't the one who walked out.'

'I couldn't take it any more, Kit. Once I found out, it started eating me away, like some sort of horrible disease.'

'You'd have got over it. I did. I had to.' She turned and shoved the bag at him, still not making eye contact. 'Take that and go down to the laundry and save us a space. We usually park ourselves over at the far end, by the door to the baths.'

'Laundry?'

'It's in the basement; it's where we all go to shelter. Go on, hurry up or we won't get our space. I'll fetch Grace and Bobby.'

'All I want to do is talk about this, Kit, before I have to go on my next trip. It's driving me out of my bloody mind. I don't know what way to turn. I miss you so much, you and the kids.'

'Stop feeling so sorry for yourself, Dan. These raids are no joke. Take that bag down to the laundry and I'll get the kids. If you can't find the spot where we sleep, just mention my name. Anyone'll show you.'

Dan reluctantly started down the stairs with the overnight bag. He had almost reached the second floor, caught up in the press of people flooding down towards the basement, when he heard Kitty shouting but couldn't make out the words.

He heaved himself back up the steps against the tide of increasingly angry residents who just wanted to get to safety.

'Kit! What? What is it?'

When he got to the fifth floor, his wife was standing on the landing with Bobby in her arms. Her shouting had scared the little boy so badly he was wailing inconsolably.

'It's Grace, Dan. She's not here. And my coat's gone.'

'Perhaps she went down as soon as the warning went?'

'No. She never goes anywhere without telling me. She's not like Freddie. I'll know he'll be all right, but she acts more like ten than fifteen. It's my fault, I've kept her so wrapped up . . .'

'Calm down, Kit.'

'Calm down?' Kitty looked at him as if he were mad. 'She must have heard us rowing and run off. This is our fault. *Ours*. She's Gawd

241

knows where, and who knows what might happen to her when the bombs start falling? Listen to them, will you?' She looked up at the ceiling as though she could see right through the plaster and into the dark skies, like the searchlights shining their beams through the clouds, picking out the glint of enemy metal. 'The planes are so close, Dan, listen. Listen!'

'All right, Kit. Don't panic.'

He watched, unseeing, as his wife jiggled the still-yelling Bobby over her shoulder.

'Look, if she's already gone down to the laundry, you're getting yourself in a state for nothing. So we'll go down, nice and calm, and have a look for her. And if she's not there *then* we'll decide what to do.'

Kitty nodded, terrified by the images in her mind of Grace alone in the blackout with bombs falling all around her.

Dan took a deep breath and nodded at the wailing child. 'So that's—'

Kitty pressed her lips together to stop herself from crying. 'Mmm.'

'He's got big.'

She nodded again, murmuring. 'What have we done?'

Dan went ahead, carrying the bag, pausing every few steps to make sure that Kitty was managing to negotiate the stairs with a bawling child in her arms.

At the bottom of the main stairwell, she pointed to the other flight of steps that led down to the basement. Dan stood to one side to let her go first.

'That's all we flaming well need.' Ada greeted Kitty from her deckchair that was, as usual, set in prime position next to Lil who, also as usual, was knitting. 'A screeching kid.'

She leaned in closer to Lil, but didn't bother to lower her tone – if anything she turned up the volume a few notches. 'That's her old man, you know.' She sniffed bronchially. '*Meant* to be away at sea. There's a story there, I'm telling you, a right bloody story. It's these modern women, getting up to all sorts, working in factories, rouging their cheeks and smoking if you don't mind. Unnatural, that's what it is.'

Kitty and Dan ignored the faces that had all turned to stare at this welcome distraction from the raid and didn't even hear the whispers that followed. All Dan could do was watch as Kitty scanned the room.

She sighed in relief. 'Bella . . . that's the friend she's made since we moved here . . . isn't down here. Grace'll have gone to see her. That's where she'll be.'

'But I am here, Mrs Jarrett.' It was Bella, standing in the doorway that led to the bathing cubicles, toothbrush in one hand, and towel draped over her shoulder.

Kitty hurried over to her, still holding Bobby who was now only snivelling quietly. 'Have you seen her? My Grace?'

Bella nodded. 'Yeah.'

Kitty closed her eyes in relief. 'Thank goodness.'

'I saw her running down the stairs. She looked funny. Her coat was too big or something. Then the warning went. I called after her to wait for me, but she didn't say anything, just kept running. I thought she'd be down here, but . . .' Bella turned down her mouth. 'Sorry, I don't know where she is.'

Kitty looked about her wildly as if seeking something no one else could see.

'This is all my fault,' she said bitterly to her husband. 'I should have thrown you out as soon as I set eyes on you in that kitchen. I've got to go and find her.'

'What, with him?' Dan jerked his head at the now hiccupping child in her arms. 'You'd risk that?'

'I'll mind him for you, Mrs Jarrett,' chipped in Bella, thinking that such a kind offer to his mum might make her look good when she told

Freddie what she'd done to help out – and would be something nice to talk about when they were at the dance. It would be *Bella to the Rescue*, like a serial at the flicks.

'No, thanks all the same,' said Dan. 'No one's going out looking for anyone. It'll have to wait till the all clear sounds, then I'm the one who's going looking.'

He steered his wife over to their roll of pillows and eiderdowns by the door to the bathing area and gently sat her on the ground while he set about making up her and Bobby's bed for the night.

Kitty's head drooped until her chin touched her chest. 'Aw, Dan, I'm so frightened.'

'Me too, Kit.' He folded the top eiderdown back so that she could get between the downy layers, his head turned away from her. 'And feeling as guilty as bloody hell.'

Kitty's eyes closed once or twice but she had no sleep. All she was waiting for was the all clear, the signal that she could go and find her daughter.

She was on her feet the moment it sounded.

'I'll have to get Bobby changed and fed, then we can start looking.'

Back upstairs, Dan said nothing as he fumbled his way around the kitchen of number

55, opening drawers and cupboards, looking for the things to make them a pot of tea.

His body should have ached from sitting leaning against the cold laundry wall all night, but if it did he took no notice.

There was the sound of a key in the lock then. Kitty hurried out of the bedroom, leaving a half-naked Bobby on the bed, and Dan almost dropped the teapot on the kitchen floor in his hurry to get out into the passageway.

'Freddie,' said Kitty, disappointment dripping from her like the grimy snow melting off the surrounding rooftops.

Then suddenly the feeling of urgency returned. She grabbed the lapels of his overcoat. 'I'm really glad you're okay, Fred, but have you seen her? Have you? I won't be angry if she told you to keep it a secret.'

Freddie bridled. What did she know? Nobody knew about Li and him, nobody. He was sure of it. And it was over anyway. 'What are you talking about? And while we're at it, what's *he* doing here?'

'Never mind your dad. It's Grace . . .'

'What's this, a party game?'

'Freddie . . . son.' Dan so wanted to hug him, but knew that he couldn't rush things if he was to stand any chance of making it up to him. 'Grace has gone missing.'

'How do you mean, missing?'

'I can't explain now, but she got a bit upset when I got here last night and—'

'That's great, that is. You turn up and she goes missing.' It was all Freddie could do to stop himself from lashing out. 'She's like a kid. She's got no idea about how to look after herself. You must be very proud, Dad, turning up and causing all this.'

'Please, you two, please! Just shut up, will you?' Kitty could hardly speak through her tears. 'Grace is missing, and it's our fault for rowing. We drove her away.'

For what seemed an age, no one spoke.

Finally Dan broke the silence. 'You'll have to stay here, Kit.' He couldn't bring himself to say: *to look after Bobby*, so instead he said: 'In case Grace comes back. She'll be in a state. She'll need you.'

Freddie, almost as tall as his father, stuck out his chin like a prize fighter taunting a weaker opponent. 'I can find her by myself. We don't need your help.'

'I can't let you do that, Fred. I've got to see her before I go back to sea. When I saw the old house, I thought I'd lost you all. Anything can happen to any one of us while all this is going on. Don't let's be like this, son.'

Freddie turned and made his way along the passageway. 'Bobby's crying, Mum,' he threw

247

over his shoulder as he flung open the front door.

Kitty looked imploringly at her husband. 'Just find her. Don't let me have this on my conscience as well.'

Dan and Freddie Jarrett stumbled their way through the chaos of the post-raid streets, asking rescue and demolition squads, fireman and WVS workers – anyone they came across – whether they'd seen Grace.

'She's got brown hair,' said Freddie to one woman who was taking a tray of tea round to soot- and brick-dust smeared volunteers, 'but not as dark as mine, and right pale skin.'

'Can't help you, young man, I'm afraid. I'm on the mobile unit, and I only just got here.'

'But maybe as you were driving along?' pressed Dan.

'Sorry.'

They moved on, picking their way over hoses, piles of rubble, and bits of broken stuff that could have been just about anything.

Freddie tripped on a loose cable, only saving himself from falling flat on his face in a puddle of filthy melting snow by grabbing the arm of an annoyed-looking warden.

'Oi, d'you mind, sonny?' The warden shook him off as if he were a dog who was trying to be over-friendly.

He took in Freddie's expensive-looking over-coat; he was clearly earning a fair whack for a kid – but how? 'There's people doing important work here. Now move along, go on. Give us a chance to get on with it. We don't need no sight-seers standing around gawping.' He narrowed his eyes and added ominously: 'Or looters.'

Freddie put up his hands in apology. He should be more careful, he knew, all he needed was for people to start getting curious about where his money was coming from. 'No offence.' He moved off again, picking his way along what had once been an ordinary Wapping sidestreet.

'Mum said she feels guilty about Grace taking off like that, but this is no one's fault but yours,' he said viciously to his father. 'No one's. Got it? You already tore our family apart once before. Nearly broke Mum's heart, you did.'

'How can you blame me?' puffed Dan who was having trouble keeping up with the sixteen-year-old. 'I didn't do anything.'

Freddie stopped and spun round to face him. 'Didn't do anything? What about all the rows, the shouting and the accusations? And then walking out on your own wife? You reckon that's *not doing anything*?'

'I couldn't help it, Fred.' Dan didn't want a quarrel, he wanted his son to understand. 'Once

I'd found out about – you know – I couldn't carry on.'

'I thought you were meant to be an adult?'

'I couldn't cope with it. I just couldn't.' Dan couldn't think what else to say.

They moved on in silence through the hellish landscape of yet more destruction, fires, warnings about unexploded bombs, and officious ARP wardens and police officers refusing Dan and his son access to any place where Grace might be.

Suddenly, Freddie froze. 'Oh, no, Dad,' he said, forgetting all the venom he'd been spitting at his father only moments before. 'Look, over there.'

An ambulance worker, who looked as if he would far rather have been at home in front of the fire with his slippers on and smoking a pipe, was kneeling on a pile of bricks – some of them still held together by mortar, others powdered to nothing but dust. A pale hand was sticking out of the rubble. It was the hand of a young woman.

Dan and Freddie moved closer, struggling with a row of wardens who were holding them back.

'Let us get through, mate, we can help dig her out,' tried Dan.

'No, get back now.'

'Then why don't you help?'

'Can't. There's a broken gas main. We could have the rest of the street down. Got to wait for the experts.'

'Can we wait here then, please? We think we might know her.' The look in Dan's eyes made the man consult one of his colleagues.

'You can stand there, but no nearer. Got it?'

'Got it. Thanks, mate.'

Dan and Freddie stood shoulder to shoulder, their arms actually touching. They could hear the ambulance man talking to the girl.

'Don't worry, my darling. We'll have you out of there before you know it.'

He looked about him, willing the rescue squad to get to them before it was too late.

'Stay with me, my darling. Don't close your eyes, now. Tell me, what's your name? I'll bet it's something pretty, just like you.'

A sound came from inside the rubble.

'What did you say, my darling? Tell me again. Go on, try. Stay with me . . . stay with me. Don't close your eyes.'

He put his ear to the bricks.

'Pearl!' said the ambulance man. 'That's more than pretty, that's beautiful.'

As it dawned on Dan and Freddie that it wasn't Grace under the rubble, the ambulance man let out a low groan that sounded as if he was mourning for the whole of the world.

'No, Pearl. No . . . don't do this to me. Please, don't. I can't lose another one. I can't!'

Still on his knees, he reared up, snatched off his tin helmet and smashed it to the ground. 'What's the point of all this? What's the fucking point?'

Dan tapped his son's hand and indicated with a jerk of his head that they should leave. 'Let's get moving. We've got to find your sister.'

'Say that had been Grace, Dad?'

'Poor kid. I can't even begin to think what her parents are going to feel or do when they hear. That's why we've got to find your sister, so I can talk to her, tell her that the rows between me and your mum are over. No more. Our lives are going to get back to something like normal again, even with all this going on around us. I've got to do something right for once, something to make amends.' Dan took off his knitted seaman's cap and scratched his head. 'But where to look next, eh, Fred? Where next?'

Freddie threw up his hands in despair. 'I don't know. I really don't.' But then it was as if a light had been turned on. 'Maybe back home in Poplar?'

Dan nodded. 'She still knows people there.'

'That's where she might be – with one of the old neighbours.'

'Let's give it a try.'

It was now coming up to half-past three in the afternoon and Dan and Freddie felt that they were rapidly running out of people to ask and places in Poplar to search for Grace.

'Excuse me, officer.' Dan raised his chin in weary greeting to an equally weary-looking policeman – everyone seemed to be so tired these days. 'We're looking for someone. A fifteen-year-old girl we think might be sheltering around here somewhere. Anywhere you can suggest?'

'Have you tried the public shelters?'

'We've tried them all as far as I can tell.'

The policeman jabbed his thumb over his shoulder. 'How about the factories along the Limehouse Cut? Spratt's has loads of people sheltering there of a night. It's got a good deep basement, see. But,' he looked at his watch, 'if she was down there, she'd have left hours ago.' He looked up at the sky. 'Might be back in a bit, though.'

Dan turned to Freddie. 'What d'you think?'

'Got to be worth a try, Dad.'

'You could be wasting your time,' warned the officer.

'I know, mate,' said Dan over his shoulder, already sprinting along Burdett Road, fresh hope giving him a second wind, 'but we've got to try.'

They'd got as far as the factory gate when an old boy who looked as if he might have fought in the Boer War, let alone the Great one, barred their way.

'Passes.'

'We don't work here.'

'What do you want then?'

'I'm looking for my daughter. I think she might be sheltering inside.'

The man's face lit up like a gas mantle as an idea occurred to him. 'How old is this daughter of yours then?'

Dan threw a look at Freddie. 'Fifteen.'

Freddie joined in. 'That's right. Pale skin. Brown hair, not as dark or wavy as mine. She's shy but she chatters a lot to cover it up.'

Dan leaned towards the gatekeeper, willing the man to know where his daughter was. 'That's right, that's her exactly.'

'And she's wearing a coat that's too big for her.'

'That sounds like her . . .'

'Where did she go when she left here? Have you any idea? Think!'

'Who said she went anywhere? I'm only too pleased that someone might know who she is.'

Impatient to find his girl, Dan was losing track. 'I don't—'

The man pushed the gate wide open and nodded them through. 'I'll get someone to take you to her.'

A young woman, all smiles and lipstick and Veronica Lake peek-a-boo hair, led them through the massive factory to a small clerks' office. They looked through the glass door and saw that two wingback armchairs had been pushed together into a makeshift bed. There was a bundle of blankets piled on top of someone.

'There she is,' said the young woman, pointing at the bundle. 'I'd better come in with you, in case she . . . well, let's say, she's used to me.' She smiled at Freddie. 'I got two of the fellers to bring the chairs through for her. So she'd be nice and comfortable.'

'That's very kind of you.' Dan sounded impatient. 'But tell me – is there something wrong with her? Has she been hurt?'

'No, but it's a bit sad. She got knocked out in a raid and lost her memory. She came staggering in here, with no idea who she was or where she'd come from. We called the ambulance people, but what with all the calls on their time, they told us to keep her comfortable until they could come for her.'

As the young woman spoke, the bundle moved. Grace's face, as plain as day, looked directly at him. Immediately, she pulled the covers back over her head.

'You don't need to worry about her, miss. She knows exactly who she is.' Dan pushed, as politely as he could, past the young woman. 'That's it, Grace, there've been enough lies. We're going home. The three of us – together. It's time we were a family again. I'm going to sort this out, if it's the last thing I do. There'll be no one running away again – no one. And I'm going to make sure everyone knows that.'

Not much more was said as Dan, Freddie and Grace headed back to the Buildings – no recriminations, no tears, just Dan steering Grace gently by the elbow, enquiring every now and then if she was all right. It was almost dark, and they had just reached the archway that led into the courtyard when the siren started.

'You two might as well get straight down to the basement. I'll go up and get your mum and Bobby.'

Freddie and Grace were too worn out – physically and emotionally – to argue with their father.

When Dan reached the landing, he saw Kitty, red-eyed and even more exhausted-looking than the kids.

'We found her, Kit, we found her! She's fine, she's well, and she's gone down to the basement with Freddie. But, best of all, I've found all of you again. My family. I swear to you, on my life, I promise I'm going to make it up to you.'

A watchful Ada nearly keeled over in disbelief. *'Found his family?* Whatever bloody next?'

Down in the basement the buzz of news about the Jarretts' new arrival was still doing the rounds, despite most people having seen Dan the night before – at least it made a change from the usual gossip.

Ada and Lil were speculating on what had been going on all day – Kitty staying at home, her husband and elder son out somewhere, and not a sign of Grace until the warning went. Ada just hoped that Bella was doing a good job of pumping her friend for information.

She was.

'So did you really run away then, Grace?'

She nodded. 'My mum and dad were arguing and I wanted to get away. I hate it when people row.'

'You did a good enough job when you had a go at my nan the other night.'

'I didn't like how she was talking about my mum.'

Bella tutted. 'That's nothing. You should hear what she's got to say about mine.' She smiled sweetly at Freddie who was sitting on the other side of Grace, flicking through a day-old paper. 'I'm really looking forward to Friday, Fred.'

'Good.' He put the paper down and closed his eyes. 'Me too.'

Grace watched as her mum jiggled Bobby in his pushchair, her dad squatting by their side, looking for all the world as if he'd never been away.

Eventually, everyone – even Ada who had been doing her best to keep an eye out for any further developments with the Jarretts – had fallen asleep. Everyone, that is, except Dan and Kitty themselves.

'We need to talk properly before I have to go away again, Kit,' he said softly. 'About all sorts of things. And I've only got tonight and tomorrow before I sail.'

'It's not easy, Dan, not with all these people round us.'

'The kids are asleep. We could leave them down here and go up and have a cup of tea.'

'It would be too much of a risk.'

'Not one worth taking?'

She shook her head. 'No. If something happened to me, who'd look after the kids? But like you say, we have got a lot to talk about. How about if we go out to the sheds? No one'll be out there at this time of night.'

'What sheds?'

'They're on the ground floor of the block across the courtyard. Every flat's got one. And at least they're protected by the Buildings on top of them. Not so dangerous as being up on the top floor.'

'Good idea, Kit.' Dan got up carefully, doing his best not to disturb anyone. 'Fetch your coat and wrap yourself in one of the eiderdowns. It'll be freezing out there.'

Kitty and Dan skidded across the icy yard, the strangeness of being together making the searchlights, the droning planes, the whistles and crumps of the bombs falling down by the docks, seem almost normal.

Kitty snapped open her handbag and took out a small torch, its dim light shaded by a little cardboard collar. 'Let's find the keys.'

Dan followed her into the shed. 'Is there a light in here?'

'No, and I can't leave this torch on either. I need it to get me home in the blackout after work. Here, take my hand, so you don't bash into anything.'

She switched off the torch and smiled in the dark: his hand felt warm, strong – familiar.

'You know, you're lucky, Dan, that Bobby's asleep in his pushchair down in the laundry.'

'I don't understand. Why's that?'

''Cos that contraption of a pram they gave us down the rest centre after ours got destroyed in the bombing – it might have its uses, and it might have been very generous of them, but the rotten thing's exactly the right height to bash you in the shins. I know, 'cos I've done it enough times when I've come in here looking for stuff.'

'I hate to think of you hurting yourself, Kit. But most of all I hate to think about how badly *I've* hurt you. I can't say how much I hate it. Or how much I've missed you.'

She turned on the torch again and shone it in his face, looking into his eyes. 'I didn't think I'd ever say this but I've missed you too, Dan. We were happy once, weren't we?'

'We could be again.'

'Could we? I don't think so. It's too late after – you know – everything.'

She turned off the torch again.

'Kit, I want more than anything in the world for us to be a family again. I'll do whatever you want. Just tell me what you want me to do?'

He pulled her to him.

'*Dan, don't.*'

But he wouldn't let her go.

'I have missed you so much, Kit, I thought my heart was going to break.'

Before she could say another word he had covered her mouth with his, and it was as if they had never been apart.

'And where have you two been?' Ada was sitting in her chair, trussed up like a parcel, staring at the door to the laundry. 'I never heard no all clear going.'

'That's because there's not been one,' said Kitty, tucking the covers snugly around Bobby in his pushchair.

'So, where were you then?'

Dan looked at her. 'If you must know, me and my wife have been over in the sheds, acting like a couple of lovebirds.'

Kitty blushed scarlet and shoved him in the ribs. *'Dan.'*

'What? We've got nothing to be ashamed of.' He looked over to Grace and Freddie, both still sound asleep, and then back at Kitty. 'None of our family has. Not any more, I hope.'

'I don't want you to go, Dan.' Kitty stood at the door of number 55, with her husband's duffel bag in her arms and tears spilling down her cheeks.

Freddie and Grace were behind their mother,

261

hair tousled and faces flushed from sleep; Bobby was dozing in Grace's arms.

Dan was on the landing, dressed in his heavy woollen peacoat, scarf and thick, knitted seaman's cap. 'And I wish I could stay, Kit.' He stroked her cheek, which immediately provoked a loud tutting noise from across the landing.

'Morning, Mrs Tanner,' said Kitty, head high. 'It's hard when your loved ones have to leave to go and do their bit, eh? Still, good job there's brave men like my Dan.'

He took Kitty's face in his hands. 'Kit, me and Freddie have had a long talk, and we've worked out a lot of things. He's going to look after you while I'm away.' He turned to his son. 'You'll be the man of the house, won't you, Fred?'

Freddie nodded, not trusting himself to speak without his voice breaking. How could anyone trust him? He took illegal bets, ran blackmarket goods, and had hidden a girlfriend he'd now lost because of all his cheating and lies. How could he look after the family?

'This is the one it's going to be hardest to say goodbye to.' Dan ruffled Bobby's hair, making him wriggle in his sleep. 'He's going to be growing so quickly, I'll hardly recognise him when I get back. Make sure you send me plenty of pictures of him.'

'Aw, playing happy families. How nice,' said

Ada, nastiness oozing from her every word.

Dan turned and looked at her levelly. 'Well, dear, he is my grandson. What do you expect?' He kissed his daughter on the cheek. 'Look after your little one, Grace. You might not be as lucky as me and get another chance to show him how much you care about him. I'm blessed, and I know it. Make sure you know it and all.'

'Here, hold up there a minute.' Ada's eyebrows had shot up so high, her curlers almost exploded. 'Did you just say *grandson*?'

'That's right, Mrs Tanner,' said Grace. 'Bobby's my little boy. Beautiful, isn't he?'

She kissed Dan on the cheek. 'Keep safe, Dad, because I'm going to be telling Bobby every night that his granddad's coming home to see him very soon. And I don't want you to let him down.'

'Nor do I, Gracie, and I won't. You can guarantee it.'

Chapter 15

Bella shivered as she walked briskly along Stratford High Street towards the Broadway. It was freezing, but at least she had the satisfaction of knowing she looked gorgeous in her powder blue crêpe-de-Chine frock. Okay, the dress probably wouldn't last for more than a few wearings – after all, she had made it out of a cheap remnant she'd bought from a stall in Crisp Street market – but the colour really suited her. And while the lightweight material might have been more suited to spring rather than the middle of winter, the bodice clung to her body just so, and the skirt had enough of a swing in it to look really good when she moved. Freddie wouldn't be able to take his eyes off her when they went on the dance floor. She was only glad that she'd had enough foresight to – let's say – *borrow* her mum's fur coat to protect her against the icy wind; even though she hadn't asked permission.

But it was all right, her mum wouldn't notice, she was far too busy sitting in the front room working her way through the bottle of gin that the woman next-door had brought in for them to share. Before Bella had left home, her mum and the neighbour had got to the point when it looked like they'd only need about another half a glass each before they'd either be sound asleep or weeping like babies for their brave husbands away in the forces. It was strange the effect that drinking gin had on those two. Without it neither of them seemed in the least bit worried about their menfolk when they went to the corner pub to 'comfort' any 'poor boys' home on leave. But after a few glasses, you'd think they were married to a couple of genuine war heroes.

Bella caught a glimmer of light as someone slipped inside the door of the department store. This was it – ready or not – here she was. She pinched her cheeks to give her skin a pretty glow, stuck out her chest and looked around for Freddie. He'd had to go to work so they had arranged to meet up here.

It was sometimes difficult to make out who was who in the blackout, but her eyes had become accustomed to the dark during the long walk – and there was no mistaking Freddie Jarrett, with his big broad shoulders and his lovely chiselled chin. She ogled him appreciatively. He was gorgeous; if he looked like this now, he could be in the films by the time he was eighteen. Not like her brother Alfie – he got more like a girl every day.

'Hello, Fred. All right, are you?'

He was leaning against the wall of the store, a cigarette shielded in his hand so as to hide the glowing tip.

'Yeah, hello, Bella. Coming inside? It's bleedin' brass monkeys out here.'

'Love to,' she said, smiling up at him.

He ground his cigarette end out under his heel. 'Come on then.'

'We've not seen my dad for months. It was nice that yours got a few days' leave.'

Freddie nodded. 'You're right, Bella, it was. You've no idea how nice.'

Inside the door, a smiling young woman sitting behind a desk looked Freddie up and down. 'Coats over there, by the lavs,' she said, batting her lashes as she pointed, and earning herself an angry glare from Bella. 'Stairs down to the basement over there. You'll hear the band playing. And if you need anything else –' another flirty look at Freddie '– just ask. The name's Vi, Vi Thompson.'

Vi Thompson? Bella couldn't believe it. The bloody brass neck on her! Cheeky mare, talking to her feller like that, giving him her name.

Unlike Bella, Freddie didn't seem at all surprised; he smiled back at the girl – as much out of habit as any real interest. 'I will, Vi. Thanks.

Thanks a lot.' Girls took to Freddie, they had done for as long as he'd been old enough to notice, it was just a pity it was never the right one. Why couldn't Li have been more keen on him? More like Bella and the girl at the desk?

Still, Bella seemed like a laugh – maybe she'd help him forget Li once and for all.

As they entered the big open space that had been cleared out under the department store to transform it into a dance hall – by special request of a local councillor to his friend the store owner, as a boost for the blitz-fatigued residents' morale – Bella gasped. It was so beautiful; she'd never seen anything like it. With Christmas only a few weeks away they had turned the place into a winter wonderland. Nothing like the murky slush left by the melting snow up in the real world, this was warm, cosy, romantic.

White crêpe paper had been cut into garlands of snowflakes and hung down all the walls; cotton wool snowballs were piled into pyramids around the room, and colourful Chinese lanterns dangled from the ceiling at different heights. As a final touch, pinky-red material had been draped over the lamps to give the light a warm, sensual glow.

The far end of the long, rectangular space had been given over to the musicians – a proper band with men sitting behind sparkly stands and a woman singer in a slinky, sequined, floor-length evening gown, her platinum blonde hair cascading over her shoulders. Next to the band was a run of trestle tables covered in pure white cloths. Spread all over were plates piled high with sandwiches, glass jugs of fruit squash, and posy bowls full of holly sprigs dotted with red berries.

And as if that wasn't enough, Bella had Freddie by her side. It was almost too good to be true; she didn't think she could have been any happier.

'Fancy a dance, Fred?'

'Not yet, eh?'

'Please, Fred, go on. I mean, listen to what they're playing – "When You Wish Upon a Star". I love this song.'

'Do you?' Freddie was looking around the room, seeing if there was anyone there who knew him. He hoped not. He didn't even really know what he was doing here. If someone did see him and Li somehow found out, he didn't know what he'd do. It'd be bound to ruin any chance he had of getting back with her. It didn't matter how hard he tried, she was the only one he could think about. Why couldn't he just get used to the fact that she didn't want him any more?

'Are you listening to me, Fred?'

'Yeah, 'course.'

'It's out of that film – *Pinocchio*. I loved that as well. Did you see it?'

'Not really my sort of flick. I thought it was more for kids.'

This wasn't how it was meant to be. She should have been in his arms by now, twirling around the dance floor like Ginger Rogers. For goodness' sake, even his name was right – Fred. But he was proving to have as much in common with Fred Astaire as she had. Bella smiled brightly. 'So what exactly do you do on the railways then?'

'This and that.' He knew he was being rotten to her, but he couldn't help himself.

Silence. Bella dug around for something else – anything else – to say. 'I don't care about Grace being Bobby's mum.'

'Who said you did?'

'Well, you know how people are. But I think everyone has their own little secrets.'

'Not me,' he said instantly.

'No?'

His voice rose angrily. 'I said – *no*.' Then he touched her on the shoulder. 'I'm sorry, Bella, I didn't mean to shout.'

'Then why did you? What have I done that's so wrong?' Momentarily, Bella felt deflated, but she soon recovered when she spotted a group of snooty girls from the turning around the corner from where she lived. She could see how surprised they all were that she was with Freddie. And why wouldn't they be? There weren't that many young blokes around at the moment, never mind handsome buggers like Freddie Jarrett. At least she could impress them with the bloke on her arm – even though it seemed he didn't actually want anything to do with her.

If this was going to work, Bella had to get a move on.

'Here, Fred, let's have a couple of dances, then we can go outside, if you like, and . . . you know, have a little cuddle and that. Don't know about you, but I'd really like that. I'd like it a lot.'

Freddie considered for a moment. Why would anyone be stupid enough to put up with him when he was acting like such a bastard? He dropped his chin. It wasn't her fault; she hadn't done anything wrong. It was him.

He thought for a long, uncomfortable second about his mum and dad and the unhappiness that had erupted between them, then he smiled at Bella.

'Why not? Come on then.'

By the time she and Freddie had gone round the dance floor to 'Bésame Mucho' and then to

'A Nightingale Sang in Berkeley Square' – and all in front of the coven of witches from around the corner – Bella was ready to do whatever Freddie wanted, soaring pride and a sixteen-year-old's hormones blocking any fear and all reason.

'Ready to go outside for a while now, Fred?' she breathed into his ear.

'If you want to.'

Bella couldn't help it, she just couldn't stop herself from smirking as she and Freddie walked out to collect their coats – arm-in-arm – right past the girls from around the corner *and* the girl behind the desk.

She, Bella Tanner, was with Freddie Jarrett – not them.

As they emerged from the warmth of the store and stepped out into the blackout, the cold air hit them.

'Least it's stopped snowing for a while, eh, Fred?'

'Yeah, makes a change.'

'We can go down here, if you want.' Bella took him by the hand and led him down the narrow service road that wound round the back of the store, not quite knowing what to expect but hardly able to stop herself from breaking into a run, she was so excited.

Safely away from the main road, Bella

leaned back against the wall, not caring what the sooty bricks would do to her mum's fox fur.

'Give us a kiss then, Fred.'

Freddie lowered his head to move in on her, but stopped short of actually kissing her.

'What's wrong, don't you like me?'

'It's not that, Bella, you're a nice girl. Pretty.' He chucked her under the chin and she almost burst into tears.

'I don't know what to think, Fred. You've got me all mixed up, you really have.'

'I can't, that's all.'

'But why?'

'It's not you, honestly it's not. Look, Bell, I've got to get going.'

'But you can't. Where? Where're you going?'

'Work. I can't be late.'

'But we've only been here for about half an hour and you told me you were at work earlier – that's why you met me here.'

'Double shift. I can't get out of it.'

'Fred.'

'Railways are important at a time like this.'

She twisted away from him. 'Go on then. Go. See if I care.'

As Freddie padded off into the night, Bella stood there in the cold, her dreams melting like so much slush in the gutter.

Freddie stood on the pavement behind a woman who was conducting a seemingly never-ending conversation through a slit in the blackout curtain covering the window of a little house in Pennyfields. Would she ever stop talking and just take her food?

'See you, Mei, and tell your gran I'll see her next week.'

About bloody time! He took her place by the window, ducked his head and almost sighed her name. 'Li, I've got to talk to you.'

'Freddie.' Mei snatched a glance over her shoulder at her grandparents who were busily cooking, just as they did every night. 'What are you doing here? You know I told you it's over between us.'

'I'm going to wait for you up by the Eastern. I don't care for how long, I'm not moving from there until you come and at least talk to me.'

'Say there's a raid?'

'Say there is? I'd rather be with you – the girl I love – if my time's up.'

'You love me?'

'Of course I do. I've tried to get over you, but I can't do it.'

'Freddie, you mustn't say that. I told you, I can't see you any—'

'Mei, are you taking that young man's order?'

273

her grandmother snapped at her in Cantonese.

'Yes, grandmother. Noodles for one.'

'Huh! That will not make us rich.'

'I mean it, Li.' He thrust some coins into her hand. 'I'll be waiting. And I won't move from there until you come.'

'You came!' Freddie threw his cigarette on to the ground and took Mei in his arms.

'Careful.' She held up a shopping bag. 'I can only be here for a short time. I pretended I was delivering this food to my friend Linda's family.' She let the bag drop to her side. 'I don't even know where I'm going to get the money from to pay for it. I'm going to get into so much trouble with my grandparents if they find out I've been lying. So much trouble.'

'Don't worry about that. I'll give you the money.' He took the bag from her and put it on the ground. 'I can't say how pleased I am that you came.'

'Freddie, we have to talk about this. I honestly don't know how it can ever work, not when there's this—'

Before Mei could finish, the air raid warning sounded. She looked up into the sky. 'We're being punished.'

'Don't be afraid, Li.' Freddie grabbed her hand and they began running.

'Over to Spratt's,' he panted. 'They've got a shelter there.'

They didn't make it to the factory. They only got as far as the corner of the street when the now all-too-familiar sight and sound of a bomb falling close by brought them to a halt.

'They've only hit the bank!' Freddie, still holding Mei's hand, began hurrying towards the damaged building, pulling her along behind him.

'Don't, Freddie, it's dangerous.'

'Dangerous? There's a bank here with no doors or windows, and no one guarding the money! We can help ourselves and run away together.' He turned to her, grinning. 'I told you I'd give you the money. Now I can get you as much money as you want, and we can go wherever we want. Somewhere nobody knows us. Start a new life. Get married.'

'You're acting like a madman, Freddie, don't!' Mei tried to stop him, but he was too strong for her. He dragged the shattered door to one side so he could get inside.

Mei paused for a moment, whispered some words in Cantonese and then followed him into the bank.

Freddie struck a match and groaned. In the pale, sputtering light it was clear that the damage was only superficial. There wasn't even much dust on the polished counters or on the marble floor, just a lot of glass. It was as if someone had gently removed the windows and then absent-mindedly let them fall to the ground before kicking open the door as a half-hearted afterthought.

'You'd have thought it would have blown at least some of the money out of the safe and it would be floating around all over the place.'

A sound coming from the doorway behind them made Freddie drop the match.

'What's that light in there?' they heard someone say, and then saw an ARP warden shining his torch about the banking hall.

The beam played around the room, just missing Freddie's face. He squatted down, dragging Mei with him. He rolled on to his side, tucking them in close to the counter.

'Looters!' hollered the warden, and then blew three loud blasts on his whistle. 'Police! Help!' He lunged forward, surprisingly quickly for a middle-aged man, but misjudged the distance and instead of grabbing Freddie as he had intended, tripped himself over and went crashing into the solid wood counter, missing Freddie completely, but knocking himself spark out. It was as if he'd been thrown a haymaker by Joe Louis.

Mei snatched up the torch and shone it on

him. There was a trickle of blood coming from his nose. 'Is he dead?'

'I don't know. But if he's not, do you think he got a proper look at us?'

'I don't think so. But I can't be sure.'

'Right, what to do? Think. Think. Looting . . . but maybe he's dead. OK, Li, this is what we do. You make a run for it before the police get here.'

'How about you?'

'I'll wait to make sure he's OK. I can't just leave him.'

'Then I'll stay with you.'

'No.'

'Yes.'

'Li, it makes no sense for us both to get into trouble.'

She started towards the door, moving slowly backwards, her eyes fixed on the warden on the floor. She watched as Freddie took off his overcoat, rolled it up and put it under the man's head.

Within moments there was the sound of heavy boots running along the pavement, and then a policeman stood framed in the doorway.

'Whoever's in there, don't move.'

'So, you two risked coming in here to help that man?' The policeman handed Freddie back his overcoat as the stretcher bearers carried the still unconscious warden away to an ambulance. 'You did a good job. Plenty of other youngsters would have been in here trying to fill their pockets, yet you two chase off looters, stay to help this man, and all without a thought for your own safety. Well done.'

Freddie shrugged himself into his coat and shook his head, barely able to control the urge to flee. 'We did what anyone would do. We were trying to be good citizens, that's all.'

'That's the spirit, lad, that's what'll beat them Nazi bastards. Excuse my language, miss.'

Outside on the pavement Mei touched Freddie's cheek and sighed regretfully. 'Look what nearly happened to us in there. It's always the same when we're together. It's like fate warning us that it's not meant to be. You have to leave me alone, Freddie. Never see me again. You have to promise.'

'We can still run away together. I don't need to steal money for us. I'll work hard, save up.'

'You're talking rubbish, Freddie Jarrett, and you know it. Listen to me, will you? It's over. It has to be. There's nothing either of us can do. This is just not meant to be. You know what people think of foreigners, but have you got any idea what it would do to my grandparents if they found out I'd been lying to them?'

'No, you're wrong, Li. If you won't come away with me, we'll be honest with everyone. Tell them about us. They'll understand. They'll have to when they realise how much I love you.'

'If only it was as easy as that.' She stood on tiptoe and kissed him. 'Freddie, it's over. And, if you think anything of me, you'll let me go.'

She stroked his face a final time, turned and ran off into the darkness.

Freddie stood there, defeated, his arms dangling by his sides. Li didn't want him.

Why did this happen to him? He knew he didn't always do the right thing, but there were plenty of others who did far worse. Was he really such a bad person?

Maybe he was.

His parents were sorting themselves out; his dad had accepted Grace and the baby – whoever would have thought that would happen? It seemed that everyone around him who could was getting on and doing their bit for their country. And what was he doing? Working for an illegal bookie and blackmarketeer.

He hung his head and started snivelling.

The policeman poked his head out of the bank doorway. 'What are you still doing out there, son?'

'Leave me alone.'

The policeman tutted. 'Same old story – had

words with your young lady, I suppose. It'll be the shock. You've been through a lot tonight, the pair of you. Here, if you don't mind sheltering under the table in here, you can step inside with me and get out of the cold. I can't leave till they send someone round to patch the place up. We can be company for one another.'

'I said, leave me alone, all right?'

'We all have our bad days.'

'Bad days? If you only knew the half of it!'

'Look, I've seen this plenty of times before. I'm telling you, it'll be the shock. You thinking that feller had copped it. It's enough to put the willies up anyone.'

'Do I have to tell you again?'

'When they send the repair fellers round, there's bound to be a mobile canteen. You can have a nice cup of sweet tea and a slice of cake or a biscuit or two. You deserve it.'

'Me? I deserve nothing. Nothing at all. Not unless I start putting things right, I don't.' Freddie's voice was growing louder, spittle bubbling in the corners of his mouth. 'Other people can do it, so why can't I? What's wrong with me, eh? Tell me that.'

'No need to get shirty. You want to pull yourself together, lad.' The policeman ducked back through the doorway as a basket of incendiaries fell across the street. 'There's no point brooding,' he called from inside the bank. 'Who knows what's going to happen? To any of us. Now, if you don't want to come in here with me, you get yourself home and sort yourself out. Act like the decent young man you were a quarter of an hour ago and not some grizzling kid.'

Chapter 16

Kitty sat at her workbench, wishing she was anywhere but in the clothing factory. The noise of the sewing machines was making her head throb; the background buzz of women trying to talk over the machinery was like a hive of a million angry bees, and the thoughts that were going around her head were like needles being driven into her brain.

Another hour and ten minutes to go, and that was if there was no overtime that *had* to be done – she'd soon learned that the extra hours were more about earning Harry his bonuses than anything to do with helping *our brave boys*. She honestly didn't know if she could last the ten minutes, let alone the other full hour. She did know she should be happy, what with Dan coming back and everything, but she felt awful. She switched off her machine, let her head drop back and closed her eyes. Everyone was tired, of course they were – how could they not be with the hours they were working, the nightly raids, dealing with the blackout and the never-ending queuing for food? – so she shouldn't complain, but she really was totally worn out.

She shuddered as she felt an arm slip around her shoulders, and didn't have to open her eyes to know who it was. She could smell the sickly combination of hair oil, stale cigarette smoke and boozy breath from his regular *swift half* – two pints more like – taken after he'd had his meal and his dinner break, of course. It was Harry the flipping nuisance of a supervisor. Harry with his creeping fingers and wet lips, his insinuating words and total disregard for his own wife, at home caring for their children. He made Kitty want to vomit.

'And what's wrong with my little sweetheart this afternoon then? Had a late night, did you? Found yourself a bit of company to help pass the long winter nights? Kept you up, did he?' He squeezed her shoulder. 'It wouldn't surprise me if a pretty woman like you had no sleep. But you are looking tired, girl.'

Kitty peeled his arm off her shoulder and stood up. She stared frostily at him. 'So, looking tired, am I?'

'Don't you get all obstreperous with me.'

'Why not? Pregnant women are allowed a bit of leeway – or so I thought.'

'What?'

'Aw, clear off, will you?'

Joyce, who was sitting across from Kitty, did a double take. 'What did you say?'

'I said: I'm pregnant.'

A woman further along the line mouthed: 'What did she say?'

'She's only flaming pregnant.'

'Do what?'

'Knocked up.'

'But ain't her old man away?'

Like a stack of dominoes falling, the machines all went quiet.

'He came back on leave, didn't he?'

Joyce raised her eyebrows. 'Aw, yeah. He did, didn't he? You said.'

Kitty tore off her overall and whipped it down on to the bench. 'That's it, I've had enough of everyone talking about my business. I'm going home.'

'Hello, Mum, you're early.' Grace kissed Kitty on the cheek. 'Everything all right?'

'Yeah, everything's just fine, sweetheart. Is Freddie home yet?'

'No. Well, yeah. Sort of. He came home and went straight out again. I'd made a nice neck of lamb stew for us all as well – dumplings and everything – and he didn't want to know. I hope he's all right, 'cos he looked a bit humpy.'

'Did he? What was wrong, do you think?'

'I don't know, but you know Fred, he'll be fine. So get your coat off and I'll dish yours up for you in a minute, Mum, it's nearly ready. It's only the dumplings that have got to fluff up a bit more.'

Kitty felt her insides heave – she couldn't even face a cup of tea at the moment, let alone a plate full of greasy lamb and suet dumplings. 'I'll leave it for a while, if that's okay with you, love. I just want to get a letter to your dad started before I settle down for the evening.'

She could only hope that her stomach would settle down as well.

'You're a good girl, Grace. I know I don't always say so, but I'm grateful for everything you do indoors for us all. I know how hard it must be for you – a young girl having to stay at home all the time.'

Grace didn't know what to say.

Kitty went into the sitting room, sat at the table and took a sheet of paper from the cardboard stationery box that she kept – usually unused – in the sideboard. She made sure the rest of the paper and envelopes were tidy, and then checked there was ink in her pen – twice. It was far easier messing around than knowing how to begin the letter.

Okay. This was it. She'd make a start. Now.

My dear Dan . . . she began.

No, that wasn't good enough, but she felt as shy as she had when he had taken her to the pictures on their first proper night out – and on the night when they had crossed the icy courtyard together and gone over to the sheds.

She had to get this right.

My dearest Dan ...

That was better.

I cannot tell you how much I loved seeing you and knowing that we are going to be a family again. It will be Christmas soon and then the New Year will be with us. It makes me think of our new life together. There is also something to make our new life even better, Dan. I am going to have our baby. I am so happy and I hope you are too. Please, keep yourself safe for us all, my darling, and come home to us soon. We are so lucky to have been given this new start, I can hardly believe it. Write to us when you can, and let us know you are well.

I will stop now and write a longer letter to you tomorrow as I want to get this off to you with the good news.

God bless, my love.

Kitty xxx

She held the paper against the envelope and

judged where to fold it, popped it inside and then licked the flap. She wished she hadn't then. The taste of the glue made her feel queasy. She had no idea how she was going to eat that stew.

As she stood up from the table the warning siren went. For once it came as a relief – no stew, for a while at least.

'Here we go, Grace,' she called through to the kitchen. 'You get Bobby and I'll bring the bag. Is the flask ready?'

Not that Kitty was sure she could hold down even a cup of weak tea, the way her stomach felt.

Across the landing in number 56 Ada Tanner wasn't feeling quite so organised. Usually she had Bella running around getting things ready for her. It was strange, Ada hadn't heard from her granddaughter for a few days now, and couldn't help but feel a bit concerned. She wasn't a bad girl as kids went.

Her next thought was to grab the vase where she kept her money, and then to put in her false teeth. Her afterthought was to shout through to the bedroom where her husband was trying to catch up on a bit of sleep.

'Albert, wake up and carry this stuff down to the laundry, will you?'

He groaned and turned over.

She stormed into the room and started

shaking him. 'What is going wrong with this family? You lazing around; no sign of Bella for days on end.' She paused, thinking over the past few days. She knew there'd been no bombings over that way – she'd made sure to check on that – so there had to be some other reason for Bella going amongst the missing.

'And as for that Alfie,' she went on, 'I don't even want to talk about that one. And Gawd alone knows what that mother of theirs is up to. What would our boy say if he knew about all these shenanigans going on while he's away at sea?'

She closed her eyes, too drained to think about it any more, and then bent forward and bellowed into Albert's ear: 'Will you get up? Right this minute, or I'll leave you here and you'll get blown up. And then what'll you do?'

He yawned and rubbed his eyes. 'I never knew you cared, Ada.'

She straightened up. ''Course I don't,' she said briskly. 'I just want you to carry the stuff down for me, that's all.'

Albert threw back the covers. The old girl was missing Bella more than she was letting on. Maybe he should pop round and see his granddaughter, have a word.

Bella sat resolutely at the kitchen table, pouring herself yet another cup of tea, while her brother Alfie tried to persuade her to see sense.

'Let's go over to the shelter, Bell.'

'No, thanks.'

'Why not?'

'For a start, I hate them surface shelters, they give me the creeps. And second, I don't like them cows from round the corner who use it. They all think they're the right business.'

'They're pretty enough girls.'

Bella looked at her brother as if he'd lost his mind. 'Why would you care whether they're pretty or not?'

'Don't be snide, Bell, I was only saying.'

'Well, don't bother wasting your breath. I couldn't care less what you think about them cocky tarts.'

There was a loud crash outside, making them both jump. 'If you won't go over to our shelter, then why don't you go round Nan's and get down the laundry?'

'What, are you my dad now or something?' Just the thought of maybe bumping into Freddie Jarrett made her recoil even more than the sound of the explosions going on around them. She had felt so humiliated that night, getting left behind at the dance like a spare part, after she'd been showing off and flaunting Freddie in front of those girls.

'I'm not leaving you here. Them bombs are getting bloody close. Come on, Bell, why don't you let me take you round Nan's? I won't stay, there'll be no row.'

'Shut up, will you, Alf?'

'Where's Mum?'

'In the pub cellar with her next-door.'

'Right. That's where I'm taking you.'

Alfie took his sister by the arm; he was slight but strong, and hauled her to her feet. 'And I'm not taking no for an answer. Someone in this family has got to start acting responsibly.'

Bella and Alfie's grandmother, Ada, had settled herself in her usual spot down in the laundry next to Lil and her ever-clicking knitting needles.

'You do know my Bella's not been around, don't you?' she said rather than asked. 'And all because she'll not want to be seen with the likes of her.' Ada, who had at last come to what she decided was a satisfactory explanation for her granddaughter's absence, stabbed a thumb towards Grace. 'My Bella offered that girl the hand of friendship, and what happens? I'll tell you what, shall I? She turns out to be nothing more than a right little trollop. Fancy my granddaughter making friends with a dirty little mare who got herself pregnant at that age! Disgraceful carryings on, if you ask me. What a family.'

Kitty bristled like a lioness protecting her young. 'So what does that make me then, Ada? A bad mother?'

'You said it,' she sneered, pouring herself a cup of tea from her flask. 'You said it.'

Mary held up her own flask and gestured towards Kitty. 'You and Grace fancy a cuppa with me and Joe, Kit? And little Bobby can play with the kids till he drops off.'

Kitty's eyes filled with tears of gratitude; she knew it was the pregnancy, but she still couldn't control it, her emotions were all over the place. 'Thanks, Mary, I'd love that.' She turned to her daughter. 'Bring them biscuits with you, Grace, so we can share them with Mr and Mrs Lovell.'

Then she twisted round and looked directly at Ada Tanner. 'And make sure you bring your little one's blankets with you. You don't want your son getting chilly, do you, love?'

'No, Mum,' said Grace, following her mother's example and looking Ada right in the eye. 'I don't. It's important to look after your children, isn't it?'

Nell and Martin hadn't gone down to the laundry, it was their turn to be up on the roof of Turnbury Buildings fire-watching. For a change the incendiary bombs were being dropped closer to Bow and Stratford tonight rather than in the docks, and although they had to keep alert they still felt relaxed enough to talk about everyday matters – well, matters that counted as everyday for some people.

'Martin, you know how good Sylvia and Bernie were to me when I got chucked out of the Foundlings' Home?'

"Course I do, and I'll always be grateful to them for that. They're good people. And think how they looked after Dad and all. He couldn't have been more down, what with having no job and no hope of one. The thirties were hard for a lot of people, yet Bernie took him on, gave him back his pride. I'll never forget that.'

'And I'll never have a better friend than Sylvia in my whole life. I often think that if I'd listened to her when she was trying to give me advice, then you-know-what would never have happened – you know, with him, Flanagan. And you wouldn't have had to go away like you did.'

Martin frowned. He wasn't sure what this was leading to. They never usually talked about that bastard Flanagan, and what had happened that night down by the river.

Martin touched his lips to hers. 'But then you'd never have had Tommy and Dolly, Nell, and I'd never have met you, would I? And we'd never have had our little Vicky.'

She dropped her chin. 'Like I said, I know all that, but we're talking about adults who can make their own choices, Martin. I know I was young and naive when I went to live in the Hope, but I never got, you know, involved in anything that wasn't *on the level*, as Bernie would say. Sylvie always made sure of that. What's worrying me now is Freddie Jarrett. He's getting in right thick with Bernie, and while I'm sure he's no fool, and I'm sure he knows what he's doing – the betting and blackmarket and that . . .' she threw up her hands '. . . does he know he could really get into big trouble? He's so young, he probably thinks it's all excitement and easy money. He's not shrewd or experienced like Bernie.'

'Shall I have a word with him, Nell? Me knowing Bern, and the lad's dad not being around.'

'I'm really not sure, Martin. I think Kitty's had more than a bellyful lately, and who knows how he'll react if we go poking our noses in?' She sighed – so tired of all the things that were going on around her that she couldn't do anything about. 'Maybe if the right moment comes along.'

'Yeah, that's my girl. Good idea.' Martin gave her a cuddle. 'You always know what to do for the best, Nell.'

'I only wish I did, Martin. With all my heart.'

'Come on, Nelly, cheer up. Look at the good things that are going on around us. Think how Mum's settled into running the shop, like she was born to it.'

'I suppose so.' She threw back her head and watched as a line of enemy planes made their way along the river towards the City. 'But the next thing you know, Mary and Joe, they'll be wanting to leave the Buildings and make their home in the shop. Then what will we do, Martin? Everything's changing, and I hate it.'

'Say they did move to the shop? It's only round the corner, Nell.'

'But nothing's going to be the same again – I just know it. It's like someone's grabbed hold of the world and given it a great big shake and then everything in it's gone and fallen back down in all the wrong places and nothing makes any sense any more.'

'Come here, you.' Martin held out his arms. 'We're supposed to be guarding the roof, not worrying about ourselves and our own little problems.'

That was too much for Nell – she burst into tears.

Tommy watched, biding his time as his nan and granddad made Kitty welcome to their little encampment in the far corner of the laundry, settling her down with a cup of tea and thanking her for the biscuits – Mary not feeling bad about taking them, knowing full well that she'd be replacing them from the shop in the morning.

The three adults were soon deep in conversation and Tommy turned his attention to Grace, Bobby and his sisters. It didn't take long for them to have improvised a game that involved hiding Bobby's knitted bear under the blanket, him trying to find it, and lots of squeals of girlish laughter.

This was it: his big chance – especially with his mum and dad being up on the roof. Perfect. They hadn't let him do it when he'd asked before – because of that bash on his head – but this time he would show them all what he was made of, what he was capable of.

He knew that the work his granddad did – delivering the coal – was really important, and they'd tried to kid him that being a van boy was just as vital to the war effort, but Tommy knew better. He'd seen Freddie Jarrett from across the landing, going out at all hours to work on the railways. Freddie was sixteen, just a bit more than two years older than him, yet he didn't need his granddad with him. It was about time Tommy Lovell showed everyone what he was made of. He'd be just like those scouts he'd seen on the newsreels.

He stood up carefully, anxious not to attract attention.

He should have known better. He'd taken just one step before she spotted him.

'All right, Tom?'

'Yes, thanks, Nan. I'm going to the lav.'

Mary smiled as Tommy made his way between chairs, blankets and camp beds with Bradman sticking close to his heels. 'That dog follows that boy everywhere.'

In the bath block that led off from the laundry, Tommy went into the first of the two lavatory cubicles, leaving Bradman to sniff around the baths, wagging his tail happily at the rich mix of carbolic and human scent.

Tommy climbed up on to the wooden toilet seat and stretched up so that he could reach the top of the china cistern. After a bit of a struggle he managed to grab hold of something and haul it down, almost toppling himself backwards on to the floor in the process. He smiled in satisfaction as he held up the brown paper carrier bag – still printed with the names of Sarah and David Meckel – that his nan had brought home from the shop.

He stepped back down on to the red

quarry-tiled floor and sat on the lavatory seat.

He opened up the bag and pulled out his top coat, a torch with a cardboard collar shading the bulb, and a paper bag containing two slices of bread and jam. He felt in the pocket of the coat. There it was, exactly where he'd put it, the key to the shed.

'Here, boy.' Tommy patted his leg. 'Time to go. And no noise.'

Tommy hesitated for a few moments in the entrance to the Buildings, looking out on to the courtyard. He could hear action going on – bombs whistling and falling, ack-ack guns firing, and bells and whistles sending their warnings and signals for help. And he could see searchlights shining and barrage balloons gleaming against the tar black sky, but it seemed that nothing too bad was happening close by – not at the moment anyway. This was a good time to make a dash for the shed.

He fumbled along in the dark until he counted to the tenth shed in the row – then he felt in his pocket for his torch and the key. Once inside he hauled out his beloved bike from under its tarpaulin. He always took great care of it – polishing it and covering it up – ever since he had been given it as a surprise present on his last birthday before the war had started. He took out Bradman's white-trimmed dog coat from the basket clipped to the handlebars. The coat had been made especially by his nan for when his dad or granddad walked the little terrier in the blackout, so that he stood out in the dark and wouldn't get lost.

'Stand still while I get you ready, boy. Then we'll be off and we can do our bit, just like I told you.'

Bradman hated the coat with a passion and Tommy wound up leaving the fastenings hanging loose so as not to annoy him. He then put the terrier in the front basket where he sat obediently, only wriggling occasionally to try and get rid of the coat.

Tommy took a final look round before wheeling his bike across the courtyard, desperately trying not to make any noise. All he needed was for his parents to hear something and then spot him from where they were on watch up on the roof.

Safely outside on the road, Tommy threw his leg over the crossbar and started pedalling furiously towards the ARP post that had recently been erected just around the corner by the shop.

'That's it, Brad,' said Tommy, his breath coming out in steamy clouds in the freezing night air. 'We're on our way. We're going to be proper scouts at last and run messages for everyone. They're all going to be so proud of us.'

'Where's Tom?' Joe looked around the laundry. 'He never took a biscuit.'

Vicky's lip wobbled as she stifled a little sob. She was sure she'd seen her brother creep up the stairs, but she knew it was wrong to tell on someone – Dolly had told her often enough. And say she'd been wrong and hadn't seen him after all? She hoped so, because it was dangerous to go out before the all clear sounded – everyone knew that . . .

Mary leaned towards her husband and said quietly: 'He went to the lav, Joe. And you know him, he'll have taken a book or a comic in there with him.'

Tommy reached the end of the street and turned the corner to where the shop stood. In the dark he never noticed the patch of ice. The back wheel skidded from under him and he went skating across the cobbles, grazing his knees and cheek.

Bradman yelped in pain as he was flung from the basket, leaving his unfastened coat behind him. But he didn't complain for long. His nose twitched with pleasure. A river rat.

He scooted off towards the irresistible scent, oblivious of the ambulance that was racing along the road towards him.

It was the sound and the feel of the impact that alerted the driver – a crunching thump – as his vehicle smashed into the terrier's little body. Bradman didn't stand a chance.

The driver opened his window and looked down. 'Aw, shit, we've only gone and hit a dog. What shall we do?'

'Hard as it sounds,' said his colleague from the passenger seat, in a clipped, middle-class accent, 'there are people waiting for our help. So I really do think a dog has to come some way down our list of priorities, don't you?'

'You're right, Gerald, 'course you are, mate. But I know how I'd feel if it was my poor old Trixie laying there. Shouldn't we at least take it with us, so's one of the medics can look at it later?'

'We are on an emergency call here, Arthur.'

'Yeah. Yeah. But, bloody hell. Makes you feel a right bastard, don't it?'

Tommy stood there, numb, as the ambulance pulled away. Then, once it had disappeared into the blackout, he slowly walked towards the little terrier.

He knelt down beside him. 'Don't worry, Bradman, I'll get you home. Dad'll know what to do. You'll be all right, boy.'

Tommy took off his coat and wrapped it around the dog. Then he picked him up in his arms and started walking home, forgetting his treasured bike completely as the tears rolled down his cheeks.

Martin spun round as he heard the trapdoor to the roof open. No one but the fire-watching shift was allowed up here during raids. This could mean trouble.

'Who's there?' he demanded, stirrup pump ready to knock the intruder over the head.

'It's me, Dad.'

'Tommy?' Martin sounded confused as he strode over to him. 'What do you think you're doing? You know you're not meant to come up here.'

Nell moved as fast as her husband. 'Get back down to that laundry this minute, Tommy Lovell, or I'll . . . Hang on. Why are you crying? What's happened to your face? And what have you got wrapped up in your coat? Have you been—'

'Let the boy talk, Nell.'

'I'm sorry, Mum, Dad. I lied to you. I said I was going down to the basement with the girls. And I did, but then I went out. I wanted to be a scout, like on the newsreel I saw with Granddad. But him and Dad wouldn't let me because I got that bash on the head down in the docks. But everyone else is doing stuff as well as their jobs, look at you two. And now look what's gone and happened.' He held out the scruffy little brown and white terrier. Apart from a trickle of blood around his snout, Bradman looked as if he were sleeping.

'Is he hurt bad, do you think, Dad?'

Martin glanced sideways at Nell as he took the dog from Tommy's arms. 'Leave him with me, son. You get yourself down to the basement.'

Tommy held out his arms. 'I'll take him with me. If he's hurt he should be down there with me, so I can look after him.'

Again, Martin looked at Nell. He shook his head.

She reached out and stroked her son's cheek. 'Darling, he's more than hurt.'

Now it was Tommy who shook his head. 'No, he's not. He's all right. I'll clean off the blood and he'll be running around trying to get at the chickens and rabbits in no time.'

Martin bit his lip and sniffed. 'I'm sorry, son, but Bradman's dead.'

Chapter 17

Freddie made his way over to Pennyfields in the dying light of the December afternoon. He was determined that this time nothing was going to stop him. Despite days having passed, try as he might, he couldn't get those ARP warden's words out of his mind – the words that he'd had drummed into him when he'd stood outside the bombed bank: *You want to pull yourself together, lad. There's no point in brooding*.

Freddie had tried to dismiss those words, but he knew that the bloke was right. It was obvious. Who did know what was going to happen to them, what with the way the war was going? What was the point in hanging around like an idiot, waiting while happiness slipped through your fingers? There just wasn't the luxury of time any more. So he wouldn't leave it. He'd insist that Li at least listen to him, give him a chance to explain how much she meant to him. He had to try. She wouldn't refuse him that, surely?

'My grandparents are going to think that Linda's family are turning into Cantonese people, what with all the noodles and shrimps they're supposed to be eating.'

Li looked up and down Pennyfields as if the enemy were threatening to advance. 'And that they've got really lazy because they don't ever come and get it for themselves any more. If ever any of them find out what I've been doing, I'm going to be in so much trouble.'

Li Mei – a fat parcel of steaming Chinese food in her arms – stared down at the pavement rather than risk looking into Freddie's eyes. 'You do know that this has to be the last time I use this excuse for leaving the house, don't you, Fred? It's getting stupid. They're going to find out. It's obvious. They might not speak much English, but they're not fools.'

'Then why use an excuse any more, Li? Why not go back to the way it used to be – us seeing each other whenever we can? And then, when we get together, we can work out a way to make it more permanent. Find a way to make it work. Think about it. Life is so short, Li, with all this madness going on around us. I want to be happy while I can, don't you?'

'I want to be happy with you more than anything, Freddie, but it can't be. Not between us, it can't. It's impossible.'

'Why do you keep doing this to me? You know how much I love you.'

Slowly, she raised her eyes and looked at him. 'Let's get away from here, Fred. I feel uncomfortable.'

They started walking down towards Narrow Street, the road that ran parallel to the river.

'Why should you feel uncomfortable? Your grandparents don't go out after dark. They won't see you.'

Mei scratched her head nervously, biding her time. 'It's not them I'm worried about. It's this boy . . . Peter.'

Freddie let out a loud mirthless peal of laughter as a look of furious realisation clouded his face. 'What's wrong with me? I might have bloody known. A beautiful girl like you, why should you care? You've got someone else already, haven't you? I bet you've been taking me for a mug all along. A right bloody mug, running along behind you like a little puppy dog, while you've been lying to me like I'm an idiot.'

'No, Freddie, I swear I've not done anything like that. It's this Peter. It's him. He won't let me see you. I told him I won't have anything to do with him, but he won't listen. And now he's scaring me. He just appears out of nowhere.'

Freddie clenched his hands into fists, nails digging into his palms, furious that he'd let himself be so stupid – and over a girl of all things. 'Oh, yeah. Right. Peter, you say. Peter who?'

'He used to live around here. Now he's come back and is staying in lodgings.'

'He's come back here to stay in lodgings, you say? In these raids? What is he, round the bend? Who'd come and lodge round here?' Freddie folded his arms and stared at her. 'Why are you bothering lying to me, Li? You've got another bloke and you can't even be decent enough to say so.'

'I am not lying to you, Fred. I don't lie.'

'You lie to your grandparents.'

'That's only to protect them.'

'Do you ever *stop* lying?'

The sky was dark now and they edged their way along the high blank walls of the riverside wharves, unable to see each other's face but avoiding looking anyway. They ducked into an alley between two of the tall buildings, stopping at the top of a flight of ancient waterman's stairs that led down to the river. They stood there listening to the tide going out below them.

'Li, I can't tell you how I feel, I can't find the words to explain, but this is killing me.'

'That's what Peter said he would do to both of us, if I kept seeing you. He follows me; he knows what I'm doing all the time. He's like a ghost, an evil spirit.'

'Save your breath, Li, and don't start with all that Chinese stuff. I've never seen this bloke.

You're either going with him or making him up as some sort of daft excuse.' Freddie jabbed a finger at her face. 'Tell you what, Li, I've had it with you and all this messing about. I'll see you back safe and sound to Pennyfields and then let's forget it.'

'Whatever you want.' Mei heaved the parcel of food into what she thought was the water below, but it just burst on to the muddy foreshore, sending noodles and shrimps up in a firework arch.

'Can't I do anything right?' she shouted at the river, and then burst into tears.

Freddie closed his eyes and drew her to him. 'What's going on with you, Li? Just tell me. We can do something about it, but you've got to tell me the truth.'

'It's Peter, I promise you, Freddie, with all my heart – I am telling you the truth. We knew each other when we were children. His father was Chinese and his mother was English. He told me that he'd hated them because of what other people said about his family. Some of the people round here, they called him a mongrel. And he said that they called his mother a—'

Her words faded away as the warning siren sounded, and the distant drone of bombers approaching had them staring up at the sky.

'Bloody great timing.'

'I have to get back, Freddie.'

'No. We've not finished. We'll find some-where to shelter here.'

'Please, no.'

'I'm not taking no for an answer, Li.'

'But my grandparents . . .'

Freddie wasn't listening; he took Mei's hand and pulled her down the steps to where a tarpaulin-covered barge wallowed on the dirty sand of the foreshore.

'Under there,' he said, lifting up a corner of the smelly cover.

'That's not going to protect us from the bombers.'

'It's close to the wall. We should be all right.'

'You don't sound as if you care what happens to you.'

'Why would I care what happens if I can't have you?'

'Let's try to get to a public shelter, Freddie. Please.'

Bewildered, he let go of her hand; he didn't have a clue what to do next. 'You're confusing me, Li. Do you or don't you trust me? Do you want to be with me or not?'

'Freddie, this isn't the time or the place, and it's nothing to do with any of that. I just don't know what my grandparents would do if something happened to me. Who would care for them?'

He drew her to him and, despite the icy December air, the heat rose in her body.

'I love you, Li.'

'And I love you, Freddie, but nothing is straightforward, nothing's—'

'Get your filthy hands off her, you bastard!'

Freddie and Mei spun round. Someone was standing watching them from the top of the waterman's stairs.

'Who's there?' called Freddie to the shadowy figure, keeping his voice calm and assertive when inside he was quaking – the blackout meant that anyone could be at risk from thieves and even lunatics, there were always stories going around about unsolved murders and rapes.

'It's him,' whispered Mei. 'Peter. He must have been following me again.'

Freddie squared up. 'So, it's you, is it, *Peter*? Right, let's sort this out. Now. Come on, stop frightening girls and stand up to someone your own size.'

Freddie bounded up the steps to confront him but Peter didn't back away; instead he barged straight into Freddie, knocking him off his feet and throwing him down on his back against the icy cobbles of the road.

Mei screamed and hurried up the steps to help him, but she wasn't fast enough. Peter had pulled out a knife from under his coat.

'Get away from him, Mei,' he commanded. 'If you don't swear now, this minute, that you're going to give him up for good, then I'll do what I promised: I'll kill him. And I'll kill you too.'

Freddie scrambled to his feet, his eyes focussed on the blade. 'So, Li, you were telling the truth after all. Except you left out the part about him being mad.'

Mei was too scared to say anything.

'Okay, Li,' Freddie continued. 'I want you to get away from here. Run as fast as you can and go in the first shelter you come to. I'll find you, don't worry.'

Mei shook her head. 'No. I'm staying here with you, Freddie.'

'Didn't you hear what I said?' Peter turned to her, his face twisted with disbelief. 'I warned you, Mei. I gave you every chance . . .'

It was the split second Freddie needed. He spun Peter round by the shoulder, threw back his own head and then whacked his forehead – smack! – down on Peter's nose. Peter reeled backwards, hitting the back of his head on the brick wall beside the steps. Freddie had the knife off him before he knew what was happening.

He was about to thrust it into the semi-conscious man's ribs when Mei threw herself at him.

'Freddie, no! You'll kill him. Don't, please.'

Freddie straightened up. He could see the blood from the wounded man's nose congealing in dark clots on his face. The sight made him gag. Slowly he backed away.

Peter shook his head and staggered to his feet to come at him again, taking a wild swing, but all his strength was gone.

'Now it's me warning you,' Freddie panted. 'If you don't leave Li alone, it's you who's going to be sorry. You'd better get on that boat tonight or they'll be finding your body down an alley somewhere. And, believe me, you won't die quick. I'll make you suffer, just like I've been suffering, and enjoy every moment of it.'

Mei shook her head. 'Don't talk like that, Freddie. You're as bad as him.'

'It's all the likes of him understand,' he growled.

Mei could barely recognise this man, with his fierce face and bloodied knuckles, as the boy who had won her love with his gentleness and devotion. It was as if he had turned into a stranger before her eyes. Stifling a sob, she ran away into the pitch-dark maze of streets that surrounded the docks.

Freddie started running too, not thinking about where he was going but unconsciously heading for home.

There was a loud crash from somewhere to his right and a building burst into flame. The sweet smell of burning rum filled the air as the leaping flames turned the dark night almost as bright as day. He stood rooted to the spot, watching as fire, rescue and ambulance squads arrived. He didn't know how long they had taken to get there; he had lost all sense of time, all sense of anything but his own confusion and remorse. If Li hadn't been there, what might he have done? Would he really have been capable of killing someone?

What had happened to him? Pulling dodgy strokes for Bernie Woods as though it was normal; thinking it was a good idea to rob a bank; now beating up a Chinese bloke and threatening him like that.

And lying to his mum about just about everything.

What had he become?

'You'd better get that looked at, lad.'

'What?' Freddie, pulled himself back to the present, trying to understand what was going on. He was squinting into the face of an ambulance man who was staring in concern at his forehead.

'Your face is covered in blood. You injured anywhere else, do you know?'

'I'm not injured,' he spat back, rubbing the

back of his hand across his forehead. 'It's not my blood. I was helping someone, that's all. It's not mine, all right?'

'Okay, calm down. Good lad for helping, but don't you go taking any risks. Leave that to us, eh?'

Freddie felt so humiliated – the lies came so easily to him – he couldn't bear to answer. He ran off, seared with a shame that felt hotter than the flames from the burning warehouse.

Somehow, Freddie got back to Turnbury Buildings, through the mayhem of bombs falling and the false promises of wrong turnings in the blackout. Despite the fact that the planes overhead were still raining down their bombs over the East End, he started climbing the stairway to the top floor rather than sheltering in the laundry. He knew he couldn't face anyone.

As he reached the second-floor landing, he felt his legs buckle and had to admit that it was all too much for him – he couldn't go on. He didn't care what happened to him. This was it.

He sank to the floor, leaned back against the wall, rested his elbows on his knees and buried his face in his hands.

Up on the roof, Nell and Martin looked out over the burning docks. It was the worst night in weeks, the bombers bent on destroying the warehouses which stored much of the food the country imported to keep its people fed.

'How much longer can we keep doing this to each other, Nell? Look at it out there. And it's not just us. Their people must be suffering as much as we are. Struggling to go about their ordinary lives – caring for their families, trying to protect them, not knowing what's going to be thrown at them, day after day. And all the while, the blokes in fancy suits and posh uniforms – on both sides – are ordering us to bomb the buggery out of each other.'

'Caring for our families – what more can we do, though?' Nell looked out over the fires and felt the sight drain all the strength and hope from her. 'Mind if I nip down to the laundry for a minute, Martin? I won't be long, but I'm ever so worried about how Tommy's taking losing Bradman. I only want to check on him, see if he's managed to drop off for a few hours. Is that okay?'

'Do you have to ask?'

'I'll be as quick as I can.'

Martin kissed her. 'You do whatever you need to.'

'I won't be long.'

'Mind them stairs.'

*

As Nell rounded the stairway, shining her torch down at her feet, she almost fell over Freddie, who was still sitting there, huddled against the landing wall.

She squatted down beside him. 'Anything I can do, Fred?'

He sniffed loudly and shook his head.

'What's that on your forehead?'

'I had a fight.'

Nell took out her handkerchief. 'Spit on that,' she said, holding it out to him, and then rubbed the blood off his face.

'You should watch yourself, you know, Freddie. I've seen what can happen when people get caught up in things they don't really understand. It can be all too easy for them to start going down the wrong path.'

'I'm all right.'

'You might think you are, but don't you reckon your mum's had enough to put up with?'

'She doesn't care about me.'

'Don't talk like that, Fred, of course she does. It's just that we've all got so much to cope with, we sometimes forget to tell other people – the ones we love and care about – that we know what our priorities should be, even if we don't always show it.'

She looked away then, thinking about Tommy and Bradman, and how much her son was suffering. And what was she doing? Sitting here with someone who was little more than a stranger to her.

But how could she walk away? If it wasn't for Sylvia – a complete stranger – taking her in all those years ago, where would she be now?

'I'll help you, if you like, but you've got to be strong, make a decision to change the way you're living. I know I'm Sylvia and Bernie's friend, and perhaps I shouldn't be saying all this, but they're older than you, and they've made their decisions. You're young – what, sixteen? – with every opportunity to make a different future for yourself and for others. Don't let lies and secrets ruin things for you or before you know where you are, your life will be out of control and there'll be nothing you can do about it.'

He raised his head and looked at her. That was exactly what he'd been thinking. 'How do you know?'

'Take my word for it – I know. I know all too well what secrets can do.'

'Everything's in such a mess. Say it's too late?'

'It's not. Really it's not.' Nell tapped her chin, thinking. 'Right, how about your mum? She doesn't know what you're doing with Bernie, does she?'

He shrugged dejectedly, hardly caring any more. 'No, 'course not. I'm not stupid.'

'Have you got a girlfriend you can talk to? I bet you have, a nice-looking kid like you.'

'Girlfriend? Me?' he laughed, the sound completely devoid of humour.

'Freddie, I know this is easy for me to say, but sometimes when the very worst is happening to you and you can't see any way out, it's then that something just turns up, out of the blue, and things work themselves out. Not always in the way you expect them to, Fred, but they do. Believe me they do.'

'Why should I believe you? Why should I believe anyone?'

'Because otherwise, what point is there in going on? What point is there in anything?'

'I'm not sure there is any point for me,' he said in a low voice.

'Please, Freddie, you have to think about your family, but you also have to think of your future as well. When all this is over, you can do whatever you like with your life – help rebuild this world we all seem so intent on destroying. You can do something worthwhile then, something you can be proud of.'

He swiped his nose with his palm. 'How can I when everything's all gone rotten? Every stinking bit of it.'

This was going nowhere. Why did Nell ever think she could help? 'Fred, I'm sorry, but I can't stay here much longer, there's something I've gotta do.'

'You go.'

She still couldn't bring herself just to leave him there. 'Tell you what, would you mind doing me a favour? My son . . . you know, Tommy? . . . his little dog got killed last week, and it's really upset him. On top of that he's feeling guilty about losing his stupid bike, of all things. Right sad he is. I've tried getting through to him, but it's useless.'

Nell stared down into the dark stairwell, picturing the face of her son when he'd heard that Bradman was dead. 'Maybe if I'd have been paying more attention to what he was up to it wouldn't have happened.' She turned to Freddie. 'He's not fourteen yet, Fred, and like all kids his age he looks up to older lads. So would you do me this favour and come down to the laundry with me? And if he's not asleep, would you sit with him, talk to him for while?'

'Why don't *you* go and sit with him?' growled Freddie.

She rolled her eyes. 'Because I'm meant to be up on the flipping roof, protecting us all from the Nazi bombers.'

'You?'

'Yeah, I do regular shifts with my Martin. Why not? I got the time. I only work in the corner shop for a few hours – you know, with Martin's mum – and apart from that there's just the flat and the kids to look after, so I'm one of the lucky ones.'

'My mum does war work.'

'I know she does. Kitty puts in the hours, all right.'

'I should be doing something – something worthwhile.'

'Well, you can start right now, if you like. Come down with me and sit with Tommy, eh?'

Freddie shrugged. 'If you want.'

'Thanks, Freddie. I really appreciate it. And I know Tommy will too.'

Chapter 18

The Lovells – Mary, Joe, Martin, Nell and the kids – were all sitting around the Christmas dinner table in the upstairs front room of the Hope and Anchor pub in Whitechapel. Bernie Woods, tongue poking out between his lips, was carving great chunks off a plump, glistening goose and slices from a golden, crackling-covered shoulder of pork, while Sylvia – done up to the nines for the occasion – made sure that everyone had a drink in front of them.

'There you are, you gorgeous girl, and I've given you a drinking straw and everything.' Sylvia put down a glass of lemonade by Dolly's plate then turned to Nell. 'You didn't have to bring us that pork over, you know, Nelly. Although it's a lovely bit of meat – that pig club of yours did really well, Martin, especially with everything that's been going on over there in the docks. A bloody miracle you ever managed to keep them there, really. But you know me and Bernie, we've always got plenty of grub.'

She shoved Joe playfully in the back as she walked past to fetch him a bottle of pale ale.

'You lot are going to have to take most of it with you when you go home tomorrow, you know that, don't you?'

'Well, I think it's smashing, you cheering us all up by laying out such a big spread on the table,' he replied. 'After what everyone's been through these past few months, we could all do with having a proper jolly for once.' He turned to Tommy. 'And how are you doing, boy?'

Tommy stared down at his food, wondering how he was going to eat a single mouthful when all he could think about was how much Bradman would have loved a bit of the pork crackling to gnaw on. 'All right thanks, Granddad.'

'That's a good boy. Here, pull this cracker with me. You're the only one without a paper hat on. Look.' He pointed at Martin. 'Even your dad's got one on. Mind you, it does look more like a pimple on a pig's bum than a paper hat. But that's the trouble when you've got a head as big as his.'

'Flipping cheek,' said Martin. 'But if I have got a big head, then we all know where I got it from, don't we, Tom? Did you see that Granddad had to split his up the back just to get it on that big old nut of his?'

'Will you listen to them two, Dolly?' Mary put on a look of mock displeasure. 'Your dad and granddad are like a pair of naughty little schoolboys.'

Tommy tried his best, but he couldn't find a smile for anyone.

'Shall I let Tom have this shandy, do you think, Nell?'

'Go on, why not? It is Christmas after all. But make sure there's plenty of lemonade in it, eh, Sylv.'

"Course I will. We don't want our boy getting tipsy, now do we?"

Sylvia gave Tommy his drink, a quick squeeze and a kiss on the top of his head. 'I know you feel a bit blue, Tommy my love, but try and cheer up for your Auntie Sylvie. We've got our presents after dinner, remember. Now, let's all get stuck into this lot before it gets cold.'

She winked at Vicky. 'And I reckon no one will even notice if you don't eat all your sprouts, love. Not today they won't.'

'Well, I hope you don't eat them all,' said Bernie, patting his big round belly. 'Or we won't be having no bubble for breakfast tomorrow morning, will we?'

Back at Turnbury Buildings it wasn't such a jolly affair in Ada and Albert Tanner's flat – they were the only ones sitting at their Christmas table.

'This is lovely grub, Ada,' said Albert,

admiring the plate of pork and veg that she had grudgingly produced. 'Seems a shame there's no one here to share it with us.'

'Shame? I should say it's a shame. It's a crying shame, that's what it is. But no one can say I didn't try. Two separate notes I sent round to that daughter-in-law of yours, inviting her round here. Two, if you don't mind. And ha'penny a time I gave that kid to run them round there to her.'

'Hold up, Ada. What do you mean, daughter-in-law of mine? Don't you mean *ours*?'

Ada ignored him and carried on with her monologue. 'Two notes I sent. And did she even bother to reply to either one of them? No, 'course she didn't, not her. Spiteful cow. It'll be her keeping Bella away from me.'

Albert chanced his arm. 'And how about our Alfie, is she keeping him away too?'

Ada wouldn't give Albert the satisfaction of an answer. What did she care about some nancy boy who'd only bring shame on her?

'I knew how to treat my elders and betters when I was her age,' she said. 'I wouldn't have dreamed of being so rude. Gawd knows what my boy's going to have to say when he finds out she wasn't round here for Christmas dinner.'

Albert's eyebrows shot up like barge sails unfurling in a gale.

'Manners, that's what she needs. She could do with taking lessons from the likes of me.'

And on and on she went.

Albert wisely decided to cock a deaf 'un and carried on enjoying the luxury of a full roast dinner, cheered further by the thought of the crate full of Mackeson he'd been collecting over the past few weeks and had stashed away in the back bedroom ready for after the Christmas meal. Albert loved the stuff, but if she'd stop talking long enough to draw breath, he'd even sacrifice a bottle or two to Ada.

Bella Tanner was having about as festive a time as her grandmother. Like Ada, she too had cooked the meal – her mum had claimed that she had had one of her 'heads' come over her, and the heat of the kitchen had proved altogether too much – although it hadn't seemed to spoil her appetite in any way. Her plate was all but licked clean.

'Mum, are you going to go in next-door for a Christmas drink?'

Bella was stacking up the dinner plates as she watched her mother concentrating on her reflection in the mirror over the fireplace. She was putting on a thick layer of the deep red lipstick that she had taken to wearing since her husband had gone away to fight for freedom. She drew her head back and admired her handiwork –

turning her head this way and that and pressing her lips together tightly – then she bared her teeth and rubbed off a smudge with her little finger before starting the process all over again.

'How could I refuse?' she said between swipes across her mouth. 'It was so nice of her to ask me in, I thought I should at least show me face and keep her company for a while.'

Bella picked up her brother's plate. 'How about you, Alf? You got any plans to go next-door?'

'What, in there? You talking through your braces again, Bell? I don't think that old trout would let me over the step, let alone into her front room – even if I was stupid enough to want to go and look at her ugly mug all night.' He took out a packet of cigarettes and lit one, releasing the smoke in a perfect circle. 'Anyway, I said I'd meet up with a friend of mine later on.'

'Nice, is he?' whispered Bella.

'Shut up,' said Alfie, flashing her a warning glare.

Bella went and stood behind her mother. 'Be all right if I pop out as well then, Mum? Seeing as you and Alfie are off out.'

Her mother stopped applying her lipstick and looked at Bella's reflection in the mirror. 'Where would you have to go?'

'Only round a friend's.'

She sighed dramatically as if she were being put on – *yet again*. 'Don't you be late then, Bell. I don't want people talking about me. Saying I let my daughter run fast and loose.' She tossed her head at Alfie. 'It's bad enough having to hear what they all have to say about him. So, nine o'clock. Right?'

Bella hated it when her mum got like this – all proper and motherly. She had to get out – her granddad had taken the trouble to come round and make her promise she'd at least pop in and see her nan on Christmas Day. But she also had to know the rules – or rather the ones her mum decided were to be observed this particular afternoon. The last thing Bella wanted to do was upset her.

'Say there's a raid, what should I do then?'

'Aw, I don't know.' Her mother waved the lipstick like a wand. 'Go in your mate's shelter or something. Do I have to sort out everything in this house?'

Bella had never got ready quicker and had never felt quite so nervous.

Across the landing from Ada and Albert Tanner, Kitty, Freddie, Grace and little Bobby Jarrett were still eating, although Freddie wasn't actually doing much more than moving food listlessly around his plate.

326

It was no good, he couldn't sit there any longer, pretending to his mum and sister that he was enjoying himself; he felt as if he was about to burst. 'I'm ever so sorry, Mum. It was a smashing meal but I can't eat any more, I've got to go out. I wouldn't go, not if it wasn't urgent.'

Kitty looked disappointed. 'But you've hardly touched your dinner, Fred. And it was such a treat, being given all that lovely pork. It was really generous of Martin and his friends.'

'I know, but I'll have it later. Just leave it on the plate in the kitchen.'

'But all that meat . . .'

Grace touched her mother's arm. 'Don't let's row today, Mum. Let Freddie go out if he wants, and I'll clear up while you put your feet up. The blackout's all been done, and the fire's stoked up. You can have a nice rest.'

Kitty's eyes widened. *A rest? What did Grace know?* 'Why should I want to put my feet up?'

'Because you work so hard, and because you cooked us all a lovely dinner and bought us all presents – that's why. I wasn't being rude or anything.'

'I'm sorry, Grace. I'm just missing your dad, I suppose. Now things are getting back to the way they used to be – the way they're supposed to be – it doesn't seem right that he's not with us.' She smiled wistfully at her daughter. 'But we're not the only ones feeling like this, eh, Grace? There are plenty of people who won't ever see their families again. We should remember that we're the lucky ones.'

Kitty turned to her son then. 'Your sister's right, Fred, you go out and have a good time. But you will watch yourself out there, won't you? Even if I don't always say so, I do worry about you when you're out in the dark.'

'I'll be careful, Mum. Happy Christmas. And, well, you know, thanks.'

Kitty could hardly believe it when he bent down and kissed her on the cheek.

She and Grace sat in silence as they listened to Freddie striding along the passageway and then slamming the front door behind him.

Kitty widened her eyes at Grace. 'Here, do you think Father Christmas has gone and swapped our Freddie for a new one?'

'I don't know, but something's happened to him.'

'It must be the Christmas spirit.'

'Yeah, and it's good, innit?'

'Yes, love, really good.' Kitty stood up. 'And I think we'd better make the most of all this goodwill. So let's clear up together, eh? We'll get it done all the quicker that way, and then we can sit down with a cup of tea and a nice slice of that cake Mrs Lovell put by for us.'

'She's such a kind person, isn't she, Mum? Always ever so good to everyone.'

Kitty took a long, deep breath, wondering if this was the moment she'd been waiting for. What the hell? She had to tell her daughter sometime.

'She is kind, Grace – a really good woman.' Another deep breath. 'Here, do you remember what Ada said that time, about me not being a good mother?'

'How could I forget? But everyone knows it's not true. You couldn't have been a better mum to us, not the way you stood by me, risking everything you had, and then how you've helped with me Bobby. I'd never had managed without you. You've been smashing, Mum.'

'I hope you're right, Grace, and not just being kind.' Kitty's words came tumbling out then double speed. 'I really do, because – this is so hard – because . . . I'm having another baby. There, I've said it. And I'm ever so happy about it, and I've written to your dad and I know he will be too. But what's really important to me, Grace, is that you're happy too.'

'A baby?' Grace held out her arms and hugged her mother. 'I couldn't be happier, Mum. It's smashing news.'

Bobby, still sitting in his high chair – wearing a good portion of his chopped-up pork and potatoes in his hair – started gurgling cheerfully, completely unaware of what was going on, of course, but enjoying the fun.

'I'm so glad you feel that way, Grace. After all that happened with you, you know, getting sent to that place – I thought you might feel different.'

Grace, her mood suddenly less joyful, dropped back down on to her chair. 'While we're talking like this, Mum – just the two of us – can I tell you something? Will you listen to me? Really listen?'

Kitty's smile had faded too. 'This sounds serious.'

'It is. And it's something that I've wanted – and really tried – to say to you for such a long time.'

Grace looked over at Bobby, who was still playing with his spoon and bowl, totally unaware of the new turn of events in the kitchen of number 55 Turnbury Buildings.

'*Raped*? But why didn't you say something before? Who was it? I'll go to the police right now, and have the bastard put away. No one's going to get away with doing that to my little girl.'

'I told you then, Mum, and I told Dad, and I was telling the truth, I swear on my life: I don't know who Bobby's dad is. I didn't know who he was then, and I don't now. I know no one believed me and that that only made the rows worse, but it was true.'

'But—'

'Please, Mum, let me tell you.'

Kitty bowed her head. 'Yes, sorry. Tell me everything.'

'I was coming home from school, and this man . . . he came up to me and started saying things . . . horrible things. I didn't really understand them, but I knew they were wrong.'

Kitty shook her head. 'No, this can't be true.'

'It is, Mum, I swear to you.'

'So—'

Grace couldn't help being rude and interrupting her mother, she had to get the words out once and for all. 'But then he said *you'd* asked him to come and meet me because you'd had to go out. He said I had to go with him, so I did, and that's when he . . .'

Kitty drew her daughter into her arms as the tears rolled down their cheeks.

'Why didn't you say anything before?'

'I told you I didn't know who he was.'

'No, I mean about . . .'

Grace pulled away. 'Because I felt ashamed, that's why. I didn't understand what had happened to me or why he did those things. I

331

just knew they hurt and that they were bad. You'd always warned me about boys, that I should be careful, but I didn't know what you meant. You never said what I should be careful of. Or why.'

'But when we went to the doctor's, when we thought you were ill and he told us what was really wrong, why didn't you say something then?'

'How could I talk to you and Dad once you knew what that pig had done to me? And then I felt even more ashamed when you two were both so upset you started rowing all the time. It was all so horrible.'

Grace sniffed and rubbed her nose on the sleeve of her cardigan. 'That made me feel guilty as well as ashamed. You'd never rowed before. We'd all been so happy. And then you sent me away to that awful place, to punish me.'

Kitty handed her a handkerchief; she could hardly speak. 'It wasn't to punish you, my little darling. I'd never do that. I'd always done my best to protect you, to keep you wrapped up in cotton wool away from the big, bad world.' She looked about the room as if seeking something she'd lost long ago. 'Grace, you need to know that we were rowing because we panicked.'

She rested her elbows on the table and

covered her face with her hands. 'Me and your dad . . .'

'What, Mum? What is it?'

'We had Freddie . . . We had Freddie when we weren't a lot older than you are now. I was barely fifteen, and your dad was sixteen.'

'Is that why you'll never say how old you are? I thought you were just having a bit of fun.'

'It was no fun, Grace, believe me. Kids, we were, and our parents didn't want to know when they found out.'

'Did they send you to a place like you sent me to?'

Kitty couldn't face her daughter. 'No. They threw us out on the street instead. On the same day we told them. They've never wanted to see us since.'

'I've got grandparents?'

Kitty nodded. 'All those lies over the years . . . I'm so sorry, Grace. I would have told you about them, but you have to remember that they were from a different era, with different beliefs. We've tried getting in touch since then but they don't want to know. And you have to remember that that's the reason you've never seen them – because of what me and your dad did – nothing to do with them rejecting you. It was *us* they didn't want to know. But sod the lot of them! We were all right. I was lucky to meet someone as good as your dad. It was only because he was such a grafter that we managed to survive. We got this room in a house over in Hoxton, and your dad worked night and day to get us a proper place of our own.' She dropped her hands from her face and shook her head sadly. 'And then that got bombed out.'

Kitty looked down at the serving plate with the remains of the pork on it. 'I wonder what sort of dinner your dad's having today. I hope it's something nice.'

Then she raised her eyes and looked at her daughter.

'If you went through all that, then how could you have done what you did to me?' asked Grace.

'I don't know, Grace, but I do know I'm not very proud of it.' She picked a piece of potato off the tablecloth and put it on the pork plate. 'You do realise what all this means, don't you, Grace?'

'I'm not sure, Mum. I'm not sure I know anything any more.'

'Me and your dad, we didn't get married till you were five and Freddie was six – we weren't old enough. So we were living over the brush when we had you. I am so sorry I lied to you, Grace, and that we never listened to you, but when we found out that you were expecting little Bobby, it was like there was something bad we'd passed on to you. I'd tried so hard to be strict, to make sure it never happened to you, to keep you out of harm's way. But now, looking back, I realise I suffocated you instead of protecting you. Maybe if I'd been less harsh you'd have been able to speak to me about things, and I could have taught you how to defend yourself against animals like that – whoever he was.'

'It's not your fault what happened.'

'No? Then whose fault is it? And I wonder sometimes what secrets Freddie's hiding from us. I'm the opposite with him, letting him come and go as he pleases, because I've not been able to face hearing what he might be up to. Him with all his nice clothes and money in his pocket.' Kitty covered her face again. 'What have I done to my children?'

Grace looked at Bobby in his high chair, knowing that she'd die rather than let anything bad happen to him. 'You've loved us, Mum, that's what you've done.' She stood up. 'Here, fancy a slice of that cake?' She didn't know what else to say.

Kitty reached out and stroked her daughter's hand. 'Thank you, darling. Thank you.'

Freddie was standing at the bottom of the stairwell, pulling up the collar of his overcoat, preparing himself for the snowy two-mile walk. He was glad he'd put his boots on.

With a shudder he stepped out into the courtyard.

'Oi! Mind me bike!' Someone had walked right into him.

'Hello, Fred.' Bella didn't know whether to carry on talking to him or to race off up the stairs as if her tail was on fire. It had taken all her courage to come over to the Buildings to see her nan after what had happened with Freddie, but her granddad had asked her especially, and she really missed coming to see them – it was about the only attention she got, even if her nan did act like she had the rats with her most of the time.

And as she'd already made a complete fool of herself with Freddie Jarrett, what did she have to lose now?

'*Mind me bike!* That's a good 'un, Fred. You're walking, but you still said it – *Mind me bike!* You should hear my granddad laugh when that bloke on the wireless says it: *Mind me bike!*'

'Sorry, Bella, I can't stop. I've gotta go.'

Think, Bella. Think. 'Yeah, it's freezing out. Going somewhere important, are you, Freddie?'

'Work.'

'On Christmas afternoon? You must be ever so important.'

'Someone has to do it.' Freddie started

tramping off across the snow-covered court-yard. 'Keep the railways open.'

'See you later?' she called after him.

'What?' He turned briefly and looked back at her. 'Maybe. Yeah, I suppose so.'

Bella could now only hear the sound of his boots scrunching away from her but she was beaming with pleasure, not even noticing the cold as the snow settled on her head and shoulders.

He'd said he supposed he was going to see her later. Well, all right, he'd said *maybe*, but he'd still said it.

'That was flipping lovely, girls.' Bernie pushed his plate away from him, his paper hat tipped wonkily over one eye. 'Drop of port or brandy, chaps?'

Joe looked at Mary, who smiled back at him indulgently. 'A drop more can't hurt after the amount you lot have been pouring down your necks.'

'I won't say no then, Bern.'

'How about you, Martin?'

'Wouldn't want to seem rude by refusing you, Bern, now would I?'

Sylvia rolled her eyes. 'Typical. Us girls get to do the washing up, while them three sit in here on their backsides, knocking back the grog.'

'If the fellers are going to start on the spirits, Mary,' said Nell, 'I wouldn't mind if you stayed in here with them. Then you can keep an eye on the kids.'

'You sure?'

'Yeah, I don't want them giving the kids any hard stuff.'

'No chance with me watching over them.'

'Good, then me and Sylvia can manage in the kitchen, can't we, Sylv?'

Sylvia hadn't reckoned on Mary not being there to help them out; this sounded far too much like hard work. 'Tell you what, Nell, why don't we leave it for now? The cleaning woman's coming back tomorrow. She can do it then.'

'No, we don't want this lot hanging around; it's miserable having a sink full of dirty pots. Come on, Sylv, you know what a good worker I am. We'll have it done in no time. Or I will, because I don't know about you but I'd love a cuppa. You can put the kettle on, if you like.'

Sylvia brightened at the thought of making the tea rather than getting her hands stuck into a bowl of greasy water. 'Nelly, you're on, girl.'

Despite the slippery pavements and the blackout, Freddie took less than half an hour to reach Pennyfields. This was something he had to do while he still had the nerve. But try as he might, and despite all the effort he'd made, he couldn't bring himself to carry it through. He stood there outside Li Mei's house, staring at the front door like a confused postman trying to find a missing street number. Why hadn't he thought this through before he'd left home?

'What the bloody hell?' he snapped. Someone had shone a torch right into his face. He screwed his eyes shut and raised his arm to cover them.

'What are you up to there, matey boy?' the man with the torch asked.

'I might ask you the sodding same. Creeping up like that. And shade that torch, can't you?'

Freddie dropped his arm and opened his eyes, blinking in the light.

Aw, no, it was only a copper – and an irritated-looking one at that, his expression stern behind his snow-sprinkled moustache. He obviously didn't like being out and about in this weather on a Christmas evening.

'I'll have you know that this torch is very much shaded,' he boomed, turning it off. 'But more to the point, I don't recognise you from round here, do I?' He was leaning in so close that his nose was almost touching Freddie's. 'You wouldn't be taking advantage of the blackout to get up to some sort mischief, now would you?' His voice dripped suspicion. 'Standing around

in this weather, it don't seem right to me. You up
to no good, are you?'

'No. No, I'm not. I've come to visit a friend,
that's all. No law against that, is there?'

'Who's this friend then? I've been on this beat
for years and I reckon I know everyone living
round here. So what's his name?'

'Mickey,' said Fred.

'Mickey?' The policeman straightened up and
thought for a moment. 'Mickey who?'

'Mickey Mouse.'

'You saucy little bugger! You'll find yourself
in trouble if you're not careful, talking to me like
that.'

'Get in trouble, will I? You don't know
anything. Nothing at all,' shouted Freddie as he
legged it up the street.

He was off and away into the pitch dark
before the well-upholstered officer even had a
chance to get his whistle out from under his
cape.

'Right, I'll make that pot of tea then.' Sylvia
reached around Nell to get to the sink. She
turned on the tap, but instead of filling the kettle
just stood there letting it run. 'How long have I
got to wait?'

'Wait for what?' Nell was rolling up her
sleeves, ready to start on the washing up.

'How long have we known each other, Nelly? Don't bother to answer, 'cos I'll tell you – long enough for me to be able to read you like a bleedin' book, and a not very hard one at that. So you might as well just spit it out, because I don't intend hanging about the kitchen while that old man of mine polishes off that bottle of brandy.'

'I never could keep anything from you, could I, Sylv?'

'No, you couldn't. So what are you waiting for?'

Nell turned off the tap. 'It was what you said about always having plenty of grub . . .'

'Now I've got even less idea what's up with you. Here, you're not going hungry, are you? Not with Martin in the docks and Mary in the shop? Because that'd be ridiculous.'

'No, Sylv, we're not hungry, not after that dinner anyway. No, it's about you and Bernie.'

'What about us?'

'It's just that you've got a way of life that's – how can I put it? – different from most people's.'

'And?'

'Sylv, this is really hard for me to say – what with how good you've been to me and my family over the years, and how you're the best friend I could ever wish for – but I don't think young Freddie Jarrett should be involved in that life.'

'No?'

'No. You see, his family, they've been suffering, and I don't think it would help any of them if he wound up getting himself in trouble.'

'Nor do I. He's only a nipper. He should grow up and learn which way the world turns. After that . . . well, then it's up to him what he does.'

'Do you mean that?'

''Course I do. Did I ever let you get involved in anything a bit near the mark, Nell? No, I never did. When you were living here, I kept you well away from all that. It's not your world. And, truth be told, Nell, if I wasn't such a greedy mare, who loves all the dresses and jewellery and that, it wouldn't be mine either.' Sylvia turned the tap back on and filled the kettle. 'Plus there's the little point that I fell in love with bloody Bernie Woods, the great daft sod, so it wasn't like I had any choice, really. If I wanted to be with him, I had to accept him and his way of going about things. He wasn't going to change. So I've had to spend my life with him pretending I haven't got the first idea what he's up to – well, you know how it is with me, when it suits me I can do. But I still sometimes put the fear of God up the old sod.'

'Then you wouldn't hate me if I talked to Freddie about what he might be getting himself into?'

'What do you think? You know me, Nell, and you know how much I value you as a friend. You know how much I'd have loved having kids of my own too. Why would I want young Freddie Jarrett getting caught up in things he's not really up to yet? That'd look well with Bernie's contacts, that would. And say he did something wrong and got my Bern in schtook over some stupid mistake? So, 'course I wouldn't mind you talking to him. But, for Gawd's sake, be a bit tactful about what you say, and you must never, ever let Bernie know what you've done. You know what he's like, I'd never hear the bloody end of it.'

Nell was now apparently focussing all her attention on scraping the sticky residue from the roasting pan. 'Good, I'm glad you said that. And I'll definitely never, ever let Bernie know what I've done,' she said, going at the goose grease with a wad of wire wool and a good shake of scouring powder. 'Because I should let you know, Sylv, that I've already spoken to Freddie.'

As he headed towards Whitechapel, Freddie slowed down. The last thing he wanted was to fall and break his leg and spoil all his plans before he'd even had a chance to put them into action. Maybe that copper had done him a favour, stopping him from knocking on the door. Before he spoke to Li, he would make sure he had something to offer her, something to prove he meant it when he said he loved her – a decent life and a way to show he was going to make himself worthy of her. Nell Lovell had been right: he did have choices, and he was going to make sure he made decent and proper ones from now on. Or how could he ever deserve Li's love and respect?

'Happy Christmas, Nan.' Bella kissed Ada and then Albert on the cheek. 'Happy Christmas, Granddad.'

Albert winked at her. 'Good girl for coming, Bella,' he whispered so that Ada couldn't hear him.

Bella held out two little parcels wrapped in plain brown paper. 'They're not much but I wanted to bring you something over.'

Ada took both the gifts and put them on the sideboard. 'We'll look at them later, won't we, Albert?'

He rolled his eyes at his granddaughter. 'If you say so, dear.'

'Where is she then, that mother of yours? I sent her notes – two of them – asking her over. It's what your father would have wanted – us being together at Christmas time.'

Bella blushed. 'Mum had to go next-door because the lady's been feeling a bit down – she's missing her husband and that – and Alfie went out somewhere with a friend.'

Ada tried not to smile, but couldn't stop a little twitch of pleasure from playing around her mouth. So, their son's wife really was a useless mother, and her little Bella had had to come running to her nan for a bit of comfort after all. This was perfect ammunition to store away for when her beautiful boy came home from the war and wondered how they'd all got on during these terrible times. She'd tell him all right!

Sylvia came back into the front room, with Nell carrying the tray of tea close behind her.

'There, that's all done.' Sylvia poured herself a brandy as Nell set the tea tray on the table. 'Until we have to start cutting the sandwiches for our supper, eh, Mary?'

Mary, who was sitting on the floor with the children doing a jigsaw puzzle of the King and Queen in full regalia, groaned loudly. 'Don't talk to me about food, Sylv. I might pass out.'

'Glad to hear it,' said Sylvia. 'I'd hate to think anyone had gone hungry in my home.'

'Some chance of that,' grinned Joe, raising his glass to Sylvia.

She was about to give him a saucy answer when, hearing a loud knocking on the door downstairs, everyone turned towards the window that overlooked the street.

'Who the hell can that be?' Sylvia went over and lifted a corner of the blackout curtain. 'I can't flaming see who it is, but if it's them sodding doctors from across the road, and they think we're opening up tonight . . .'

Bernie made a half-hearted show of standing up.

'You stay where you are, Bern. I know how soft you are with customers. You'll have them all in here.' She stuck her fists into her waist. 'I'll deal with this one.'

'I've no doubt you will, my little turtle dove,' said Bernie, grimacing in sympathy with who-ever had been foolish enough to disturb his wife's Christmas.

Sylvia knocked back her brandy and stormed out of the room.

They heard her complaining loudly as she trotted down the stairs to the bar. 'All right, all right, I'm bloody well coming as fast as I can. Stop that bloody racket, will you?'

Then they heard her opening the door, some muttering, and the sound of the door closing again and two sets of footsteps coming up the stairs.

Sylvia appeared in the doorway to the front room with Freddie Jarrett close behind her.

'We've got a visitor, Bern.'

'So I can see.'

It hadn't occurred to Freddie that all the Lovells might be there. 'Hello, Bern.'

'Hello, stranger, more like.' Bernie's greeting wasn't a warm one.

'I've come to wish you and Sylvia a Happy Christmas.'

'Have you, Fred? Well, you're a bit late, ain't you? We've not seen hide nor hair of you for days. And do you know how busy we've been, with the market workers and the hospital and everything?'

'I do know, Bernie, and I'm sorry about that. I should have come round to see you, but better late than never, eh? Something came up. You see,' he glanced over to Nell, 'I've been doing a lot of thinking lately. And I thought it was about time that I did my bit for my country. So I'm joining up, as soon as they'll have me, even if I have to lie about my age.'

Nell's smile was as bright as a Christmas candle. 'That's smashing news, Fred. We'll be worried about you, of course, but we've all got to pull together to win this war.'

'Yeah, well done,' said Joe. 'Your mum and dad must be right proud of you.'

'I hope they will be when I tell them, but I thought it was right to tell Bernie first, what with him giving me a job and everything.'

Sylvia edged over to Nell and whispered, 'Seems you haven't got to worry yourself about young Freddie after all, Nelly darling.' Then she held up the bottle of brandy to Freddie. 'Fancy staying for a drop, Fred, to celebrate your news, and to show there's no bad feelings that you're leaving the Hope? You can watch the kids open their presents.'

Freddie saw Bernie's expression and inwardly squirmed. 'Thanks, but I'm not sure . . .'

'Go on, Fred,' said Nell. 'A quick one to celebrate your new life.'

Sylvia nudged Freddie in the ribs. 'I might need you here for moral support when Nell sees what I've got the kids.'

Everyone went down to the bar and Sylvia sat them down at one of the big round tables.

'I'm giving out mine first,' she said, all giggles and flapping hands, and went behind the counter to drag out an onion sack full of brightly wrapped parcels.

'Here you are, Nell. It's not your biggest present, but it is special to me – it's a card I had done for you. I saw the words in a magazine and thought they were so lovely that I got one of them sewing girls from down Brick Lane to embroider it for you and Martin.' She put a fat, Manilla envelope down in front of Nell – just the first of the cornucopia of gifts she was about to distribute. 'I don't half hope you like it because I think it's beautiful.'

Nell took the envelope and was about to open it to show it to Martin when she was distracted by the miraculous sight of Sylvia somehow managing to produce a couple of presents for Freddie, including one very boldly striped tie that Nell could only guess had originally been intended for inclusion in Bernie's tottering pile.

Soon there were similarly large stacks of gifts dotted around the table – a pile in front of each of them. Each of them except Tommy.

'Mum,' whispered Dolly, 'Tommy's not got anything. Shall I give him some of mine?'

'I don't know, Doll.'

'Ask her, Mum. He's right upset.'

'Sylv,' hissed Nell. 'You've forgotten Tommy.'

'What was that you said?' Sylvia asked in a loud, theatrical whisper. 'I've forgotten Tom? How could I ever do that?'

She put her hand on Tommy's shoulder and steered him round to the other side of the counter.

'Here you are, darling. I know he's not

Bradman, but he does need a good home. And I know you'll love him to bits because you're such a kind young feller.'

At the look on Tommy's face as he came back from behind the bar with a little scrap of sleeping, brown scruffy fur nestled in his arms, Nell couldn't hold back the tears.

'You don't mind, do you, Nell? And I know he's not a Jack Russell – he's more of a cross between a house cloth and a scrubbing brush when you see him walking about – but it was the best I could do. There's not a lot of pups around at the minute.'

'Mind, Sylv? Mind? Just look at Tommy's face. I could flipping well kiss you.'

'Well, go on then. It is Christmas.'

Freddie ruffled Tommy's hair. 'You're a lucky young feller and all, Tommy Lovell. And so am I, I've realised that. So I'm going back home now to see my own family, and I'm going to enjoy being with them while I can.'

'Alfie, I know we said we wouldn't give each other anything, but . . . I couldn't help myself.' The sandy-haired young man leaned forward and took something out of the built-in cupboard next to the gas fire, his face glowing in the cosy light from the flames. 'I saw this and knew it was exactly right for you. It's engraved.'

He and Alfie were sitting side by side on the single bed, the only piece of furniture, apart from the sink and a Lloyd Loom chair, that could fit into the little bedsit.

He handed Alfie a small flat packet and kissed him on the cheek. 'Happy Christmas, Alf. Something to remember me by.'

Alfie stared down at the packet.

'Go on. Open it.'

Alfie looked up, his face shining with happiness. 'Let me give you yours first.'

'*Alfie!*' The young man laughed. 'And we said we wouldn't.'

'I know.'

Alfie unhooked his jacket from the end of the bedstead and took out a slim, gift-wrapped parcel from the inside pocket. 'So you'll have something to remember me by as well.'

They tore the paper off their gifts.

'A cigarette case,' said Alfie.

'A silk muffler,' said his friend.

Alfie opened the lid. Inside it bore the inscription: *For my darling Alfie. Forever.*

The sandy-haired young man turned to Alfie and took his face in his hands. 'Now, how about something else to remember me by?'

As they rolled sideways on to the bed, wrapped in each other's arms, Alfie thought that he might just die of pleasure.

Chapter 19

'Hello, Nan. Did you and Granddad have a good Christmas?'

Ada was standing blocking her doorway like a short fat prison guard preventing a break out, although in her case she was preventing a break in – by her own grandson.

She was a formidable sight: tight, down-turned lips; curlers bristling in her hair; pop-pom-topped tartan slippers on her feet; lisle stockings rolled down to her ankles, and a voluminous crossover apron wrapped around her bulky frame. She ignored her grandson's question and looked over his shoulder out on to the landing.

'What are you doing here? Anyone could see you. And where's Bella?'

'I told her I was coming over, and she wanted to come with me – you know how she loves coming to see you, Nan – but I asked her to let me come and see you alone.' Alfie snapped his fingers nervously. 'There are things I need to say to you.'

This was so hard. He couldn't remember

when he'd last been over here; his nan had said barely more than a few words to him in months, and when she had said something it had been to tell him to clear off or something even more unpleasant along similar lines.

He tilted up his chin and looked straight at her. 'Nan, I've been called up. And I'm so lucky – it's the Air Force, exactly what I wanted. But you know how dangerous it can be, with all these planes getting shot down, so I came over because I wanted me and you to make friends before I go. Just in case anything happens. I really don't want to leave it like this between us.'

He edged towards her. 'Can't I come in and have a word? Try and explain some things to you? I won't keep you long.'

'Why would I want the likes of you in my home *explaining* things?'

'Because I'm your grandson.'

'You're no grandson of mine.' Ada stepped back, looking as if she'd rather be cleaning the lavatory than having to stand anywhere near him. 'I'm only pleased your father's away so he doesn't have to see what you've turned into.'

'Why do you have to be like this to me?'

'You're trying to blame *me* for the way *I'm* behaving? At least I don't have anything to be ashamed of.'

'Nor do I, Nan.'

'Aw, no? Well, then, we've got very different views on shame and on the proper way of going about things. And why do you think they put the likes of you away? Because it's wrong and it's disgusting, that's why. All I wanted was a decent family around me, and look what I wound up with. You, and a daughter-in-law who don't wanna know.'

Alfie stood there, head bowed, wondering how he could get her to listen to him – how he could get her to love him. Weren't you *supposed* to love your family?

'Have you ever thought that you drove Mum away, Nan?'

'Just piss off, will you? The warning'll be going soon, and I need to get me bag ready for the night.'

'Let me carry yours and Granddad's things to the shelter for you. Where is it?'

'Do you think I'd tell a slippery type like you where our shelter is? You'd watch till you saw us all go down there then you'd come up here and rob us all blind.'

'Nan, how could you say such a thing? You know I'd never do anything like that. And especially not to you and Granddad.'

'Do I? And you can forget trying to get my Albert involved in this. Soft as butter that one. But me, I can see you for what you really are.

You were brought up by that mother of yours, weren't you? And she'd have anyone over for a ha'penny that one. Now, clear off, I've got to get me things ready.'

As if on cue, the siren sounded.

Alfie craned his neck and looked along the passageway into the flat. 'Granddad indoors, is he?'

'Your grandfather went down the pub, and, if I'm not mistaken, by now he'll be making his way down to the cellar with a glass of Mackeson in his hand, talking about flaming pigeons. Not that it's any of your business.'

A loud crash had them looking up at the ceiling, then a bright flash illuminated the court-yard outside, followed by the glass rattling violently in the landing window-frame.

'That was really close by, Nan. You really had better go to the shelter. Let me get your bag for you, I'll take you down.'

'I'd rather die here in me own home than have anyone see me anywhere near the likes of you.'

'Why? Why do you hate me so much? Why would it be so awful to be seen with me?'

'Because you're not normal, that's why. And do you think I could stand hearing people saying, "Look at her, poor old girl, her with her nancy boy grandson." I've told you, you're not normal.'

'But, Nan, I've met someone, and I really like

him. That's normal, innit? Liking someone. He's kind, and he's—'

Ada stepped out on to the landing, her fat sausage of a finger stabbing at his chest, her jowls wobbling with rage. She kept poking him until she had him backed right across the landing with his head pressed against the opposite wall.

'*You've met someone?* No, that is not normal. All you've done is let this family down. Why can't you get it into that stupid head of yours? You do know that, don't you? You've already made a right poppy show of us as it is, without you having *met somebody*. What next? You gonna turn up here arm-in-arm? You disgust me. Your poor father away at sea, doing his best for us all, whatever would he make of all this? You make me sick. He's out there risking his life, and you, what are you doing? *Meeting someone.* Get away from me.'

'Don't say that, Nan. Please.'

'Why not? Would you rather I lied to you? Said how happy it made me, you having a . . . I can't even say the word.'

Martin sprinted across the cobbles and pulled open the door. He waited for Joe to catch up and then shoved him inside the ARP shelter by the dock gate.

'That was bleedin' close,' panted Joe.

'You're telling me, Dad. You can hardly believe that Christmas was only four days ago. Us all sitting around having such a good time together – eating, drinking, laughing. Now look at it again.'

'Never mind no Christmas.' It was the warden, tea mug in hand as if no time at all had passed since that Saturday back in September when the Blitz had begun and it seemed the whole of the docks had caught fire. 'What are you two doing back in here again? I told you last time: this is an official post this is. It's not meant for no civilians.' He looked down suspiciously at their feet. 'Or dogs.'

'Don't worry yourself, we've not got any dogs with us this time.' Joe glared at the warden's hand, clasped around the mug. 'But, as you say, this is an official ARP post – so why aren't you out there doing your bit?'

'What do you expect me to do?'

Joe's lip curled in disgust. 'How about your official duties? That'd be a bloody start.'

'I don't see you two doing much to help.'

'At least we offered.'

'Yeah, I bet you did. Brave men like you. That's why you came running in here like a pair of frightened rabbits.'

Joe shaped up, ready to punch the man on the nose.

'Leave it, Dad.' Martin held on to his father's shoulder, preventing him from making what could be the very serious mistake of hitting an ARP warden – no matter how annoying he was, the man was an official. 'He's an idiot. You hit him and you'll only wind up getting nicked. He's not worth it.'

Emboldened by Martin's words, the warden lifted his chin. 'You still haven't explained why you're in here, you pair of cowards.'

'If *you* hadn't been such a coward, and had gone out there to see what was going on, you'd know that there's a neap tide, and the water's far too low for the fire brigade's pumps. There's nothing we can do.'

The warden bristled. 'That still don't explain why—'

'We ducked in here to shelter on our way home, if you must know,' said Martin. 'The planes are coming over the East End and the City like no one's seen them in months. It is genuinely horrible out there. Frightening. We offered our help to the crews, but they said there's nothing anyone can do. Not for a few hours. So we're going back home to take over the fire-watching for a shift or two. Then we won't feel like a pair of spare parts, will we? Not like some people I could mention. Now what's your excuse?'

'I don't have to answer to the likes of you.'

'No, your sort don't answer to the likes of anyone.' Martin threw open the door. 'Come on, Dad, let's make a run for it.'

Out of breath from running the eight hundred yards across to Turnbury Buildings from the river, and then up the five flights of stairs to the top landing, Joe stood there not knowing where to look. He turned to Martin and slid his eyes in Ada Tanner's direction. She had some poor young feller backed up against the wall and was hollering at him like a lunatic.

'All right, Ada?' Joe greeted her.

'What did you say?' she snarled back at him.

'Nothing, Ada, nothing.' He pointed over to the vertical metal ladder that led up to the trapdoor that opened on to the roof. 'Fire-watching, that's all. And if I was you, I'd get down and shelter with the others. You've never seen nothing like it out there. It's bad, I'm telling you.'

'Well, you're not me, are you? And all I can say is, Thank Gawd for that.'

Up on the roof, three exhausted women from the fourth-floor landing gratefully accepted Joe and Martin's offer to take over their watch.

'Good luck,' called the last one as she

disappeared through the hatch and pulled the trapdoor shut behind her.

'And I reckon we're gonna need it, son,' said Joe, tightening the strap on his tin helmet as he surveyed the horizon. 'Will you just look at it out there? This really has to be the worst raid since that first one back in the autumn.' He started checking that there were enough buckets of sand and water. 'But I think I'd rather face this lot than stand up to bloody Ada Tanner. She was going off alarming at that poor kid. He looked terrified.'

Martin stood riveted to the spot, watching the waves of bombers coming up the river towards the very heart of London. It was an awesome sight, but he knew that the carnage they were capable of unleashing was terrible. Martin looked over to where his father was busily checking the buckets. He'd aged. Martin had been surprised when he'd heard him puffing and panting as they'd been running across from the dock.

It was hard to admit that his father wasn't a young man any more.

'Dad, why don't you go down in the laundry with Mum and Nell and get some sleep for once? I can manage up here.'

'And so can I, son. Now, come on, let's be having you. Get that stirrup pump ready, it looks like we're going to have our work more than cut out for us tonight.'

Down below them the three worn-out women they had taken over from had reached the bottom of the metal ladder and had just stepped down on to the fifth-floor landing. Tired and anxious to get to the shelter as they were, they couldn't resist pausing for a mesmerised moment to gawk at Ada. She was on cracking form tonight all right, carrying on at some poor young bloke who looked close to bursting into tears. Gawd knows what he'd done to set her off.

'I don't want to interrupt you, Mrs Tanner,' one of the women said, her exhaustion forgotten at the sight and sound of Ada in full flow, 'but it really is bad out there. You should get yourself down to the shelter as soon as you can.'

Alfie was given temporary respite as Ada spun round to face the three women. 'Why is it that everyone thinks that they can tell me what to do, and when I should do it, all of a sudden?' She drew her finger across her throat. 'I've had it right up to here with you nosy, interfering load of bastards.'

The women recoiled, unused to hearing such language from a woman, especially one of Ada Tanner's age.

'Suit yourself,' said the one nearest the steps.

'But you must have gone doolally tap if you'd rather stay up here with all that lot being chucked down at us. Come on, girls, let's leave the old bag to it.'

The women said nothing more, they had had their brief distraction. Without another word they started off down the stairs, leaving Ada Tanner to sort herself out.

'Nan, please, why won't you go down to the shelter with them?'

'You trying to tell me what to do as well now, are you?'

'No, Nan, I'm worried about you, that's all.'

'You? Worried about me?'

There was another very loud, very close blast, and the glass from the landing window shattered around them. The dimmed bulbs that lit the stairwell all went out with a single disconcerting pop.

'Get out of my way,' shouted Ada, pushing Alfie to one side and starting off down the stairs.

He followed close behind her. 'Careful, Nan, these stairs are steep and it's dark. You'll fall if you don't take care.'

'Don't you think I know it's dark? And, anyway, don't talk to me, you nasty piece of work. I don't want nothing to do with you.'

'Fine, fine, but, please, take it easy or you'll fall.'

Ada was gasping for breath and her slippers were flapping as she made her way down, but she wouldn't give in. She wouldn't let him have the satisfaction of knowing she was struggling.

They were almost at the bottom when another bright white flash of light lit up the whole of the stairwell, then there was a loud whoosh, and a blast of air picked up Ada as if she were nothing more than a yellow duster floating off the washing line in a summer breeze. It turned her over and over then dropped her – bang! – down on the concrete steps. She rolled down the final flight and came to a rest on her back on the tiled floor.

Alfie had been thrown on to his side. He'd been dazed as he hit his head, but apart from that was only grazed on his cheek and on his hands, where he'd tried to save himself from falling on top of his grandmother.

Gingerly, he made his way down the stairs, still dazzled by the sudden burst of light and so unable to make out much in the dark. 'Don't worry, Nan, I'm coming.'

He stopped as a shower of incendiaries fell outside in the courtyard and his surroundings were lit up again like daylight.

He saw her sprawled on the floor in front of him. He wanted to lift her up, but knew you weren't supposed to move someone if you didn't know what you were doing. It might make things even worse.

'Stay where you are, Nan. I'll go and get help for you. You'll be fine, I promise.'

He stood there looking out across the empty courtyard. Where had they said the shelter was? Where had they said she should go? He felt confused, dazed.

Down. That's what they'd said. *Going down to the shelter.* Down? Where did that mean? He looked around, seeking inspiration from the dark brick walls.

They were already on the ground floor so it had to be the surface shelter. That's what they must have meant – the shelter where he'd met that woman, what was her name?

His head hurt, but he had to think of her name for some reason. What was it?

Florrie.

That was it. That was her name and that's where they'd all be. He just knew it.

He raced across the courtyard and out on to the street towards the shelter. But the door was locked. Did they lock the doors? Why would they do that? Who'd want to keep people out of a shelter?

Alfie banged on the door with both his fists. 'Let me in, someone.'

The door opened and a narrow crack of light spilt out on to the snowy street.

'Who's there?' It was Florrie Talbot, squinting out into the dark.

'Please, I need someone to help me.'

Before Alfie had a chance to say another word, Florrie had grabbed him by the jacket and yanked him inside the shelter, slamming the door behind him. 'You do know you'll get us into trouble if you let the light from this lamp out there, don't you?' She looked over her shoulder and chuckled at the man standing behind her who was concentrating on doing up his fly buttons.

'And we don't want to go getting into any trouble, now do we, you dirty old dog?'

'You speak for yourself, Flo.' The man gave her a saucy grin – he sounded more than happy.

'Please, Florrie, I really do need help.'

She turned back to Alfie. Her make up was smudged all over her face as if she'd slept in it. A moment of recognition had her smiling broadly.

'Well, look who it is, it's young – no, don't tell me, don't – it's what's your name, innit? It's . . . no, don't tell me. I know, I do, it's . . . That's it, it's Alfie – Alfie Tanner, Ada's grandson.'

'Please, can I—'

'No, you cannot. You listen to me, 'cos it's a right coincidence you turning up here tonight. I was hoping to bump into you.'

'Florrie, please, listen—'

She giggled girlishly. 'No, I told you, you've got to listen to me.' As she spoke, the man handed her a discreet wad of money that she pressed to her lips before slipping it down the front of her dress. 'I met this feller in the pub the other night. Lovely he was. A young sailor. And he was – you know – your type. He'd be just right for you. Good-looking, nice and clean, great big . . .'

'Just forget it.' Alfie wrenched open the door.

The other man stifled a laugh and slipped past him out into the night.

Alfie went to follow him, but Florrie had taken firm hold of his sleeve. 'Me and my big mouth. Sorry, Alf, I didn't mean to embarrass you, sweetheart.'

'I'm not embarrassed. Why won't you just listen to me? It's my nan, she's been hurt.' He screwed his eyes tight shut, not sure if he could go on. But he had to get help. 'She's been hurt bad.'

'So what are we standing here for then?'

'She's the same as you, she won't listen either, won't let me talk to her. And I do love her, but she's ashamed of me, Florrie.'

'Don't be so dopey. Come on, Alf. Let's go and show her what you're made of.'

They hurried out on to the street. They had just reached the archway leading into the courtyard when a massive blast had them crouching down, protecting their heads with their arms.

Florrie dropped her arms and straightened up. She stared back in the direction they had just come from. 'Blimey O'Reilly, Alf. Will you look at that?'

The whole cement roof of the shelter had risen into the air and had come crashing back down, crushing the entire brick structure beneath it, reducing the whole thing to nothing more than a pile of rubble.

Florrie threw back her head and laughed out loud as if she'd just been told the best joke ever. 'Good boy, Alf. You saved our lives, young man. You're a blinking hero, that's what you are. Think what your nan's going to have to say about that when you tell her.'

'Sod me. Did you see that, Dad? The surface shelter's been blown to bloody bits. The roof went right up in the air like someone raising a trilby hat. I hope no one was in there. They wouldn't have stood a chance.'

Joe looked over the edge of the roof down on to the street below. 'No one ever uses that place, thank God. All our lot'll be down in the laundry, safe and sound.'

'I hope so, Dad, because I really don't think anyone could have survived that blast. D'you think I should go down and check? Make sure.'

'I think we should stay up here where we can do most good, Martin, because we can't risk leaving this lot. Look behind you – more stinking incendiaries. When are that lot gonna take a break?'

Florrie was having trouble keeping up with Alfie in her high heels. 'Hold up, Alf, I'm not a bleedin' racehorse. Tell you what, where we going if I lose you? I'll see you over there.'

'Nan's block. By the front door.'

'Go on then, Alf. I'm right behind you, darling.'

It was fortunate for Florrie that she couldn't keep up with Alfie Tanner. In her second piece of good luck in one night, she once again narrowly avoided being killed.

Alfie wasn't so blessed.

Florrie watched, open-mouthed, as he was thrown into the air like a toy being tossed for a dog – blown right off his feet, straight past her, back through the archway and out on to the pavement.

She tottered towards him, as fast as her heels

and the icy snow that covered the courtyard would let her, but skidded to a halt as she smelt an unmistakable stench – a gas pipe had been ruptured in the blast.

Slowly she moved closer, but the smell grew stronger.

'Bugger me, Alf. What am I going to do now?'

She knew she had no choice. Ignoring the danger, she crept forward and bent down next to him. 'Alf? Alf? Talk to me, handsome. Go on, say something. Anything. Call me an old brass if you want to. A dirty old tom. Just say something. *Alf!*'

Nothing.

Florrie swallowed hard and stood up. 'I'll go and see to your nan for you, darling.'

Florrie edged around a pile of debris in the courtyard. The sheds for the middle block had all copped it when whatever it was had fallen, but at least it hadn't damaged the Buildings themselves – not by the look of it, anyway – and she made her way over to the entrance to Ada's stairwell.

She could just about make out the shape of a body sprawled out on the tiled floor of the entrance hall.

'Ada? Ada, is that you, girl?' She knelt down and touched what she thought must be the woman's face, but immediately pulled her hand away.

'That boy loves you, you silly old bag. Your young Alfie. You do know that, don't you? And he wanted you to know it. Now he's gone and got himself blown up trying to help you.' She smoothed the sticky hair away from Ada's face. 'But how could the poor little sod have thought we could ever do anything for you? Your bloody head's been smashed open like a bleedin' fairground coconut.'

Florrie wiped her bloodied hand on her coat. 'You might have been a rotten old cow, Ada, but no one deserves this. No one. Not even you.'

She crossed herself, took off her coat and draped it over Ada. 'I'll go and get someone.'

'What's *she* doing down here?' An indignant Lil, knitting needles clacking as always, stared at Florrie as if, single-handed, she was responsible for the invasion of the British Isles.

'It's Ada Tanner.' Florrie was grasping hold of the edge of one of the laundry sinks for support. The metallic smell of blood in her nostrils was making her feel nauseous, and the realisation of the senseless waste of two more lives even sicker.

'Well, she's not down here, is she?' Lil smirked nastily for the benefit of those around her. 'So it's "Goodnight, Vienna". Sling your hook and get back where you belong.' Lil's expression hardened. 'Wherever that bug hutch might be.'

'No, you don't understand, it's Ada, she's been . . .' Florrie looked around her at the watchful faces, all full of curiosity as to why this woman had invaded their safe little world. But the faces that stood out the most were the children's: innocents, sleeping or playing. She knew what she'd like to say to some of these tight-arsed bitches, but she wouldn't upset the little ones. Nothing would ever make her do that.

She took a deep breath. 'You need to know, Ada Tanner has been hurt. She's up on the ground floor.' Florrie paused, needing to gather herself. 'And her grandson. Young Alfie. He's out there on the pavement. In the snow. And it's ever so cold, believe me.' Her eyes glistened with tears, and she really didn't know whether she could find the strength to say any more, but she knew she had to. 'Is there anyone down here with any nursing or first aid training?'

Mary stood up. 'Sorry, Flo. We were asleep over there, love, and I only heard half of that. But I'll go up and see what I can do. You look perished. Stay down here with the kids and Nell.' Mary yawned and scratched her head, then looked around and beckoned to an auburn-haired woman who had been dozing to one side of her. 'June, you used to work at the London, didn't you?'

'What? Yeah. Why? What's up?'

'We need a nurse. Come and help me. Someone's been hurt. Florrie, get yourself a cup of hot tea, Nell's got the flask, and make sure you wrap yourself up in my blanket. You'll freeze in that frock. Tommy, do you think you can run round to the phone box for me and call an ambulance?'

'Yes, Nan. 'Course I can.'

'And Ginny, you're strong.'

A plump, rosy-cheeked young woman jumped to attention. 'I am, Mrs Lovell.'

'You can help and all.'

As Mary hugged Florrie, before taking her little troop of helpers upstairs, Lil actually stopped knitting for once.

The sour look on her face would have curdled milk.

Up on the roof, Joe and Martin had no idea what was happening in the Buildings below. They'd seen an ambulance roaring up in the street a few hours ago, but that was nothing unusual on a bad night like this. Now the all clear had sounded and even though dawn was already

breaking they stayed where they were, transfixed by the view over London.

'Dad, this is so terrible. How many do you
reckon died here last night?'

'Even if it was just one person, it was one too
many.'

'What are we doing to ourselves? We're all
human beings. Why can't we just put a stop to
it? All say: "No more, we're not carrying on".'

'Because that's not how things happen. And
while I don't know what we're doing to ourselves either, son, look over there.' Joe pointed
west. 'There's always hope. You remember that.'

Martin looked to where his father was
pointing.

The dome of St Paul's was standing tall and
proud above the billowing clouds of smoke
from the countless fires smouldering below.

'That's London for you, boy. They won't beat
us. They won't destroy our spirit.' Joe coughed
loudly to hide the tremor in his voice. 'Now, I
don't know about you, but I'm starving. Let's go
down and get ourselves a bit of breakfast and
see the girls. They'll cheer us up.'

Chapter 20

The sandy-haired young man in the RAF uniform waited until the last of the mourners had left the churchyard, and the sexton had returned with his shovel ready to fill in the grave, before he stepped out from behind the yew hedge.

'Would you allow me a few moments alone?'

The sexton looked surprised. The young man's voice wasn't the sort you usually heard round those parts – well, apart from the vicar's – he sounded more like those blokes they had reading the news on the wireless of a night.

He held up his shovel. 'It'll be getting dark in an hour or so. And it's bloody cold. I should be getting on.'

The young airman put his hand in his pocket and took out some change. 'Would five bob buy me a few minutes' privacy?'

The sexton smiled, displaying a set of teeth almost as moss-covered and crooked as the gravestones surrounding them.

He weighed the money in his dirt-encrusted palm. 'I'll go over to the church and have myself a fag, but make sure you don't take too long about it. I don't wanna freeze me arse off waiting about for you.'

'I won't be long.'

With the sexton safely out of the way – sitting on the church steps, rolling a cigarette so skinny it hardly seemed worth the effort – the young man opened the cone of paper he was carrying and took out a single yellow rose.

He plucked off the petals, one by one, letting them fall into the open grave. 'For you, my darling Alfie. Forever. My first love. My only love. Sleep well until I join you.'

Tears clouded his eyes as the bitter wind whipped the final petals from the rose. 'And from what they're all saying back at the airfield, I don't think it'll be too long before we're back together again.'

He unwound the white silk muffler from his throat and let it float down on to the petals. 'Goodnight, my love. Keep warm till I join you.'

'What a way to start the New Year.' Florrie Talbot was sitting between Nell and Mary in the saloon bar of the Black Dog in Wapping; she had a weak gin and orange in one hand, and a pilchard sandwich in the other. 'If you'd have asked me last week, I'd have said that Ada Tanner was completely bloody indestructible.'

She knocked back a mouthful of gin. 'And it's so sad that she never made it up with her grandson. It just goes to show: you never know what life's got in store for you. You should never take it for granted that you've got plenty of time to do things tomorrow. Do them today or they might never get done. I didn't say anything, but I sort of got to know Alfie a little bit over the past few months. He was a nice kid, and all he wanted was for his nan to accept him and the way he was.'

Mary sipped at her port and lemon. 'It's a good turn out though, Flo, especially considering this rotten weather.'

Nell nodded. 'It was a wonder the grave digger could break the ground. I can't remember it ever being so cold.'

'Look at Albert, he's like a lost soul. And such a shame that his son's not gonna hear about it till it's all over. He's out there somewhere at sea, like all the other brave blokes fighting to fetch us food and stuff, and this is happening back home. It's wicked, that's what it is.'

'I couldn't agree more, Mary. This war makes less and less sense when you see something like this.'

'Joe tried to talk to Albert earlier, but he couldn't get a peep out of him. And young Bella standing there with him – she might be like a little Ada at times, but everyone knew how much she loved her nan. And how much Ada loved her, in her own funny way.' Mary put down her glass.

'This might sound a shocking thing to say, Nell, but I'm glad Sarah and David went together the way they did. Neither of them could have carried on without the other. It would only have been half a life.'

'What a year it's been, eh?' Nell stood up. 'I'm going to nip over the road to make sure that Grace and Tommy are doing all right looking after Dolly and Vicky. I won't be long.'

Mary patted her hand and smiled faintly. 'All right, sweetheart, but don't let Dolly know she's being looked after, will you?'

Nell made her way through the crowd towards the door, but stopped when she saw Kitty Jarrett, standing alone, nursing a cup of cold tea.

'Hello, Kit. I'm popping over the road to check on the kids. Anything you want me to tell Grace?'

'Don't worry, Nell. You stay here, I'll go over. I was thinking about making a move anyway, but I didn't want to leave too soon. You never know the right thing to do on occasions like this, do you?'

'Let's both go over, Kit. I could do with a

breath of air. And you can hold my arm so you don't slip on the ice.'

'Thanks, Nell.' Kitty put her cup on the counter. 'Do you know, I can't remember ever going to such a sad funeral. When they lowered that boy's coffin down on top of his nan's . . . it was heart-breaking, them being buried in the same grave.'

'At least they're together now.'

'I wonder what Ada would have made of that.' Kitty sniffed back a tear. 'I keep coming over so sentimental lately. It must be the baby.' She rubbed her stomach. 'Nell, I've just got to go and tell Fred I'm leaving or he'll wonder where I am. He's been fussing round so much since he found out.'

'See you later then, Mum.' Freddie pecked Kitty on the cheek. 'I'll finish my drink and then I'll be over. Or shall I come with you now because of the ice?'

'Don't worry, darling, I'll be fine. I'm going over with Nell.'

Bella, who'd been standing with her distraught-looking grandfather and her increasingly pissed mother, watched Kitty leave with Nell. She had cried more than she would have thought possible these last few days. Where did tears come from anyway? Were they already there inside and when you'd cried all you were born with you were left dry-eyed?

She had no idea. She had no idea about anything much at all. Except that she wanted to talk to Freddie Jarrett. Maybe he'd be able to stop her from hurting so much.

She made her way across to where he was standing, ignoring all the '*I'm so sorry*' and '*keep your chin up*' and '*at least they're at peace now*' type remarks as she did so. She didn't have a clue what she was going to say to him, but everything was so horrible anyway it couldn't get any worse, no matter what she said or did.

'Hello, Fred.'

'Hello, Bella. I'm so sorry about what happened to your nan and your brother.'

'Me too. And are you sorry that you told me on Christmas Day that you'd see me later, then didn't bother?'

'Bella, I didn't. I never promised anything. But I apologise if you thought I did. I was on my way somewhere really important and I must have been distracted. I truly didn't mean to upset you.'

'But you did, though. You upset me a lot. And you made me feel like a fool.' She blew her nose. 'And I thought you liked me.'

'I do, but not in that sort of way. And if I made you feel like that, I can't apologise enough.' He smiled kindly at her. 'Look, this is no way to begin the New Year.'

'What, going to my nan and my brother's funeral? No, you're right, it is no way to begin the year. But I'm not talking about that, I'm talking about us.'

'Bella, there is no us. I don't even remember what I said to you exactly. But I know I would never have meant it to sound like a promise. I don't want to lead you on. I don't want to lead anyone on. It wouldn't be right. I'd only be using you.'

Freddie considered his words. He wasn't going to lie again. 'I'm in love with someone, Bell. And I feel really bad if I made you think there could be something between you and me.'

He caressed her cheek with the back of his hand. 'Let's think of this as an end to the old year and a start to a New Year when we can be friends. Could you do that?'

Bella started weeping snottily, her chest heaving. She still had plenty more tears left inside her.

'You can't go telling me you love someone else, Freddie Jarrett. Not today of all days. Not with Nan and Alfie getting buried and everything.'

'I can't do anything else, Bell. Look, I'm going to go now, otherwise it'd just be another lie, and

I'd be hurting you again without meaning to. You're a sweet, beautiful girl, and you'll find someone exactly right for you very soon, then you'll wonder what you ever saw in me.'

Mary watched as Freddie made a dash for the door and Bella dissolved in a flood of tears in the corner of the bar. 'Aw, will you look at Bella, the poor little kid.'

She worked her way through the now considerably jollier, booze-fuelled crowd. 'How're you doing, sweetheart?'

'Rotten, Mrs Lovell. Really rotten.'

'Where's your mum?'

'I dunno. She was here a few minutes ago, but she seems to have got a bit friendly with her next-door's husband since he came home on leave a couple of days ago, and I wouldn't be surprised if she's crept off with him somewhere. 'Cos her next-door's got herself too pissed to notice.' She jerked her head towards a bench where the woman who lived next-door to them lay flat on her back, snoring inelegantly.

'Yes, I see.'

Bella threw her arms around Mary's waist and buried her face in her chest. 'I'm so fed up, Mrs Lovell, I really am. What am I going to do without my nan and Alfie? I wish I could make everything all right again. I wish I could cuddle my nan.'

The snow had turned to a steady sleet and Freddie was soaked through by the time he got to Pennyfields, but there wasn't a chance in a million that he was going to take no for an answer – not this time – despite all Li Mei's best efforts to put him off. She saw him through the window of the front room and immediately came out on to the pavement.

'Freddie, do you know how much trouble I'm going to be in if you don't leave here this very minute?' she said, glancing back nervously at the house.

'I don't care. I'm going to be going away soon, and I can't let things be left like this between us. I've had time to think all this through and begin to make some changes in my life. I've decided I'm going to be open with people from now on. No more secrets, no more lies. I'm going to tell your family first, and then mine. And then it's all out in the open and no one can do anything about it. I mean, if they don't like it, what's the worst they can do?'

'But Freddie—'

'Even if that Peter bloke is stupid enough to turn up again, he'll have nothing he can threaten us with because everyone will know.'

'No, Freddie. You make it sound so easy, but you can't do this.'

'Do you love me?'

Mei couldn't bring herself to meet his eyes, knowing how hard it would be to look away again. 'You know I do.'

'Right. That's all I need to know. Now let me past.'

She shook her head. 'No, you can't come in here. I won't let you.'

But Freddie meant it – he lifted her off her feet, put her on the pavement behind him, and walked inside the house.

Mei chased him through to the front room and started gabbling away to her grandparents in rapid-fire Cantonese, but it was Freddie who had their attention.

'I apologise that I do not know how to speak your language, but if I speak slowly will that be all right?'

Mei's grandmother glared at her and pointed a finger. Mei immediately went quiet.

'Go on,' she said to Freddie in heavily accented English. 'Speak.'

'I have come to tell you that I love Mei. I am joining the army. I have no idea where they will be sending me, or even if I will ever come back. But I wanted you to know before I went that I love Mei, with all of my heart, and that if I do come back I would like to marry her. With your permission, I would like to become part of your family, and Mei to become part of mine. I will care for her – and you – in the very best way I can, and I will never do anything to make you ashamed of me. I promise you, with all of my heart.'

Mei looked at him as if he had lost his mind. 'You called me by my proper name.'

Freddie fidgeted self-consciously. 'Of course I did, out of respect for your grandparents.'

Mei's grandmother whispered something to her husband, and then pointed at Mei and spoke to her in Cantonese. 'Tell us both what he said so that we are sure we understand. And know that we *did* understand a lot of it. So no lies.'

Mei did as her grandmother asked. When she had finished, her grandparents again talked quietly to each other. Then her grandmother turned back to her.

'So this boy, he is your secret?'

'Secret, Grandmother? What do you mean?'

'You are not a foolish girl, don't try to play tricks with me. Your secret. Is it him?'

Mei felt her hands go clammy. 'What makes you think I have a secret?'

'Mei, I am your grandmother, of course I know. I can read what goes on in your head. You do know it is not easy, marrying a foreign boy?'

'Marrying?'

'Answer me.'

'Yes, Grandmother, I know.'

'Do you think you are strong enough to do this thing?'

Mei stared at her feet.

'You love him, this boy?'

Mei's lip started to wobble as she fought back the tears. 'I do love him, and I hope that that will make me strong.'

'Good, that is how it should be.'

'Good? But I thought you would be angry.'

'Did you ever ask us?'

'No, Grandmother.'

'And has this boy asked his family what they think?'

'No.'

'Why not?'

'Because we knew that you wouldn't approve, and nor would—'

'Young people can be so foolish. Mei, your grandfather and I, we won't be here in this world with you much longer; you will need someone to care for you then. Look at him. He is big and strong. That is good. It has been worrying us, what will become of you without us being here, and we knew you didn't want to go back to China. Now he can look after you.'

'Don't say that, Grandmother.'

'Li, what is she saying?'

Mei felt so confused – at once as light and bright as if she were walking through the spring meadows her grandmother used to tell her about, where everything smelled fresh and beautiful – but it was all such a shock.

'She likes you, Freddie. I think she approves.'

Freddie swallowed hard. 'Thank you. Thank you,' he said. 'I would like to take Mei to see my mother now. Is that all right?'

Across the road, in the shadows of the West India Dock, the silhouette of a young man could be seen staring over towards Li Mei's house. He had his kit bag over his shoulder and his embarkation papers in his pocket. He had to go soon, because he was about to leave on the next tide, but he wouldn't forget the boy who had actually dared to go into Mei's home.

When he came back, he would deal him, he would deal with him once and for all, and then that arrogant idiot would understand what it meant to regret his own actions.

Not far from Li Mei's home, Florrie Talbot was sitting in the public bar of the Oporto, a pub just across from the dock gates. 'Do you know what, Charlie? I'm not gonna charge you for today.'

Charlie, who was also waiting for the tide to

turn, put down his pint. 'No? Why's that then, Flo? Won a few quid, have you?'

'Don't laugh at me, Charlie. I've had a right day of it up in Wapping, and now I want to cheer things up a bit. So accept it as a little going away present.' She sipped daintily at a gin and orange – considerably stronger than the one she'd been drinking earlier at the funeral – and granted Charlie a coy little sideways glance. 'You will look out for yourself when you're away, won't you, Chas?'

'Guaranteed I will, my little mermaid, guaranteed.'

'Good. I'm glad of that. Because I've lost too many people lately, and I need you to take care of yourself and come back safe and sound for me.' She took another sip. 'I'd hate anything bad to happen to you.'

'Well, I'd better be careful then, hadn't I, Flo? And when I come back, you do know we're going to get married, don't you?'

Florrie sniffed and dabbed at her nose with her hankie. 'Aw, Chas, you silly old sailor. You can't say things like that to me. Not today of all days. You'll have me crying me eyes out again.'

'Don't do that, Flo. Give us a smile and say you'll marry me?'

'I wish I could, Chas, but it's not that easy, is it? I swear I'd love to say yes, 'cos you know how fond I've got to be of you over the years. But there's only ever been the one man in my life I would have married.'

Charlie smacked his pint glass down on to the table. 'And he's not me? Is that what you're saying?'

'Charlie, he's not you.' She shook her head, wishing so hard that she wasn't. 'I always knew he was the love of my life.'

'Can I ask who this bloke is?'

'You wouldn't know him, it was a long time ago. We were only kids. He went to Flanders. And he never came back.'

Charlie picked up his glass and took a long swallow of mild and bitter. 'I had no idea.'

'It's not something I talk about very often.'

'So how about marrying me for company then? Or friendship? All this is going to be over one day, and we're not getting any younger, Flo, you and me. We'll need someone then. Someone to be with, grow old with. If you've not got someone to share your life, what point is there in anything?'

'Who knows what's going to happen to us in the future, Chas? Who knows what's going to happen to us tomorrow even? How could it work, you and me? It can't happen.'

'You don't mean that, Flo. Me and you, girl, we can make it happen.'

Florrie's mouth went dry and she could hardly speak. 'I've been to that funeral today, Chas, and it reminded me of a very dear friend of mine – Sarah. I know she would never have settled for second best, and I'm sorry, but that's what you'd be for me. I also know that Sarah wanted me to give up what I'm doing, this way of life. So, I've decided, I'm starting this New Year with a new me.'

'I wouldn't care if I was second best, Flo. And I'm not asking to take anyone's place. I only want to know that my girl's going to be here for me when I come home. I've got a thing for you, my little old darling that I can't ignore.' He took her hand in his big rough paw. 'Marry me, Flo. Please.'

'Come back home safe, Charlie, and we'll see, eh?' She closed her eyes and touched her lips to his. 'Tell you what, when you get back, don't let's go to the pub, let's go to my flat above the shop and we can have a nice pot of tea. All proper like. Then we'll have a good old natter about what might happen next. I can't promise you anything, but it'll be a start. How about that?'

Charlie smiled. 'That'll do me for now, darling. Thank you. I'd like that a lot. In fact, I'll be looking forward to it more than you'll ever know.'

*

'Fancy coming over to the Hope, Nell? While it's still light.'

'I'm not sure, Martin. This has been such a stinker of a day.'

'All the more reason. And this lot are going to start getting a bit rowdy soon, what with all this free drink Albert's laid on. We can go in Joe's truck or get a taxi even. Come on, Sylv'll cheer us all up.'

'Go on then. I'll just go over and have a word with Albert and young Bella first – maybe suggest she goes over to sit with Grace for a while. Then I'll go and get the kids ready, if you go and tell Mary and Joe.'

'You're on.'

'Right, give me ten minutes to get the kids' coats on and I'll see the three of you down in the courtyard.'

Martin smiled at her, his beautiful Nelly.

She touched the pearl brooch that was, as always, pinned to the lapel of her coat. 'What do you think this New Year's got in store for us, Martin?'

'Who knows, love? Who knows? But let's hope that 1941 sees the end of all this, eh?'

'Yeah, let's hope so, because I really don't know if we can stand another year like last one.'

Martin looked around him. 'Hope – that's what we all need to get us through.'

'Here, talking about that, Martin, did you ever get to see that card we got from Sylvie on Christmas Day?'

He frowned and shook his head.

'It had this verse on it. She had it made for us especially, by one of the embroidery girls down Brick Lane. It's beautiful. But we've been so busy I bet you've not even looked at it.' Nell smiled and tapped him on the tip of his nose. 'And on Christmas Day itself I think you and Joe and Bernie were more interested in the brandy than in opening cards.'

He shrugged non-committally.

'You never looked at any of them, did you?'

This time Martin put on a suitably guilty expression.

'I didn't think so. But Sylvie's was so lovely that I've kept it in my handbag. Here, before I go over the road for the kids, have a quick look at it now. The embroidery's beautiful, but it's the words that I like best.'

She opened her bag and handed Martin the card, and he read out the words:

> Yesterday is history
> Tomorrow is a mystery
> Today is a gift
> That's why we call it the present

'What do you think of that then?'

'Blimey, Nell, I must be getting soft.' His voice sounded gruff. 'I wouldn't have believed a few words could make me feel like this. Must be the funeral getting to me.'

'You're not soft, Martin. You're a good, kind man. And I'm so lucky to have you.'

'It's me who's the lucky one. So here's to the future, eh, darling?'

'Yeah, here's to the future. Now you go and get Mary and Joe, and I'll get the kids. Let's see this New Year in the way we mean to go on – in peace and with friends and family. This rotten war won't beat the Lovells.'

Rough Justice

Gilda O'Neill

They loved and lost, hoped and feared . . .

The Flanagans, the Tanners and the Lovells all live on the top floor of the Turnbury Buildings – a crumbling Victorian tenement in the heart of London's East End. It's 1936 and Britain is in the grip of the Depression.

Nell Flanagan is a decent, hardworking woman, married to Stephen, a tough, heavy-drinking brute of a man, who works as a casual in the docks – when there's work available. Nell has hidden the abuse she has suffered at this hands from her young children, although most of the neighbours realise what's going on.

The Tanners think she must be asking for it, but Martin Lovell has always admired Nell. When he sees Stephen actually attacking her, he can stand back no longer, but his actions have repercussions for all the families . . .

THE POWER OF READING

Visit the Random House website and get connected with information on all our books and authors

EXTRACTS from our recently published books and selected backlist titles

COMPETITIONS AND PRIZE DRAWS Win signed books, audiobooks and more

AUTHOR EVENTS Find out which of our authors are on tour and where you can meet them

LATEST NEWS on bestsellers, awards and new publications

MINISITES with exclusive special features dedicated to our authors and their titles

READING GROUPS Reading guides, special features and all the information you need for your reading group

LISTEN to extracts from the latest audiobook publications

WATCH video clips of interviews and readings with our authors

RANDOM HOUSE INFORMATION including advice for writers, job vacancies and all your general queries answered

Come home to Random House
www.rbooks.co.uk